THE VITAL MINUTE

Further Titles by Roger Ormerod from Severn House

A CURTAIN OF BEADS
FAREWELL GESTURE

THE
VITAL MINUTE

Roger Ormerod

This first world, edition published in Great Britain 1996 by
SEVERN HOUSE PUBLISHERS LTD of
9–15 High Street, Sutton, Surrey SM1 1DF.
First published in the USA 1997 by
SEVERN HOUSE PUBLISHERS INC of
595 Madison Avenue, New York, NY 10022.

British Library Cataloguing in Publication Data
Ormerod, Roger, 1920–
    The vital minute
    1.English fiction – 20th century
    I. Title
    823.9′14[F]

    ISBN 0-7278-5152-7

Typeset by Hewer Text Composition Services, Edinburgh.
Printed and bound in Great Britain by
Hartnolls Ltd, Bodmin, Cornwall.

Chapter One

Looking back to it now, I realise that I was over-confident in the case of Mrs Trent's husband, as everything appeared to be straightforward, from the documentation I had read back at the office. Usually, it requires no more than an interview with the widow to establish the facts, and agreement on the details of the accident. I was used to it. I would simply nod and smile, having read the full details in the MO's report before leaving the office. These were the preliminaries, establishing an atmosphere in which free talk would flow. That over, I would be able to make a recommendation, later to be submitted in writing to my Manager. This decision was vital. On it usually rested the question of whether or not the widow would be entitled to an *Industrial Death Pension*. She was too young (not yet 40) for a normal widow's pension.

Three months before I set eyes on the file, her husband had died by crashing his car into a lamp-post. The question I had to resolve was simply: at that time, had he still been engaged in his employment, or had he been driving away from it, heading home? No wonder that Mrs Trent was worried about non-receipt of her widow's pension. Three months of delay.

But I was required to establish, or not, the basic fact: had the death occurred during his employment, and arising out of it? If so, she would be entitled to an *Industrial Widow's Pension*. I went to talk to her about it.

Her name was Virginia Trent. She was dark, plumply pretty in a sad sort of way, and bewildered. She could see no end to the frightening trail of uncertainty that reached indefinitely ahead. It was my job to clear up the situation.

"You do realise why you're not entitled to a widow's pension?" I asked. "You'd need to be 40."

"Yes." Her voice was dull, but a shade of resentment darkened it. "I'm young enough to work." She glanced at her hands. "It's been explained."

I looked down at the file, open on my knee, then reached for the tea she'd insisted on getting me. Anything to stop me saying the banal and insulting: "It's the law." But it was. If you're one day under the age of 40 when your husband dies – one hour – you're out. Keep him alive for the one important hour . . . that's the law. It's got to have a cut-off point, and there's no flexibility.

"So," I said, putting my cup down and trying a smile, "we fall back on Industrial Death Benefit. Which, I'm afraid, is a little tricky in this case."

"But they told me at the office it was what I'd get."

Internally, I sighed, quite certain they hadn't. But you don't argue. "We didn't know the facts at that time, Mrs Trent."

"What facts?" Sharp, bitter, challenging. Her neighbour had probably told her not to let herself be bullied. "What facts are you talking about?"

"In order to qualify for this particular benefit, the accident that caused his death would have to be the result of his work."

"Well . . . wasn't it?"

"I've been asked to come to see you and go into it fully."

"If you must," she mumbled.

"Quite simply, the accident happened in the street outside the factory, late at night . . ."

"Nine twenty-three," she told me, nodding. That moment was fixed for ever in her memory.

"So accurate . . ."

"The gatekeeper heard it. His eyes went to the clock."

"Yes. Yes, I see." Making a note. "But, you understand, for this to be accepted as an *industrial* accident, he'd normally need to have been working, on a machine, or at a desk. But he was driving."

"But I explained that. I put it down." She leaned forward, trying to read my file upside-down, jabbing her finger towards it. "Didn't I say? He was a buyer. It was *his job* to go out in his car."

I'd already thought along those lines. There were no end of legal precedents, and I'd read up a few before I'd come out to see her.

"But," I said gently, "didn't his work as a buyer finish at the moment he left the place of his last call, and head home? Just like any other employee – the journey home isn't part of the employment."

"Well . . . it ought to be!"

"And employment terminates at the factory gate or the office door."

"It's not right!"

"It's the . . ." Hell! I swept round it. "There have to be rules and regulations, you see."

If she only knew! Rules and regulations. Books packed with them; we called them Codes. Laid out, they stretched across the whole width of a desk. And as for Industrial Accidents . . .! The original Act itself is only a quarter of an inch thick. Any normal genius could understand it. But anomalies become apparent as soon as it becomes law. Borderline cases poke up their annoying heads, and somebody has to decide whether this or that circumstance comes under which section or sub-section, or doesn't. In the end, the top brain lays it down: the Commissioner. He makes a decision in a specific case, and it's called a precedent. Guiding lines. Inside ten minutes there'll be another case, *nearly* the same – but who's to say? The Commissioner, of course. So you've got another precedent.

At the time this interview was taking place the collection of Commissioner's Decisions was over an inch thick.

I did not intend to go into the ramifications of the legal definition of an Industrial Accident as one "arising out of and in the course of employment."

Clearing my throat, I said: "Now . . . if he'd been heading back to his own factory for some reason . . . but it was nearly nine-thirty and the offices would be dark and empty . . . I mean, there couldn't have been any reason . . ."

"But there *was*!"

"Ah!" I waited. Was she going to say he'd been rushing back to the factory with two-dozen nuts and bolts? This was a big firm. His buying would be entirely paper transactions.

"He phoned me," she said, and suddenly there was eagerness in her voice, seeing a chance. "From Manchester. He'd gone north to this firm – Turners, I think it was – he'd gone to see about a delay in delivering an order for castings, and he phoned to ask what the weather was doing here, because it was snowing there, and he'd got 80 miles to drive . . . and it was snowing here, too, a kind of sleet. You remember January?"

I nodded. I could remember January, all right. But not there. I'd been living and working on the outskirts of Birmingham at the time. I remembered January because of the row with Lena over the party at the Bellinghams. I nodded. "Yes. It was bad, January."

"So he warned me he'd possibly be home late," she went on. "And he said he'd got to call in at the office on the way, so that would delay him even more."

"Did he say why he had to call in?"

"Something about an order his Managing Director wanted to see."

"That late at night?"

"It wouldn't have been that late – would it – if it hadn't been for the weather," she pointed out reasonably.

"What time did he phone?"

"Oh dear, I'm not sure!" She thought, her fingers idly playing with her skirt. "Some time after four – before five."

"Late for a Managing Director, anyway, if he couldn't get there till nine."

"Mr Lorimer said he'd wait – however late Leonard might be."

"For an *order*? But you said your husband was a buyer, not a salesman."

"He definitely said an order."

Virginia Trent was now staring at me with complete sincerity, her eyes huge. Somehow she'd seen in me someone who was going to rescue her from an awkward financial situation. She couldn't know that the picture was becoming more complex with every second.

I had worked in this town for only two months, so that I'd needed to memorise the area and street maps to stand any chance of getting around to do my job. Manchester was to the north. The main road came in . . . now let me see . . .

"But surely," I said, "coming in from the north he'd hit the roundabout at Six Ways, where he'd be only half a mile from his home, here. If he was that late, he'd surely have popped home to say hello, phone in and check his boss was still waiting."

She smiled. "The weather was so bad that he'd probably made a diversion in order to miss the hill at Duxbury. Then he'd have come in on the far side of town, and . . ."

So true, so very true. That was what he might have done. I allowed her to go on talking while I thought it out.

Somebody at our office had done a good job on the file, taking it as far as anybody could on paper. That was what I was around for – when paperwork comes to a dead-end I go out and look at these things personally. So I hadn't come to Mrs Trent in ignorance. I had an inquest report, comments from the police on the accident. Yes, Leonard Trent might well have been coming in from what Mrs Trent called the far side of town. From the east, that would be. The road past the factory runs roughly east to west. Coming from the east, then, at the time of his accident Trent would have been a hundred yards short of the factory main gate. There was a small hump-back bridge over the canal, just to the east of the accident spot. Perhaps he'd gone into it too fast. The road had been a sheet of ice along there, due to the sleet freezing on frozen tarmac. He'd spun – though that was a guess – and wrapped his car around a telegraph pole. The police said he could have been going in either direction, but in any event he'd been moving fast, fast enough to reduce the car to a heap of wreckage, and him to a crushed body, dead before anybody reached him.

It was the speed of a man hurrying late home to his wife, and with every intention of driving past the factory and to hell with the Managing Director. Or hurrying to his MD, and to hell with his wife? In the first instance, he would have put himself outside the sphere of his employment.

Oh Lord, I thought, what have I got myself into? A new posting for me, this job was, and already I'd got one file on a man with a lethal spade, and another on a woman who'd blown herself off the lavatory. This one promised to be worse.

Mrs Trent was still talking, and I could've been missing something important.

". . . so I'm quite sure Philip would have been waiting . . ."

"Philip?"

"Oh, you're not listening." Philip Lorimer. The Managing Director. I said I'm quite sure he'd have been waiting. Oh, you're getting me all confused!" Easily done, I thought. She was the fluttery, lost type of woman. "Of course he was waiting. You *know* he was waiting. You've known all along."

"I'm sorry. There's nothing in my file about a Philip Lorimer."

"Not in your file!" She was becoming angry now, tearful with it. "In the newspapers, Mr – What did you say your name is?"

"Beacham, Mrs Trent."

"It was in all the papers, Mr Beacham. You can't have missed it."

"In the locals, perhaps. I wasn't working in this area in January."

"Then they should have told you. Philip Lorimer was Leonard's brother-in-law. Philip married Leonard's sister, Marjorie. What does it matter who he was married to?" She shook her head angrily, flipped her hand in dismissal. "But it *does* mean Leonard was anxious to do him a favour, which was what bringing that order was. Philip had told him – yes, I'm sure I remember this – told him the order was very important to him. But of course, Leonard was so late. Too late, as it turned out."

"I don't know what you mean."

"Philip Lorimer," she said, "shot himself that night, at his desk, and it must've been only a few minutes before Leonard's accident. Minutes! Don't you think that might have been why Leonard was hurrying, Mr Beacham?"

Those big eyes were very innocent now. She's scored a point, she thinks. But it only pushed me one step farther on the road to chaos. There I'd been, deciding that all I'd need to wrap it all up was a word with Philip Lorimer, and now Lorimer was out of reach. So how the devil was I ever to find out whether Trent had been hurrying to bring his MD an order, part of his job if you stretch it a bit, or even hurrying to save him from suicide, which could not be said to be within a buyer's normal duties?

The trouble with a Civil Servant's job is that you become so wrapped-up with technicalities, regulations, instructions, and pure cold figures, that in the end the humanity becomes drained away. As it puts it in those precedents I mentioned: "Mr T did this," "Miss Y said that." They're not people.

But abruptly I was faced with two deaths, a suicide and a car accident. Tragedies, both. I slid the file into my brief case – regulation black, "E II R" in gold on the flap – and fought my way back to humanity. I got to my feet.

"Obviously, there's more to this than I thought, Mrs Trent.

I'm sorry . . ., I see I've upset you. There was no warning."
I looked around. A neat, tidy bungalow, the furnishings
still as new as their marriage, probably mortgaged up to
the rafters, and all I could say was, "no warning." I was
excusing myself.

My eyes roamed the room, not really registering anything.
Habit. That last look round was nothing to do with the job,
it was me wondering when I'd see it again. There need not
be any official necessity, as it could easily resolve itself into
a simple disallowance, which would be no more than a form
through the post. But over the years I'd developed habits. I
liked just to call in and pass the news personally – even if it
was bad. I said: "I'll no doubt see you again, Mrs Trent,"
but she expressed no delight at the thought.

I sat in the car for a few minutes, thinking about the
contents of my brief case. It was three-fifteen. Time, still,
for one more quick visit, and the obvious case to tackle
was the spade-wielder. The only one, really, because I'd
been putting it off, putting it off. . . .

There are cases where, like an appointment with the den-
tist, you need to build up the determination. I am not made
for assault, neither physically nor mentally, nor was it part
of my duties to invite danger. I had a warrant that authorised
my enquiries. It was not bullet-proof, though, nor spade-
proof. On a visit a year before, the previous Inspector had
added a note to the file: "This man attacked me with a
spade." So I was not enthusiastic. The man in question was
a farmer, working on his own, and paid his contributions
only when visited by an Inspector from our Department,
and then only on production of a warrant card.

It would be only the third time in 12 years that I'd
flashed it.

Driving there now, turning away from the town, I was
determined to get this done quickly and smoothly. My
warrant? In my wallet.

This warrant they give us . . . it's signed on behalf of the Lord Chancellor and gives us simple powers to conduct our duties as required by the Act. In fact, it gives me more powers than a policeman has. I may enter any premises where there is evidence to believe employment is taking place. That means even a private house, if work is being done from that house. A policeman can't do that without applying for a magistrate's warrant. But policemen were created to protect property. Property first, the individual second. My duties, though, involved the protection of money. I was protecting the public's money from the depredations of the crafty and the fraudulant, and protecting the individual's legal right to money from being snatched from him by legal finagling. *That* was why my warrant was so strong. Money first, property second, and the individual third. That's how life is. Once you've got that firmly in your head, you're well on the way towards being a law-abiding and compliant citizen.

But, as I say, I'd only ever had to show my warrant twice, and never had I used it to demand entry to a private house. It's there if you need it. Like your appendix; it can sit there doing nothing for years.

Mr Fallon was running a one-man operation on 20 acres, and seemed to confine himself to dairy farming. I found him in his milking shed, hosing it down. There was a sweet-sour smell, like babies, in the air. He turned at my shadow in the doorway, the hose spurting around his gum boots, a big, florid man with a bald head. A dog ran barking from behind me. I ignored it, and it licked the knuckles gripping my brief case.

"Mr Fallon?"

He nodded.

"I'm from the Social Security office," I said. "My name's Beacham."

He eyed me up and down. The hose pipe alone would have disconcerted me.

"You'll be wanting your money," he decided.

"That was the idea."

He dropped the hose and walked over to the tap. "You'd better come in the house, then."

I followed him. It was as easy as that. Everything in the cottage was old and revered. Including his cheque book. He didn't draw many cheques.

"You sit down there," he instructed me, pointing to a chair at the end of the table, "and work it out. Make out the cheque for me, and I'll sign it."

He went to find his wife and tell her to prepare tea, then came back and sat close to me, elbows on the table, seeming awed by my ability with the calculator. When I pushed across the cheque, along with my pen, he licked its point and signed carefully. Cups were rattling at my elbow. Mrs Fallon banged down a chunk of seed cake on a plate.

"Get y'r teeth into that," she challenged, and stomped away.

We drank tea and chewed seed cake. I felt relaxed. It'd been easy. He hadn't asked to see my warrant card.

"You're new at it?" he asked.

"New here. Twelve years on the outside job, though."

"Like it?"

"I like to work on my own."

He considered that. "The last one was a bastard," he told me. "A reet bastard."

"Oh, yes?"

"Came here – every year, almost to the day. Shouting his head off, as per usual, last year. Threatening summonses."

"Did he?"

"But last year was different. The ambulance was in the yard when he come. The missus asked him to come back another time – but would he? Not on your nelly he wouldn't. So I had to persuade him."

"Ambulance?"

"My lad. Got himself stomped by the bull. Stupid bugger. Died in hospital that night."

10

I said nothing, but retired behind my cup.

"Your man," he said, looking up quickly, sharp eyes fastening on mine, "just wouldn't listen to sense. 'Let's have your cheque book, dad,' he says. Dad! So I took a spade to him. Reckon it was a good job the ambulance men were here, or I'd have brained the sod."

"Yes," I said.

"That part of your duties, is it?"

"Not exactly."

"I should say not."

I'd meant being brained, but it was equally not, in the way he meant it.

I said goodbye, shouted good-day to his missus, let the dog lick my knuckles again, and drove away. The Inspector he'd been talking about was the man I was replacing. He'd been transferred on promotion.

I wondered vaguely whether my new Manager had recommended the promotion because he admired the chap's operating technique, or whether he'd also thought of him as a "reet bastard," and had been glad to get rid of him. But I hadn't been able to make up my mind about the Manager. Paul Harkness was an enigma to me, and quite frankly it was beginning to worry me.

You need to know your Manager, and understand him. Life can be so much more pleasurable if you can work with him, and promotion comes so much more easily if you know the way he thinks. If that's what you want from life, and if you're willing to dig deeply enough for it. Quite frankly, that was why I was at that particular office – promotion. It had been sliding past me. I was 34, and stagnating, and the general idea was to try another office, with a new Manager to impress. The *general* idea? No – it was really Lena's, my wife's. Me . . . well, I could have let it ride. No push, Lena said, no ambition. All right, so maybe that was the trouble. But I'd allowed myself to be persuaded, and here I was, two months at my new office, and still uncertain where I stood with my new Manager, and he making it clear he was pushing me, to see how far I'd let him go.

Paul Harkness, Manager. One grade above me and roughly my own age, and himself only recently promoted. He was taller than me, a shoulders-back man, abrupt, and sometimes, I thought, ignorant, in the meaning of lacking manners. He had, I'd discovered, been transferred in from Regional Office, where perhaps he'd not have had staff to control. His manner with the staff was formal and terse. Nobody knew whether he was married, or where he was living. He never discussed personal matters, only official ones.

I drove back to the office, but not because it was necessary. My bed-sitter was closer, so that I could have justified going directly there. But already, on this point, Harkness had made his attitude clear. He required me to check in before going home.

So I checked in.

A new office was being built for us, just off Six Ways, but funds had dried up, so we were still in the old Victorian monstrosity with the mullioned windows and the ivy, and the single-storey extension out at the back. I had one of the front rooms with the bay window, a huge room for a single Inspector, but with plenty of space for use in times of pressure, I'd been told, when casual staff would be brought in under my supervision. At this time it was just an echoing space, with my desk in the window recess. It was, however, right next door to the kitchen, so I could always brew myself a cup of tea when a lunch break had been absorbed by a visit.

Harkness had the matching room the other side of what had been the hall, but his room had pictures and a carpet, and a glass-fronted bookcase, in which he kept all his codes and regulations and enactments. All firmly shut away to imply that he had no need to refer to them, their stores of knowledge being locked away in his head.

Every now and then I tried it out on him, going in to

12

discuss a case after memorizing the code reference numbers. These I'd rattle off at him, while he nodded and nodded, making surreptitious notes on his blotting pad, then I'd leave and shut the door behind me, and wait. And hear the glass doors slam back as he hunted frantically to discover what the hell I'd been talking about.

In my job, you needed your bit of fun.

On my desk was a note from him. "Please call in and see me. P.H."

It was ten to five. Hell to it. Ten to five on Thursday. That meant he was going to talk about my case load and my clearance percentage. Double hell. My phone rang.

"Saw you come in, Ken. Have you got a minute?"

Ken! He insisted on using christian names to the executive staff, but nobody had the nerve to stare into those grey, cold eyes and call him Paul.

"I'll be right in," I said.

I mean, it wasn't as though I had a home to return to, just a bed-sitter. Lena was still living in our semi in Acocks Green, and had no intention of budging until we had somewhere of our own in this new district. Somewhere "decent".

"Right in," I said, and banged my brief case down on the desk.

What I'd wanted to do was go through into the back extension, where the benefit sections operated, and catch them before they locked up the cabinets. I had an urgent desire to see whether we had any information on the death of Philip Lorimer, by suicide, at nine-something on an evening in January. Now Harkness was going to make me late.

And Lorimer had shot himself! For heaven's sake, pistols aren't generally available to Managing Directors, unless they were becoming standard issue for dealing with union convenors. I had an aching necessity to

find out more facts, and Paul Harkness had to inter-
vene.

I walked heavily across the parquet hall and opened
his door.

Chapter Two

Mrs Zalusky had a tall, narrow house to the west of the town, not so very far from Virginia Trent's, but whereas the Trent place was new, and regimented with the rest of the avenue, Mrs Zalusky's was in a row of elderly houses that seemed to have been tossed up haphazardly at the whim of the builders. The front garden was deep and the rear garden long, but the plot was narrow for the size of the house, which reached up like a piece of white sliced bread on edge. All the same, they'd managed to enclose the entrance door, which was halfway down the side, in a conservatory, which, having been stocked when the house was built, now presented a jungle-like obstacle to visitors.

She was my landlady, or whatever is the title for a woman who lets you have a bed-sitter on the third floor. I'd expected digs. After a month or so of my new transfer, during which I'd been on day lodging allowance and therefore had been able to afford a cheap room in a cheap hotel, I'd craved a homelier atmosphere. One of the women clerks at the office had heard that Mrs Zalusky was thinking of taking lodgers, so I'd called in there one evening on the way back from an official visit. She had changed her mind about lodgers. She'd never before had anyone living in, but on her husband's retirement from the railways the financial position had forced her into considering it. However, she was not certain that her cooking would suit a lodger. This was absolutely ridiculous, but on that first call I wasn't in a position to argue, and was told she'd prepared a room as a bed-sitter. If I thought I'd like that, she asked doubtfully. I said I'd look at it. I liked. Yes, I definitely liked. You know

15

how it is, you get a feeling. There's the smell of the place, a compound of lavender wax and ragout of something, the atmosphere of acceptance, the look in her eye. And the terms seemed reasonable. I settled on that room in ten seconds.

Mrs Zalusky was the laughing type of woman. I think of her with Polski, her Siamese cat, wrapped around her neck, with her hand outstretched towards me with fingers extended to touch my shoulder every time she laughed, and with her apron caught up in one hand supporting a hot plate under my nose. "There was enough for three," she'd say, and meals had not been part of the bargain. A year there, and I'd have been too fat to force my way through the conservatory. I wondered how her husband did it. He never said. He rarely spoke. I never actually saw him moving. For around 40 years he'd been on a footplate, said Mrs Zalusky, who didn't know steam was past, and that was what he did. Nothing else. So he sat there with his newspaper, waiting for eternity.

She was a jolly, relaxed woman. She needed to be.

I had been there a little over five weeks. That evening I wended my way through the greenery towards the welcoming wink of the large, polished knob on the front door. It was, as always, open. She heard me in the hall and shouted that there was tea made, if I wasn't in a hurry to go up. Which I wasn't. It had become a routine, though I never learned how she managed always to have a fresh pot of tea ready, when my times of return were so indefinite.

We sat there at her kitchen table and she asked me as usual whether I'd had a good day. I said I had, though the interview with the Manager had depressed me. Mr Zalusky commented on the rail strike. I sympathised, not having known we'd got one. Two cups later I thanked her, and got to my feet.

"There's a letter for you on the hall-stand," she said. I hadn't noticed it.

It was Lena's writing on the envelope. I took it in one

hand and mounted the narrow, twisting stairs, uneasy that she'd written at all. We'd arranged that she'd be driving up on the Saturday to plan our move into the bungalow I'd found. Polski trotted up ahead of me. He liked to stretch on my bed and watch me.

The room was small, or appeared so, being twice as long as it was wide. She'd had it re-papered, put in a wash-basin and a small electric cooker, an electric kettle, and an electric fire. My tall window at the opposite end of the room looked out over the slice of front garden.

I threw off my anorak, kicked off my shoes, and had a look in my cupboard to see what I might cook up for an evening meal. And decided to go out. Then I sat down on the end of the bed, one hand provoking Polski into a purr, and read my wife's letter.

Dear Ken,

You will be angry with me, I know, but I'm not coming on Saturday. That last time was enough for me. Did you *have* to drive me round the town, showing it off, when you knew I couldn't stand it? Those factories! The terraces of houses!! That frightful, horrible town square!!! Where's their pride, for God's sake? No, I just can't face it.

I know the place you've found is out in the country, as you put it, but what does that mean if it's just the same old tips and coal mines. It wouldn't be so bad if something was *moving*. Has it occurred to you – have you ever used the slightest bit of imagination in your life – can't you realise how depressing a dead coalfield can be? The whole rotten town's dead. Dying, rather. I don't want to watch it die, and you with it.

I think you will have to transfer back here. Tell them it was a ghastly mistake. Or something.

Think about it.

Love,

Lena.

I threw it on the floor at my feet. Transfer back? Did she know the complete impossibility of such a thing? I could just imagine going to Harkness and telling him that. After what had gone between us that afternoon!

It had been about figures, as I'd guessed. The Civil Service, like any other large operation, has to function on figures. It's the only way to exercise any control at all on what goes on. I can understand it. If I was a manager I'd use them, too, because my own performance would be judged on my ability to use figures, and I too would be a statistic. Factories, banks, shipping empires, small shops – they all run on figures. But it is the claim of every Inspector in our Department that *his* work cannot be assessed by figures.

A case is not a statistic.

As simple as that. One registered file comes to you as a case. It could be simple, cleared in half an hour with a single quick visit. One case cleared. An item in, an item out. But another case could involve three weeks of work, dozens of interviews, hours of paper work, yet it's still one item in and one item out. And because you're working alone, usually miles from supervision, advice, or your treasured codes, only numbers can be the judge of your performance.

Because of this, the job is wrapped around with argument over figures.

"The previous Inspector," Harkness had said, "seemed to clear straightforward cases rather more quickly."

The previous Inspector nearly got himself brained with a spade. I got a chunk of seed cake.

"And it does seem that you spend far too much time on interviews. Nearly two hours on the Sanderson woman, and the statement couldn't have taken more than ten minutes."

All right, so I like a bit of a chat. It's how I operate, and I can't help it. Some people call it public relations. Besides, Mrs Sanderson was surrounded by 17 other women, all trying to persuade her to show me her wounds.

I said: "I had to see the scene of the accident."

His eyes bogged at that. It had been a lavatory bowl. He cleared his throat. "And your routine surveys . . . you know Region expects an average of five a week."

"Routine surveys," I said, "are not supposed to hold up case work."

"But you're not even clearing your cases!" He looked down at his clean blotter, embarrassed apparently by the outburst. "I can understand that you're new to the area, and perhaps feeling your way around. But you're far from new to the job of Inspector, and though you might have operated well enough in a large city . . . we are not a city, Ken. We're a tight little town." He said it possessively, as though it was his, but he'd been a stranger to it himself only a few months before. "And maybe it's a temptation to spend some of your working hours hunting for houses . . ." He sighed. "I had to do it out of working hours."

Too true. I'd scoured the district, depending on where the work took me. But his sour tone reflected his jealousy for my freedom of movement, and his disappointment that my time schedule hadn't shown any uncovered gaps.

"If you want figures, Mr Harkness," I said, "I'll give you figures."

He smiled. With Harkness this was a movement of his jaw, as though he was chewing. I longed to provoke him to a laugh, just to see what emerged. Some hope! Perhaps the full details, previously unrecorded, of the Mrs Sanderson escapade!

"Figures," he declared, "are what I want to see."

And that was the man Lena proposed I should persuade to recommend another transfer. So soon! Regional Office would go wild. And how could I expect his support when I was about to launch a figures campaign that would prove I was the best Inspector he'd ever known?

I laughed. Polski stared at me with suspicion. I said: "Come on, now, your missus won't let you stay up here when I'm out," and reached for my anorak.

He always climbed the stairs happily enough, but

preferred to go down from the safety of a shoulder. So I put on the anorak first, and with Polski making gentle yowling sounds in my ear, went down to tell his missus I was going out.

My car was parked outside in the street. Not even having a drive was a small snag, but it was well out of town and there were no parking restrictions. All the same I'd have preferred to get it off the road. But . . . no drive. Not that anybody would think of lifting the Mini. Even if they were able to start it. That was the trouble with it – starting, which was the reason I was using it. I know that sounds contradictory. What I mean is that it was Lena's Mini. When I'd transferred I'd left her my old Cortina, because, old or not, it was reliable. The Mini, which was even older, needed understanding and sympathy. I think the condenser had gone, otherwise why did the points keep burning and the plugs oiling up? And there was something intermittent in the ignition switch, so that I'd shorted it across from the distributor to the battery, and put in a small toggle switch of my own. The result of all this was that you had to know your way around to start it. That Mini had its own built-in anti-theft devices.

So we'd decided, Lena and I, that it was best to leave her my Cortina as a runaround, and I'd have the Mini. I'd had to search for a new home with a two-car garage. On my salary! A two-car garage! Don't laugh.

It started first touch that evening. It would, because I've just been grumbling about it. I headed for the town centre.

From that direction into town the prospect is reasonably promising. It was just a long and straight road off the flats, the thousands of acres of lush farmland giving way gradually to tentative development, then the rows of Victorian town-houses, and finally the let-down.

I must admit it, the main square is not inspiring. The hills begin the other side of town and the coal-seams lurk only just below the surface. The town centre has never made up its mind what it wants to be, a market square or a grim and impressive reminder of the black treasure so very near. It is not even a square, or any other shape, just a widening where the modern shops have condescended to retreat a few yards from the dark scowl of the town hall block across the way. The public houses are squat and dim, the working men's club is pressed away into a side street. There is no form, no promise, and everywhere is grime.

I parked behind the main store and went to find the restaurant I liked. Check formica covered the tables, not laundered linen. The food was plain and plentiful. It was noisy. I liked it. When I left there, and walked again across the square, I felt it was mine. My square. Perhaps, subconsciously, it reminded me of somewhere.

The sun was going down. I dug out the Mini. It started, but misfiring on one cylinder. Didn't I say? I flicked my toggle switch on and off, and the engine smoothed out. I couldn't help laughing at it. The car gave me a feeling of masterfulness. That was just what I needed, as I intended to go and look at the little place I'd found.

Mrs Trent had mentioned Duxbury Hill, to the north of the town, and I'd known it. The road begins to rise steadily as soon as you leave the town, and the long lines of terraced miners' houses begin. They'd been built when the original shafts were sunk, and when miners had far enough to walk underground to the coal face, thank you very much, without a long trek to the pit-head from home. Lena wouldn't like the district, of course, but me . . . I'd driven her along these dismal rows without a hint of imagination. This had been new territory to me, exciting, new experiences to be explored. I'd chattered away, not realising – but remembering now – how cold and silent she'd been. Lena's parents had never even seen a miner, not in the flesh. I should have guessed.

Then the rise levels out, and Duxbury Hill faces you, steep and curving down into the valley, and it would not be at all surprising if it was impossible in the winter. And

21

down there the winding-heads raise their spindly legs and spinning wheels, the coal tips sprawl, the waste tips rise. Smoke hangs over their heads, and the yards move stealthily with conveyor belts and shunting engines. It was far from dead, as Lena described it.

I drove barely a hundred yards down the hill, then turned right. This was not much more than a track, flanked by spindly hedges and black rock outcrops. Collier's Lane. It flanked the hill, turning away from the pits. A turn left, twisting and steep, another swing right. I turned into a drive and got out.

The houses were built on only one side of the road, above it. You'd never have perched a house on the steep slope below. I stood in the drive of the bungalow, on which I already had a solicitor preparing the contract, and the sun was setting way over to my left, a red glory to mock me.

Some day, when you get a chance, try looking down over a mining valley with the sun setting at your shoulder. Watch the purple shadows moulding the pit-heads into strange, prehistoric and exciting shapes. Catch the flicker of blood-red light sparking in the spokes of the spinning wheels, and the smoke glowing and twisting, grey, red, green – where did the green come from? The light clothed the tips and softened them to glory. I watched, and breathed gently, willing it to stay, but the sun was retreating and slowly it dissolved into darkness, relieved only here and there by yellow lights from sheds and the flicker of headlights as a car rounded a distant bend.

My neighbour – the neighbour who might have been – said at my shoulder: "You've come to watch this. I knew you would." A spark flew from his cigarette.

"It's impressive."

"Yes." He was silent a few moments. They're a tentative lot around there. "When're you moving in?"

I'd liked him when we first met. He'd worked down there, all his working life, retiring as an under-manager.

22

"I don't know that I shall," I told him. "The missus isn't keen."

"Might not suit everybody."

"Is it always like this?" I asked. "In the evening, I mean."

"Never the same twice."

"I reckon not." I'd have liked to see a year of successive evenings. "A bit rough in the winter, I bet."

"Can be. We live through it, though."

"Duxbury Hill," I said. "It'd be closed by one inch of snow."

"You don't wanna believe that."

"Last winter was bad, they tell me."

"If that's what you're worrying about . . ."

It was, but not in the way he meant. "January, for instance – I hear the hill was closed."

"Never been closed," he declared. "You don't think. Listen – they dig the coal out, down there, and they deliver it to the rail-head. Wagons. Every day. You don't think they'd stop for a bit of snow! Not on your life, mate. If any road's clear, in the worst blizzard you could imagine, that's Duxbury Hill."

"Ah!" I said. "Useful to know. Generally known, is it?"

"Of course." He laughed. "It's only you who didn't know. And now *you* do."

Yes, I did, and I was wondering why Leonard Trent would have made a diversion to avoid Duxbury Hill, with that knowledge to work from.

I said goodnight. He said he hoped my wife would change her mind. Then I drove the way Leonard Trent *should* have driven, on the night of his death, to reach the factory of Crayshaw Brothers.

I circled the Six Ways junction, as I'd have expected him to do, and came to the factory from the west. It stretched for about a quarter of a mile on the left side of the road, facing across to a pressing mill and a car park that belonged to Crayshaw's. I'd seen the place, driving past once before. Now I parked the car on the westerly end of the factory and got out. There was not much to see, as it was now completely dark, but the orange streetlights shone on an empty, quiet and straight street, and I could see all the way down to the canal bridge in the distance.

This end of the factory was dark. The building beyond the iron railings was squat, and seemed new. I saw a sign, and approached it, just able to read: "Crayshaw Brothers Ltd – Administration." There was a gate, now locked, to a small car park inside. The top brass were not expected to walk across the road. Beside the gate was a smaller one, opening on a path leading to the entrance of the office block. It, too, was locked.

Down towards the main gate was a stretch of further dark shapes, with the saw-tooth roofing just visible against the sky. Lights shone dimly from a few windows, but there was no sound of machines or activity. Leaving my car where it was, I walked the length of this building, which was set back a few yards behind the railings, and came to the main gate.

This – these, rather, two huge and broad gates – were wide open. A sign warned: No Entrance For Private Vehicles – Stop At Gatehouse.

There was light in the gatehouse, its doors open. It was empty. Beyond it, extending down towards the canal bridge, was another long stretch of factory building, but in this there were lights and the hum of machinery. A loading bay was open, with lights on somewhere in the depths, and an articulated lorry was parked against it. I stood just inside the gates. At this end, the building suddenly rose starkly to a height of five storeys. But there, all was dark.

As I stood there idly, a man in uniform appeared from behind the wagon and walked towards me.

He was a strutter, head thrown back and chest out. Fancied himself. His uniform was intended to mark him as a gatekeeper, not to be smart. He resented its floppy informality, twitching his shoulders and stiffening his back to give the material a military drape.

"And what might you be doing?" he demanded.

I might have been planting a bomb while he was hiding behind that wagon. I didn't say so.

"I'm from the Social Security office."

"And the rest." He eyed me up and down and sideways. "At this time?"

"I wanted an impression of how it must've been."

"What must've been?"

"The accident to Leonard Trent."

"Took you long enough to get here. That was January."

"And am I lucky enough to be talking to the guard who was on duty that evening?" I asked.

He marched into his guard hut and shut the door behind him. I didn't think it was simple ignorance, because at once he became another man. In the door was an opening, with a small shelf below it. There you placed your credentials. He was home and safe, peering out at me from his control centre.

"Now sir," he said. "Let's see your authority."

So I did have to produce my warrant that day, after all. He looked at it, nodded, handed it back to me, and said, "You'd better come inside," then opened his door again.

At last we were on speaking terms.

"I take it you *were* on duty that night," I said chattily.

"As ever was."

"I understand the road was bad past here." I used that as a lead-in.

"A proper freak, that was. Never known it before. Never. It rained and it froze. Ever hear the like?"

I nodded. It can happen, the temperature up in the clouds being higher than the ground temperature.

"Sheet ice," he said. "Could hardly stand on it. You should've seen Mr Trotter, trying to run on it."

Trotter was a new name to me. "Who's Mr Trotter?"

"He was here with me when it happened. The crash. We both heard it. My eyes just automatically went to the clock."

There was a row of windows along the side of the hut, overlooking the street, above them a round, brass clock face. As I watched, the hand jumped to the next minute, 9.17.

"Around this time, wasn't it?" I asked.

"Nine twenty-three," he said, nodding. "Ask Mr Trotter, if you don't believe me."

"Oh, I do! I do. But who *is* Mr Trotter?"

"He's the Production Control Manager." He breathed the words as though the title constricted his chest. "The brains around here, and don't let anybody tell you different. David Trotter's been here as long as I have, and what he don't know . . . he *controls* this factory, and don't you forget it."

I nodded, giving the impression of someone anxiously committing it to memory.

"All the top brass seems to have been staying late," I commented. "The Managing Director – Mr Lorimer – he was here, now Mr Trotter, and Leonard Trent on his way."

"Or been."

I stared at him. The peaked cap he wore was low over his eyes, and the light was no more than one low-power bulb. It was impossible to read his eyes. He wiped his knuckles across his mouth as though regretting the words. "You like a cuppa?" he asked, hoping to wash them away.

I said I would. He had an ancient electric ring on a box in the corner of the gatehouse, probably serving as central heating, too, in the winter. The kettle on it was whispering steam. He added two spoons of tea to a thick deposit of old leaves already clogging the bottom of a brown teapot, and poured in water. Two mugs already waited on his bench surface.

"Is he here now?"

"Who?" he said. He was spooning condensed milk from a tin.

"Mr Trotter."

"Not at this time." Utter scorn at my ignorance.

"But he was here that night?"

"That was special, wasn't it!"

"In what way?"

"Rush job on. Could've been the saving . . ." He stopped. "Help yourself to sugar."

I did. It was perhaps the worst tea I'd ever tasted. I smiled at him in appreciation.

"The saving of what?"

"If it's not going to go any further," he said cautiously.

"I can't promise that, if it's relevant to Leonard Trent's death."

"How could it be?" He shook his head. "I'll tell you this, though . . ." He was still shaking his head, the movement apparently preventing him from telling me anything.

Gatekeepers are lonely souls, especially night-shift ones. At the same time they are the recipients of all knowledge. Not a thing goes on in their factories that they don't know. It can't get past the gates without calling in. Rumour has it that Managing Directors, when stuck on a decision, call in for a chat with the gatekeeper. This rumour, I believe, began with the gatekeepers. But they know, and they almost explode with frustration if they can't tell somebody.

I put down the mug. "Never mind, then."

"It's like this." He took off his cap, a gesture of confidence. "We're running on a tight string here, on the edge of bankruptcy. You wouldn't believe!"

I would. I nodded. He meant liquidation.

"For a year now it's been hand to mouth, one day at a time, you know the sort of thing. Mind you, there's the recession, but it ain't just that. We make carburettors here. Machine and press 'em and assemble, like. Buy the castings from a firm in Manchester."

"Which was where Mr Trent had been that day? Doing his buying job?"

"You're on the ball. Right. We couldn't afford any delays in delivery of the castings, 'cause the engine assembly plant was pushing for the finished carbs. You getting me?"

"I'm receiving very clearly." I had a thought. "And this assembly plant, who were waiting for the carbs – that's in Manchester, too?"

"Makes yer laugh, don't it! Right opposite the engine factory, that's where they do the die-casting of the carb bodies. Carcases, we call 'em. But they have to come here, 'cause we're the only place that's got the vertical millers and turret lathes and whatnot under one roof."

"Puts you in a happy position, I'd have thought. A monopoly."

"Sort of. Except for Spicer's."

"Oh yes?"

"They can do the die-casting themselves, and all they need to do is get tooled up for the machining. Mind you – big money, that'd be. But the Japs are interested. You get me. Competition coming up. So we're on our toes. Yes sir. That's why Mr Trotter was here that night."

"And the Managing Director?"

"Waiting for the latest order from the engine assembly plant."

Now I was beginning to understand. Leonard Trent had been to the die-casters, to roust them up a bit. While he was there, he'd only got to cross the road to the engine plant in order to obtain their regular order – or however these orders were worked. It was this order that Philip Lorimer, Managing Director, had been waiting for. Then why had he shot himself before he'd seen it? *If* he hadn't seen it.

Now we were back on my home ground. If Trent had been heading towards his Managing Director's office when he'd crashed, then he would have still been involved with his employment, and Mrs Trent would get her Industrial Death Pension. If he'd already seen Philip Lorimer, and was coming away, then she would not. Leonard Trent, at the moment he handed the order to Lorimer and left the site, would no longer be in the sphere of his employment. There was no point in explaining this to the gatekeeper.

"You said earlier," I reminded him, "when I was saying that Mr Trent was on his way to Mr Lorimer's office: 'or been.' What did you mean by that? I thought he was definitely on his way."

"Don't you like your tea?"

"It's fine. What did you mean?"

"Look," he said, grabbing my elbow. "Here." He opened his door and thrust me out into the night. Then he stood back and regarded me. We were standing in the open gateway, the street facing us.

"That's where the car crashed," he told me, pointing to our left. "That third lamp-post from here."

"The one the other side of the street?"

"That's it. You can see the canal bridge just past it. So . . . you say to yourself: he came over that bridge a bit too fast and hit the ice. Sure. Could've been. The car could have spun a few times. The only thing we heard, me an' Mr Trotter, was the crash when he hit the lamp-post."

"I heard it was a telegraph pole."

"Did you? No. A lamp-post. We heard it. I saw the time. We ran out, slippin' and slidin' all over the place, but there was nothing we could do. So I stayed with the car. Mr Trotter ran back and phoned the police from the gatehouse here, then he ran up . . ." He took my elbow and turned me. I was now looking to my right, towards the administrative block. "Up there. The admin block. The MD's got his office there – the corner one. You could see his light on. So Mr Trotter ran up to tell Mr Lorimer about the crash."

"Why didn't he phone him while he was in the gate-house?"

"Tried, didn't he. No reply. Well, there wouldn't be. Not with Mr Lorimer already dead. You know about that. Must do. When Mr Trotter got there, Mr Lorimer was dead in his chair. Shot himself." He shook his head in wonder. "Two dead at the same time. I tell you, there was a right panic on."

"Had you got him out of the car? Mr Trent, I mean?"

"We tried. You always worry about fire, but they say don't touch 'em. Mind you, I knew. Had my course in first aid, I have. Mr Trent was dead, no getting round that. But we tried to get him out, only it was a right tangle inside there. We got the door open, but his jacket was caught. We got him outa that – tore it, we did. But couldn't shift him. And as soon as it was certain he was dead, Mr Trotter was shoutin' 'Where's his brief-case? Where's the brief-case?' And trying to get the door open the other side."

He poked me in the shoulder. "Here – don't you tell him I said that. It's instinct, see. First thing he thought about was that order, and losing things in a fire. Not that there was going to be one, mind you."

He paused. I managed to say: "And where *was* the brief-case?"

"Turned up later, behind the seat. But he didn't spot it, and I said I'd stay with Mr Trent, and Mr Trotter went dashin' off."

"Slipping off," I corrected, for the sake of an accurate image.

"What the hell's that got to do with anything?"

"Just getting the picture. So, as I see it, Mr Trent had obviously been driving towards the admin block up there." Forget, for the moment, I told myself, the strange fact that he'd been *coming in* from the east. "Why did you suggest he might already have *been* there?"

"Mr Trotter said he heard a car going past here, just before the crash. Could've been Mr Trent."

Heading east, that would have been. "But you didn't?"

"I'd surely have heard – seen the headlights, perhaps."

"But you didn't?"

"I was mashin' tea."

"Then, if Mr Trotter's right, Mr Trent could have parked up there by the admin block, gone in to see his MD, then left and driven past here, and spun on the ice?"

"But I didn't see him come past. Or hear."

"I see. But the car was moving fast, so I believe?"

"Must've been."

"To get to any speed – and it can't be more than 200 yards from the admin block – he'd have had to accelerate like mad."

"He drove a TR7."

"But you'd have *heard* a TR7 – the sports exhaust, accelerating hard."

"I told yer, I didn't hear it."

There was something strange in the dead tone of his voice when he kept repeating it. He hadn't seen it. Hadn't heard it. And Leonard Trent had either been coming from the east, or heading towards the east, when his home was west from there.

"And anyway," he said, still in that strange, flat voice, "if he was comin' from the admin block – why was he in such a hurry?"

Was it offered in confirmation of his observation, or was something else intended?

"We don't know why, do we?"

"And never shall," he decided.

We stood there, two silent men in that night-deserted street, and it might have been January again, the chill seemed to strike me. I gave it two minutes. Then I thanked him and said I'd be round for a written statement the next evening. I began to walk towards my parked car. A minute later he ran out into the street behind me.

"You haven't finished your tea!" he shouted.

I pretended not to hear him.

For several minutes I sat behind the wheel of Lena's Mini, staring down the straight, orange-slicked street, at the lamp-post where Leonard Trent had died. Even in a TR7 he'd have had to push it hard, and on an icy surface, to reach self-destruction speed in that distance. What had been driving him to such speed? Panic? I wondered whether he could have walked in on his MD and found him dead. That *could* have produced panic. But why should Lorimer, waiting late for the order, have shot himself before Trent arrived? The whole thing was a contradiction.

I started the car, did a U-turn, and went home to Mrs Zalusky.

Chapter Three

Sitting on the end of my bed, I tried to write a letter to Lena. There was an easy chair, but it was too easy and I'd probably fall asleep. Polski wasn't there to give advice, and the letter went badly. I didn't know whether to be aggrieved and forceful, or calm and reasonable. It came out a mess, so I tore it up, and decided to drive down and see her on Saturday. After all, it was Friday tomorrow. She'd get me as soon as she'd get the letter.

I glanced at my watch. It was already Friday, two minutes into it.

Friday, the day I met Kaye, the day I became aware that I could be involved with a murder.

In the morning, the first job at the office was to provide Harkness with figures, in and out. The "in" ones I couldn't really control, but the "out" ones . . ., I sent two files, which had addresses on the outer edges of my district, to the offices the other side of the boundary, minuted simply:

Is this your area, please?
K. Beacham.
Inspector.

My newness to the district would be the justification. They would come back:

No. This is yours.
    Scribble. Scribble.
        Inspector.

Two out. Two in again.

I sent another file to Regional Office (Benefits), minuted:

> I propose doing so-and-so, do you agree, please?
> K. Beacham.
> Inspector.

They would naturally agree; it was the correct procedure.
I hated doing this sort of thing. It implied a lack of
confidence. But it was one out, and one in again when
it was returned.

I considered the next file very carefully. I'd had to go out
and obtain completion of an application form for Industrial
Death Benefit. Easy enough on the face of it. But Mrs Torini
was Italian and spoke no English. Her husband had been an
Italian, killed on a Norwegian oil-rig in Norwegian waters.
A nice one for somebody to work out, somewhere. All I
had to do was get the form completed – but it was printed
in Italian. I'd visited the woman. She was living with her
married daughter, but had been alone with a huge pot of
simmering spaghetti when I arrived. One mention of the
husband's name dissolved her into arm-waving wails and
tears, and I was helpless. I was rescued by the daughter,
dashing home for lunch, who'd taken charge of her mother
so effectively that both were in tears inside two minutes.
The daughter spoke English, but poorly through her tears.
I'd left. The job would now therefore be reasonably simple
– a visit in the evening when the daughter was home, and
all was calm. And truth to tell, I'd enjoy that. The daughter
was a classic Italian beauty.

Heavy-hearted, I sent off the file, requesting a translation
of the Italian form. One out, and one in when it came back.
But I'd have no excuse, then, for a visit when the daughter
was home. I'd ask the questions in Italian, knowing their
meaning. We'd get on fine, me and the mother. Well . . .
maybe I *would* need the daughter. Somewhere I'd have to
mention the husband's name. Somewhere there was sure to
be tears. I sent off the file, relieved at this rationalisation.

Four out in an hour. Good going. I went out with the intention of making a quick job of an FAM fraud case that'd come in that morning.

A Mrs Zuleika Quimby, living in a neighbouring district, had complained that her husband had left her, with four children, but taking her Family Allowances book with him. She'd had one postcard from him, from an address in my area. This matter was urgent, to be dealt with before he cashed too many orders.

The address given was 42 Piper's Lane, which was only a hundred yards from the office. This turned out to be derelict. Not surprising, otherwise he wouldn't have committed it to writing. But he must have *seen* it to be derelict, so probably was living somewhere close, being a stranger to the district. I walked there, giving the district a good look-over.

It had been a street of bay-front terraces, with 6ft of frontage to each and an alleyway between each fourth. The whole row was due for demolition. A hundred yards farther down, on the other side, was a grimy and uninspiring pub, the "Horseshoe". The sign indicated the luck running out. I went in. They'd just opened. I ordered a shandy, there was a long day ahead.

I leaned over the counter. "Lancelot Quimby," I said. "Sure to come in here. New to the district. You know him?"

"You police?"

"A friend."

He leered.

"He's probably Jamaican," I suggested. "With that name."

"A big bugger?" he asked.

If I was out of luck, yes. "Probably."

"Scar over one eye?"

"Wouldn't be surprised."

"The top of the street," he said. "Second house. He's on the third floor."

"You're very accurate."

"Lucy's been there."

"Lucy?"

"Our local. And look, put him away, will you? I don't like trouble in here."

"I'll do my best."

I went outside, wondering how I could stall-off this one. Not getting any inspiration, I went to look at the second house from the end.

It was just about as derelict as the rest of the street, except that the holes in the windows had been boarded across. I mounted the three steps into the hall. The patterned tiles were intact, the door unlocked, and nobody about.

"Anybody here?" I shouted.

Not a sound. The uncarpeted stairs faced me. Third floor, he'd said. Swinging my briefcase in one hand, wondering what protection it might afford, I mounted steadily into a smell of decay and stale food that gradually became stronger.

There were three doors on the third floor, two of them open onto empty rooms. I thumped on the third.

"Wha' you want?" a voice bellowed.

"Mr Quimby? Can I have a word?"

"'Tain't locked."

I went in. It was a small room, the double bed just about filling it. A large, brown man with a stubble of beard was sitting up in the bed, apparently naked but with a blanket pulled up to his stomach, watching a colour television set, which he'd rigged on a shelf fastened to the wall facing him. He was watching the West Indies playing England at cricket, thumping the bed with his fist in great excitement. Beside him, a large shape lifted a tent in the bedclothes. All I could see was black, curly hair.

I told him I was a Social Security Inspector, and I believed he had his wife's FAM book.

"You wanna watch this, or not?" he demanded.

I said not.

"That's 'cause you're losing."

36

"Am I?"

"You don't *know*? Man!"

"Do you have Zuleika Quimby's Family Allowances book?"

"Reckon I might."

"Then I must ask you to give it to me."

"It's in the top drawer."

He indicated a narrow chest of drawers, behind the door. Strictly speaking, I had no right to ferret around in his drawer. He should have handed the book to me, I should have obtained a written statement if there were any orders cashed, then I should give him a formal warning of a committed offence.

"Will you get it for me?"

"Ya want me to get outa here?"

The thought of 6ft something of naked and belligerent West Indian rising from that bed was appalling. I drew open the drawer and helped myself.

He had eight Family Allowances books in there. Lucy Quimby, Angela Quimby, Amanda Quimby, Sally Quimby . . . I stared at them and read out the names aloud. When I got to Poppeia Quimby the shape beside him stirred and her brown eyes pinned me.

"Heh, that's mine," she said.

Breathing deeply, I signed official receipts for seven of the books. I told him I was confiscating them. I issued a warning and said I would be reporting the matter.

"Heh, man!" he said, spreading his palms. "Ya want me to starve?"

When I got out on the landing he was already whooping his delight again, and thumping the bed. Or Poppeia. Then I walked rapidly back to the office.

I raised another six files in the wives' names and sent them to Registry for return to me. That'd give me six new files in. Wrong procedure, but I'd probably get away with it. I typed out a minute, leaving names blank, ran off six copies on the Xerox, filled in each lady's name, then charged all seven, including Zuleika, for each wife to be interviewed and statements obtained as to the last date of encashment, and marriage details. Seven files cleared that morning, plus the four earlier. That was eleven, and all before lunch.

The seven would come back to me. I'd then be in a position formally to charge Lancelot Quimby with fraud. Also, with the police in on it, probably with bigamy. Or septamy. But of course, he wouldn't be there, was probably up and gone before I'd completed the files. With Poppeia's FAM book, no doubt.

But Harkness had wanted figures.

Hoping to get somewhere before lunch, I went out to do some work on the one that really counted.

At 11.30 the factory was humming. The upper half, the building next to the admin block, I discovered made petrol and water pumps, presumably destined for the same assembly plant as the carburettors were. Wagons were manoeuvring to the loading bays, and fork-lift trucks prowled the yards. A new man – new to me – was on the gate, and directed me to the Production Control Offices.

These comprised the lower floor of the three-storey pile at the western end of the carb factory. Above were the drawing office and planning office, and the engineering executives. The man I wanted to see was David Trotter, and after knocking on a few doors and asking I discovered he was in conference with his new Managing Director. So I filled in by having a word with the Production Controller, Trotter's second-in-command, who was just as firmly in touch with what went on as his boss, but had the less harrowing position of not being on the Administrative Staff. This he explained to me.

His name was Terence Stone, a slim, dapper man with a forceful face and a jaw like a steel trap, to match the precision of his brain. He'd come up from the shop floor, as I understood had David Trotter, having operated just about every machine there, and had in practice taken a drop in pay to get into the office as a Job Chaser. From there, he'd worked his way up to Production Controller. It was as far as he expected to go. As he explained.

"The management usually come in with degrees to the plum jobs, and have to learn it all from scratch. They're all on yearly contracts, so it keeps 'em on their toes. Right up to and including the Managing Director. One slip-up and they're out. It's rough. Now me – I'm just on the Executive Staff. No company car, no entertainment expenses. But I should worry! If this place closes, I get redundancy pay, and at my age . . ."

He'd have been pushing 60. We were chatting at his desk, which was at the end of the room containing the rest of the Production Control staff. This was the way I got most of my work done, the informal approach, during which I'd be likely to hear the important details. But I thought he spoke with a touch of bravado, perhaps with controlled envy. He, too, would have liked to run a company car, and to hell with the risk. Even a reject from the Admin Staff would stand better future chances than an ex-Production Controller. At his age, though?

"No chance of that, is there?" I asked. "The place closing, I mean."

"Well . . . you never know. There could be new competition, working with new machines . . . D'you know, some of our Fischers have been running day in and day out for 20 years. The operators are called skilled. Copy Fishers, you see. But the main skill is in knowing where to wedge a fag packet to take up the slack."

"I don't believe it!"

"I'll show you," he offered.

He took me through into the machine shop. This was home to him. He lived on the shop floor, intimately involved with everything that went on, and weaved his way with ease around Inspectors, Tool Setters, Shop Stewards, Engineers, Breakdown Men, all of whom cluttered the gangways. He dodged spurts of oil from howling millers, ducked under swinging cranes, and happily continued to chat to me above the almost painful roar of machinery. This chatting consisted of shouting into my left ear while gripping my shoulders with both hands. I saw other pairs of men doing it, strangely like a still dance in the cacophony of a homo disco.

"Fred there," he roared. "See. Under the edge of his milling bed. That's a Dunhill packet. Two thou thicker than a Player's Number Three."

He was wildly pulling my leg, I thought, but indeed there was the gold edge of a cigarette packet.

"So how could we compete with new machinery?" he roared.

"How close is it?" I roared back.

"Trouble? It's been with us for a year. Here, come inside . . ."

His voice was tiring. He opened the door of a glass-sided cubicle, which apparently was a foreman's office. It was empty of foremen. One chair, a bench on which drawings were strewn, and with the door shut, silence. The glass must have been double. For a moment I thought I'd gone deaf.

He was continuing in a normal voice. "Things started to go wrong when the previous MD came. Chap by the name of Philip Lorimer. One of your whiz kids, only he wasn't a kid any more. You know what I mean. The edge was wearing off by the time he came to us. Or so it seemed. Of course, Trotter should've got the job. Everybody said that. Perhaps with Trotter we wouldn't have accepted orders we couldn't meet. And the breakdowns . . . you wouldn't believe."

"Hardly the MD's fault, I'd have thought."

"No. But he cut capital outlay on routine overhauls. Trotter begged him not to – so I heard."

"From Trotter, you mean?"

He smiled. "How'd you guess?"

There was a touch of malice in Stone's voice. He was

not averse to stirring-up trouble. If he spoke like this to a complete stranger, what gossip would he spread to his friends? I decided he was a dangerous man to know. It was not surprising he hadn't made it to the Admin Staff.

"It got to the point – the beginning of the year – when the warning signals cropped up," he went on. "The schedules. You can read a hell of a lot from the order schedules. And I see 'em all."

Orders for completed and assembled carburettors were broken down into work schedules. The orders covered up to nine months ahead, to allow time to vary their own orders for castings and component fittings. The schedules had begun to show a tapering-off in the autumn to come.

"So there we were," he said, "last January, with everything hanging on the order Lennie Trent was bringing back from Manchester. The MD didn't dare go home, and Trotter was here all hours, pushing the production. Nearly had a strike on his hands."

"And the order?" I asked.

"Disastrous. Hadn't you heard? Lorimer shot himself."

"Over an order?"

"What else was there?"

To this man, nothing existed except the factory. If his private life was falling apart, he wouldn't know. If his wife left him, he wouldn't notice for a fortnight.

"There can be other reasons for suicide," I suggested.

He shrugged.

"And that's the second time I've heard he shot himself," I commented. "But no ordinary people own pistols. How in heaven's name . . .?"

"He used the nail gun from the Stores."

"The what?"

He laughed out loud, delighted to have surprised me. "Come on, I'll show you."

"Mr Trotter could be back now."

"Not him. They make a session of it. This new MD's a tough nut."

"Is he?"

I'd rather gathered that the factory was not, after all, sliding into closure, so that since January some improvement must have taken place. A tough-nut MD could well be that improvement.

Stone took me out on to the shop floor again. There was a decreasing whine to the machinery, their motors dropping to a howl and then to a grumble.

"Lunch break," said Stone.

"Yours?"

"Mine's when I can get it." Proud sacrifice was in his voice.

The Stores was against one wall of the factory, a sort of extended cage of barred barriers, with several lockable windows in it, presumably where operators went to ask for new cutters or the like. The door was permanently locked. Stone rattled it, and a man came to open it for him.

"Security," he said. "If you knew how much money is locked away in here it'd take you breath away."

It seemed I was trusted. I couldn't remember what I'd said, but he appeared to have decided I was there to investigate Lorimer's death. I did not disillusion him. All this could have a bearing on Leonard Trent's death. I watched and I listened.

"Open Number Three for me, Charlie," said Stone.

The Storekeeper produced a set of keys and opened one of a row of green, steel cabinets. It was the one containing carpenters' equipment. On one shelf was a wooden box the size of a small suitcase. This, too, was unlocked for me. Stone laid it on the floor.

There were several recesses holding nails of different lengths, strange-looking nails because they had small collars. There was a compartment holding several lengths of cartridges, around .22 gauge, all blanks. There was a gun.

Stone carefully lifted it out. I know nothing about guns, apart from what I've seen people waving on the films and television. This was much like most of those, but appeared longer, and when he handed it to me it was very heavy. If real guns felt like that, I'm surprised anybody ever fired one single-handed.

He flipped open a breech, and said: "The cartridge goes in here, and the nail down the barrel. You put the muzzle . . . here, I'll show you. Charlie, can you find me a bit of wood?"

While Charlie found and brought back a piece of 12 inch, thick packing case, Stone explained.

"Only three people in the factory are authorised to use this, me and two of the assembly men. Say you want to hang shelves on a concrete wall. You put vertical laths up first. But just you try drilling concrete. Now . . . with this, you put the lath against the concrete, the gun muzzle against the lath where you want the nail, and pull the trigger. It'll bang a nail into anything, even a steel joist. It's the speed or something. I don't understand it."

When I was a kid I had a science book. It said if you fired a candle at a plank it'd go right through. Speed, you see. It didn't tell you how to fire a candle, though.

"Okay, Charlie," said Stone. "Hold it against the wall."

The back wall was the outside brick wall of the factory, lime-washed. Charlie held the slat of wood against it, and Stone loaded his gun. He put the muzzle against the wood and pressed the trigger.

The crack the gun made seemed very quiet. I'd expected more. When he removed the gun, which itself had hardly bounced, the nail was hammered home.

"This is what Mr Lorimer used," he said. "In the morning we found the Stores door broken open and this cabinet broken open, and that box broken open."

"Surely the MD would have keys?"

Charlie spoke up. "I've got keys, and my deputy's got keys. Nobody else. It's a responsible job, this."

"He used a two-inch nail," said Stone. "In the temple."

"I'm keeping you from your lunch," I murmured.

"It's all right."

"Mr Trotter could be back. Look, I'm grateful for our little talk . . ."

"You're rushing off to *your* lunch! You Civil Servants – never miss out on your breaks."

This day I was going to. I didn't feel well. I nodded to Charlie, gave Stone a smile that was probably a bit sick, and went out for some fresh air. The gatekeeper saluted as I walked past him, but all I was doing was heading for my car for a quiet sit and a quiet think.

It all sounded unreal, and there was no solid sequence of events that I could uncover that made sense. Lorimer was supposed to have hunted out that nail gun and taken it back to his office – and waited for Leonard Trent to bring the fatal order. But why should not Trent simply have phoned in the details, if it was so critical? Maybe he had done that. But in that case, why did Trent still need to drive madly to get there with the physical evidence, the order, in his brief-case?

Unless the driving madly bit had been *away* from the MD's office. In which case, why easterly, when his home was to the west?

In any event, the timing was all wrong. Assuming the MD had been waiting for the actual order from Trent, and that phoning the details had not, for some reason, been practical, then he could not have contemplated suicide until Trent arrived with it. But he'd been dead at his desk when Trotter found him, not more than five minutes or so after Trent's crash. How on earth could Lorimer have done all that breaking and entering, to get the nail gun, with a trek to and from the machine shop, in the time?

I could see only one explanation for it. Trent had arrived at the factory from the west, Duxbury Hill not having been closed off by snow, a good half hour before his own accident. Entering by way of the admin block personnel gate, he'd made his way quietly down to the carburettor shop and acquired the nail gun. *Then* he'd visited the MD, his brother-in-law, not with the intention of handing him any order form, but with the intention of killing him. And then he'd driven away in a panic.

But . . . why east? Simply because his car was pointing that way, and he did not dare afford himself the time to do the U-turn? Certainly it would explain how he came to reach such a speed in such a short distance. It even went some way towards explaining how he'd come to lose control of the car.

Suddenly I hated the case. Murder was not in my line. All I wanted was evidence for or against an Industrial Death Benefit claim from Mrs Trent. All right. Forget my nasty suspicions, and I could simply report that Leonard Trent had died on his way to see his MD with important documents. Mrs Trent would get her pension, and that'd be that.

One file cleared, and nobody would query it.

I drove back towards the office with that intention in mind.

Chapter Four

I usually managed to avoid facing, head on, the question of what the hell I was doing with my life. You drift along, operating to the correct signals and reacting instinctively to the few obstructions. Usually you steer round them. That's how it is for everybody. In the Civil Service you're a tiny component locked inside a chip, which is itself part of the larger component, itself a computer programmed and fed by an indefinite outside body. Every now and then you're taken out and polished, and if you haven't broken down under the pressure, or in some way shorted the system – thereby causing a malfunction – you're replaced in a slightly more important part of the circuit. Until you begin to falter, when you're discarded. There is no alternative to this uncompromising procedure. You exist, and that's it.

But every now and then something happens to disturb the small flow of signals reaching you. A flicker of alternation in the current, perhaps. You blink, and you look around, and realise that outside the solid metal structure surrounding you there's something else going on. Of course, you're always aware of it; you're programmed to observe and note and act accordingly. But what is outside there is life in all its facets, and it's likely, suddenly, to slap you in the face and shout *this is real!*

Reality was a 2 in nail in the temple.

I threw the brief-case on to my desk and went next door into the kitchen. Call it a canteen if you will, but we had no cook, so it was a kitchen. I'd landed right in the middle of the first lunch period. It was bedlam. By the nature of things, the Civil Service was attracting more women than men. As I was working alone, and not supervising one of the sections, I came in contact with them only rarely, and then it was while they were presiding like queen bees at their desks, fighting helplessly against a growing pile of incoming paperwork. Once released from that restriction, they were noisy. Most of the men were older, and went out to lunch, as I did usually. The ladies brought sandwiches, packed into the kitchen, and chatted.

All I wanted was a cup of tea. I had a box of tea bags in the cupboard, a half bag of sugar, a bottle of milk. I fought my way to the stove and checked there was water in the kettle, and turned up the gas beneath it.

"Good man," said Harkness behind my left shoulder. "Just what I've come for."

He'd eat his sandwiches in the protracted silence of his own room. He hadn't come for tea, he'd come for people and noise.

"Brought your mug?" he asked. He waved his own. "Can I borrow a tea bag?"

I showed him the box. "I shan't want it back."

I was shaking the jelly-like deposit in my milk bottle. I was out of luck. We stood and watched the kettle, which was not boiling fast enough for my liking. He smelt gently of a very expensive after-shave.

"It was very crafty," he murmured, "but I'm sending three of the files back to you."

"Oh?"

"The two area queries – I've checked by phone, and they're definitely ours."

"Oh . . . that's good! I'd have hated to lose them."

"And the query to Benefits section at RO, I've authorised your suggested action. You were on the right lines."

I felt him squeeze my shoulder, I hoped in praise. But he could keep his praise. The clever bugger had realised how I'd react to his little lecture the evening before, and had kept his eyes open. I'd given him the opportunity of authorising a procedure which he knew was quite safe. It indicated his knowledge and his confidence, and his signature would be there in the file, confirming it.

"I had an idea I was," I told him.

"You were just checking, though?"

"Exactly."

"Perhaps . . ." He paused. "A slight lapse of confidence, was it?"

"The kettle's boiling."

He held out his mug for me to fill it. Not looking up, he said: "And the Italian one – no need for a translation. That dark young woman over there, in the corner . . ." He didn't glance that way. ". . . she's Italian. But of course, you wouldn't know. I'm going to ask her to pop in on her way home – time off it'll be. She can get the form completed."

I gauged the level exactly. Not so full that he'd suspect I was rattled, and had miscalculated; full enough that he couldn't carry it far without spilling it down his slacks. I was proud of the steadiness of my hand. It was a deliberate insult, taking the file from me like that.

"So it'll be *one* cleared," he said. "Would you care for some of my milk?"

"I'll owe you."

Then he looked up into my eyes, and actually smiled. With pleasure? I couldn't tell. Malice, perhaps. Surely not approval, in spite of what he said next.

"But the action with the FAM books – very quick and very efficient. I liked it. I really did."

Then with a nod he was gone, and the level in his mug was as steady as a rock.

When I turned, the dark-haired girl was there. Her eyes were dark, too.

"Did he tell you he's asked me to do one of your files, Mr Beacham?"

"He mentioned it."

"I hope you don't mind."

"Lord, no."

She tried a little smile. "I'm a bit nervous, really. It's the first time I've been visiting."

"Good experience for you. You'll do fine." Then I grinned. "As long as she doesn't start crying. She'll probably get you at it, too."

"Perhaps I'd better tell him I'd rather not."

"Not on your life! I was pulling your leg. You'll be all right." I turned to the door. "Ciao!"

She laughed. But my face was straight the moment the door closed behind me. I went into my own office and sat down with my cup of tea, and stared at last year's calendar on the wall.

He was deliberately trying to undermine me. The compliment had been delivered reluctantly, and only because he realised his criticisms had been too blatant. He'd *known* I'd try to fiddle the system. He was challenging me. I hate being condescended to.

But there was one I could slip past him, an Industrial Death Benefit claim I could write up, and on which I could recommend allowance. It wasn't cleared, not by a long way, but Harkness wouldn't know that. An allowance was safe. There'd be no appeal. Half an hour would get it off my list.

Yet I knew I was equating the Trent case with the paltry, childish fiddles I'd committed in order to produce figures for him. Was that all that Virginia Trent was, a figure? Was the death of Leonard Trent no more than a question of whether it fitted a legal slot? Had Philip Lorimer hammered a nail into his skull simply to provide me with a statistic?

I took out the file and stared at it. Inside the brief case were left another four files I'd hoped at least to make a mark on that day. I took them out and locked them away in my cabinet, and went out to ask David Trotter, Production Control Manager, who by now should have finished arguing with his MD, a few facts about that fatal order.

Feeling better all round at the decision, I found time to

49

stop for a chips-and-egg at the local caff, before driving to the factory.

Trotter had an office just along the corridor from the Production Control main office that I'd already visited. He was not pleased to see me. He stared at me above a desk covered with technical drawings, and glared.

"Can't I get *any* peace?"

He was well into his forties, a bull of a man, forceful and forthright, and carrying with him all the drive that had hauled him up from the shop floor to a reasonably high position in the Admin Staff. Not quite as high as he'd like, perhaps. The post of Managing Director was in his eyes – just out of grasp, perhaps, but within his sights. Yet he also carried with him the rough harshness of the shop floor, and belligerence was in the deep-set eyes, determination in his low, wide brow, and resentment in the set of his mouth. To Trotter, he would always be a failure. Always there would be a target just a little way out of reach.

But he, of all people – workmen, office workers, staff – he knew most of what went on in this factory, how it went, why it went. I could have told him he was destined to remain where he was – he was too good at it. And he knew it. You could see that awareness in his eyes, the despair against which he was fighting. He had his head down, working his head off to make a good impression, and yet knowing he was proving no more than that he was indispensable in his present position. Besides, he was not a University man.

"I'm from the—"

"I know you are. Stone told me you'd seen him."

"Some questions . . . A few minutes."

"Stone told you all there is." He returned his attention to the desk. Apparently our meeting was over.

"If it's inconvenient," I said, "I could call and see you at home. This evening, say."

"This evening I'll probably be here." Without looking up.

"Then I'll see you here."

"Now what," he demanded, with two hands spread on his drawings and his jaw jutting, "would I be doing here, if it's not working?"

"I thought the pressure was over," I told him.

"It's never over." For him, it wasn't.

"I mean, even on that night in January . . . and you know which one I mean . . . even then you had time for a chat for a few minutes with the man at the gate."

"Am I expected to explain my movements to you?"

I slid into a seat. It swivelled, but I held it steady. I was prepared to argue all afternoon, if that was what he wanted.

"By no means," I protested. "You can tell me to go to hell, if you like, but then I'll only have the gatekeeper's word to go on, and I could go away with exactly the wrong impression."

I'd thought his brows were low already. He managed to project them even more. "What impression?"

"Simply that Leonard Trent came over that canal bridge, from the east, and crashed before he passed the main gate."

Now I could relax. I had him involved. He came round from behind his desk and stood looking down at me with his hands on his hips.

"Has that fool been shooting off his mouth?"

"You make it sound as though he was supposed to be keeping secrets."

"He's been here since doomsday. Thinks he owns the place. When I get the time, I'll have him sacked."

Big talk, that, management talk. I shrugged. "He sounded bright enough to me. He's still got all his marbles. And he's sure Trent hadn't driven past the gate."

"Of course he had."

"You're certain?"

He stared at me, then slapped his forehead with a palm.

"You actually saw it going past?" I asked.

51

"Not see. Not actually see, like in look out of the window and *see*."

"Well then!"

"But I got an impression. The change of light in the corner of my eye. You know. Hell, why am I wasting time arguing with you?"

"Are we arguing?"

"You come here – you people – and think nobody's got anything better to do . . ."

"Did you hear it?"

"How could I . . .?"

"A sports car, moving fast. Accelerating."

"Listen, friend." He turned, and slapped the table all over until he located a cigarette pack under his papers. He turned back, waving it. "You just want to spend all day on that shop floor, half the night too . . . and I can tell you, you wouldn't . . . you wouldn't . . ." His mouth wouldn't stay still long enough for him to insert the cigarette. "Wouldn't be able to hear anything. And if you did, you'd think it was the damned factory din again."

The cigarette got lit. I could understand his impatience with me; I was absorbing his precious time. But there was something else. He was evasive.

"I'm going to see him this evening," I said. "Your gatekeeper. I'll be getting a statement that as far as he's concerned Mr Trent did not drive past the gate. He was coming in from the east, and he didn't reach his MD."

"You want a statement from me . . .?"

"I shall."

". . . you can have it. I *know* he reached Mr Lorimer."

"Perhaps we could get some times tied down."

"You're not bloody-well listening."

"I am. I said . . ."

"I told you I *know*."

But his knowing was all impressions. It would not make a useful statement. My thoughts were now that I could just about close down my file, as I'd intended, with a clear conscience. All I needed was some timing that would completely exclude Leonard Trent from Lorimer's death. Then I could walk away from it.

"How long," I asked, "d'you think you were with the gatekeeper?"

"Changing the subject?" he tossed at me.

"The crash was at 9.23. We know that."

"Oh . . ." He waved an arm. "I was there from around nine."

"Twenty minutes? You could spare 20 minutes from the hustle and noise of your factory floor?"

His smile was twisted, teeth showing at one edge only, the cigarette cocking in the other. "Good point. But *that* night . . . don't go by what he told you at the gatehouse . . . that night I was there for the same reason as Lorimer – that damned order Trent was bringing."

"It mattered that much?"

"To Lorimer, it did. Hell – for a year, since he'd been here, things'd been going down the Swannee. We needed an uplift, just one hint from the new orders. You know. Or don't you? You people in the Civil Service, nice and secure, you can't imagine the pressure. Lorimer knew if that order didn't show a lift, he was finished."

"And you were anxious, too?"

Again that grin, this time mocking. Self-mocking. "If he was out, I reckoned I'd be in."

"But you're not. He killed himself, and they brought in a new man."

"You trying to say something?"

"I'm suggesting you're too valuable where you are."

"Stone could have my job."

"But could he do it?"

"Like hell! What are we talking about? You're too bloody tricky for me!"

"Sorry. I was just getting the picture. Both of you waiting for Trent . . ."

"I was in Lorimer's office till nine. Talking it through.

Wondering how we could push up profits even if . . . it was if that and if the other. All a waste of time until Trent came. But he said Trent had promised, if he couldn't get through – there was bad weather."

"I've heard."

"If he couldn't get through, he'd phone by nine. He hadn't phoned by nine, so I couldn't stick it any more. Lorimer was like a taut spring. Driving me crazy. So at nine I walked down to have a word with Geoff, on the gate."

It sounded fantastic that Lorimer, in that 20 minutes, would have gone out to get the nail gun and then killed himself, with Trent clearly on his way.

"But surely . . ." I said. And stopped.

He'd been edging round his desk, back to his drawings. My hesitation caught his attention, and he looked up. "Surely what?"

"You'd be expecting him to come by way of Duxbury Hill and Six Ways."

"Would I?"

"In that case, he'd come in from the west. That'd get him to Lorimer's office without having to pass the gatehouse. You'd expect that. So – by going down there and talking to Geoff – you wouldn't know whether Trent had come or not." I raised my eyebrows. "And you so anxious?"

"I don't know what you're getting at!"

"Just that you seem to have expected him to come from the east, over the bridge, past the gatehouse. You wouldn't miss him then, you'd see him drive past. Wouldn't that explain your impression, when something *did* go past? You had the impression of a car, but going the wrong way, the wrong way from your expectation. So it didn't really register."

He laughed, a bitten-off bark of sarcastic laughter. "Is that what I'm wasting time listening to? My God, what a life you must lead, you lot! You have to make up these fantasies, just to kill the boredom."

"But you *did* expect him to come in from the east. After

54

the crash, you were hunting for Trent's brief-case, as though you reckoned he was just arriving."

He lost his temper. "Write it down then. A statement. Do you have to warn me, like the police?"

"In different circumstances, yes. The same wording, as a matter of fact."

"Then do it."

"We're sliding away from the point."

"Which is?"

"Why you expected Trent to arrive from the east."

"What does it matter! How can it possibly matter! We *know* he didn't. He came in from Six Ways and parked outside the admin block and went in to see Lorimer."

"But, you see, all I'm interested in is the legal aspect of an industrial accident. No personalities. I can't prove which way Trent was driving when he had his crash."

"But I *know* he must've been driving away from Lorimer's office. I know it now, even if I didn't think so at the time. And I can prove it."

"Can you? That's interesting."

He stared at me stonily for a moment. Then he got up and went to a cabinet at the side of his office. He slid open a drawer and produced a thick folder. Impatiently, he swept aside his papers and banged down the folder.

"These are order forms," he said. "You didn't ask – I've been waiting for you to ask – what happened to the orders Trent was bringing. Well . . ." He flipped through about half an inch of flimsies. "Well, here they are."

This order I'd been hearing about was not a simple sheet of paper. There were 17 in the set, all around 12 in × 14 in. Each sheet was for a separate design of carburettor. The order forms had columns for the months of delivery, this set running from January to October, with three columns for each month headed: "Previous Order", "Arrears", "Current Order".

"If we could only cut down the arrears," he said. "They spread the arrears forward, which makes it more difficult to maintain the new calls, and see here . . ." He glanced at me. "This is confidential information, you know."

"I operate under the Official Secrets Act." It meant nothing in this context. It referred to Official secrets – not his. But he nodded.

"All right. But you can see – January 8,297, February 6,262, March 4, 729 . . . and October 1,207. Now *that's* what was worrying Lorimer."

"But you were going to tell me . . ."

"When Trent crashed, me and Geoff ran out. The thing was to get him out of it. But we couldn't. His jacket was caught on something. I reached in and got it off his shoulders, but the steering wheel . . . He was dead. Geoff had a look, and he was dead. So I ran back. Ran! Slipped and slid back to the gatehouse and called the police, then tried to phone Lorimer on his extension. Nothing. So I had to run up there. You've seen?"

"Yes." I'd seen that he'd have had to run the length of the pumps factory.

"And there he was – spread out over his desk with the nail gun by his hand and his head sideways. I could *see* that bloody nail. Christ! I leaned over him. You never know. Not much blood, d'you see. But he *had* to be dead. So I backed off – God knows what I was going to do – and there was Peterson behind me in the doorway."

"Peterson?"

"The night foreman. Looking for me, he told me later, 'cause a machine had broken down. So we both just stood there, like fools, but I heard the police car going past . . ." He took a breath. The memory still affected him. "And there they were, under Lorimer's arm, this same set of order forms, folded into four."

"Folded? You mean he hadn't even *looked* at them?"

"How the hell do I know what he'd done?" he shouted. "Don't talk so stupid! The fact was that they were there. Peterson saw them too. Under Lorimer's arm."

I pulled at my lower lip. Something was niggling at me,

but I couldn't tie it down. "These same orders?" I asked, my brain still not up with it.

Not saying anything, he turned up the edge of the last order sheet of the batch. There was a small brown stain on it.

"I told you – there wasn't much blood," he said.

So now I had evidence that Trent *had* reached Lorimer's office, and left again. He had left his sphere of employment, and Mrs Trent was out of luck.

But I still had difficulty believing that Lorimer would have fetched the nail gun, intending to take his own life, yet had waited for Trent with hope . . . but had not waited until he arrived. If that was what it meant. Surely, if suicide had become necessary it would not have become so until after Trent came. *Then* he would have gone for the nail gun, and probably not even have returned to his office with it.

I raised my head. Trotter was strangely quiet, sitting now behind his desk, head lowered, eyes just visible beneath his heavy brows.

"You realise what you're saying?" I asked quietly.

"If you're asking me if I think it was suicide, the answer's no."

"Did you say that to the police?"

"My ideas don't matter. They knew what they were doing."

Hmm! I nodded. "So you think Trent arrived here before nine, got hold of the nail gun . . ."

"Look," he said, palms firmly on the desk surface. "Look – does this matter? To you. To this damn claim you've got."

"Maybe. I haven't thought it through." It was definitely not part of Trent's duties to kill his MD – his brother-in-law! "But there's something . . ., Trent blinding off into the night . . . why would he drive straight past the gatehouse? He could be spotted, and he wouldn't have wanted that."

"Panic?"

57

"Panic to get *clear* away. Not to be seen."

"If you say so. Look – I've got work to do."

"Why should he race away, in the opposite direction to his home?"

He flapped his drawings. "Do you mind?"

"Why go east?" I asked.

"Do you *mind*!"

I got to my feet and took up my brief case. I turned back. "Because . . . if you know anything . . ."

"For God's sake!"

"You do, don't you?"

"Look – it's not my business. You go and ask Kaye."

"I don't know a Kaye."

"My sister, damn it! She's over the paper shop in the Macklin Shopping Centre."

"That's east of here."

"So it is."

I nodded. "That's Kaye Trotter? She's not married?"

"More's the pity," he said sourly. "Me neither, if you want to know."

Geoff the night gatekeeper, wouldn't be on until later, but all the same I called in there. This one was a big, slobby chap with an air of vagueness, but he did know that Peterson was still the night foreman. Probably I wouldn't need to speak to Peterson about what he'd seen when he walked in on Trotter and his dead MD, but it was useful to know where to find him.

I threw my brief case in the back of the Mini, and drove out east to Macklin.

It had been a village in its own right at one time, but now there was no break between village and town, and Macklin was merely a suburb. I knew it already. It was there that I'd interviewed Mrs Sanderson at Morton's, the washing-machine firm. It was from one of Morton's toilet seats she'd been blown. Parking my car in the shopping centre, I could see the glinting glass roof of the factory, and winced. It had been a traumatic experience. For me, I mean.

The shopping centre wasn't much, just a block of shops around an open square, which was parking area, but if you looked carefully you could discover all the necessities of life, several of the premises doubling up to make ends meet. The butcher was selling potted plants, the greengrocer had a sideline in sliced bread, the post office was renting video tapes, and the newsagent was trying-out a display of factory-reject pullovers. It was at the newsagent's that I asked a girl.

"Kaye Trotter?"

"She's in the flat above. The door just at the side there."

I thanked her. The door at the side was open, and faced a flight of narrow stairs. At the top they became a narrow corridor, left and right. Two doors, two flats. One of them had a hand-written card sellotaped to it. "K. Trotter." I pressed the bell-push beside it.

"Who is it?"

"I'm from Social Security," I shouted back.

A slight pause. The lock clicked and the door opened.

"You're from *where*?"

I was face to face with Kaye Trotter, and this was another experience the village of Macklin had to answer for.

Chapter Five

She was around 5 ft 4 in, and plumpish, I supposed. It was difficult to tell, because she was wearing a kind of loose smock that came down to her shins. Bare feet – very neat, small feet. Small hands. Oh . . . and glasses. I never discovered whether she wore them of necessity, or as a kind of camouflage, something that enhanced her face and gave her restless hands something to do. Even as she stood there, she was pushing them back up her nose with her forefinger, big, round glasses with a retaining chain around the back of her neck, giving her a bit of a school-marm look. Sometimes – I discovered – they slid all the way down and off her nose. Hence the chain. But her stature required that she should forever seem to cock her head, chin up, in order to stare at me. I topped her by 6 in. At the moment she was jutting that chin at me, her mouth doing something that was very like a struggle not to smile at me – even laugh – and her clear grey eyes were challenging me from under high, arched eyebrows. She was ash-blonde, her hair swept back and caught in a restrained tangle at her neck. She had a smudge of green paint on her small, sharp nose.

"Social Security," I repeated. "I wonder if I could just have a word?"

She stood back, looking me up and down, still with a suppressed glee, as though I'd come there just to amuse her. "You're real! I heard you people exist, but it didn't seem true. And the brief-case, too! Oh, do let me see! Can I see your brief-case? Please!" She spoke like a retarded teenager, but she was well on in her twenties.

I'd encountered every sort of welcome, from the violently abusive to the cringing self-deprecation. But derision was new. I wasn't sure what to do about it, but took her attitude for an invitation to enter, and did so. She walked all round me.

"I don't think I've met one before," she explained.

"I'm sure you have! Buy a stamp and you meet one, at least, used to be, but the same thing. The police are Civil Servants, really, servants of the public."

"That's what you are, a servant of the public?"

"I'm what they call an Inspector."

"And you've come to serve me?"

"Not exactly the phrase I'd use myself," I told her.

I had, I decided, discovered the correct mood of levity with which to approach her. She blushed faintly, pouted, and said: "Then sit down, and tell me what it's all about."

"I'm interrupting." I gestured.

"A work of art," she said scathingly. "It's of no importance." A cocked eyebrow. "What do *you* find that's important enough to bring you here, Mr . . .?"

"Beacham, Miss Trotter. Ken Beacham." Why did I give her my christian name?

"So we are Ken and Kaye. Two k's. How exciting. You didn't tell me what's more important than a work of art."

"A death."

I had thought we were playing word games, feeling for amusing advantages of a trifling kind to alleviate the boredom. Truly, she welcomed me, as a break from solitude. Something about me had triggered her mood. But I saw that I'd genuinely shocked her. The finger went to the bridge of her glasses again, and she turned away.

"This," she said dully, "is the work of art in question." But she was not looking at it.

She had an easel near the window that overlooked the yard behind the shops, inspiration apparently flowing from the dustbins, the rubbish, and the empty boxes. On it was a sheet of thick plywood, on which she was working in oils. I thought I should be polite, so approached and considered it with a critical air, giving her time to recover. An elephant was marching through jungle, one of those box things on its back. There were figures in the box, guns in their hands.

"It's good."

"Then you're no art critic. I'm doing the same thing both sides, for a pub sign." Her voice was still lifeless. "The 'Elephant and Castle.' That's the castle thing on its back – I think. I'm assuming that. How else would elephants be connected with castles?"

"You're probably right."

"It's about Lennie Trent, isn't it?"

I turned to face her. "Yes, it's Mr Trent I want to talk about."

"Is it going to take time?"

"I don't know."

She shrugged, and began to swill her brushes in a jar of turps, and wipe them off. Then she stared at her hands. "I'm filthy. And I stink!"

"No – you're fine."

"Give me a minute?"

Then she whisked away through a door, and left me standing there, wondering what to do with myself.

All I knew about her was that she was David Trotter's sister. Perhaps a couple of questions and two straight answers would see the end of it, but I was hoping it would need more. She intrigued me. The facetious welcome had not been completely fun. Part of it she'd meant. I was encountering opposition, and something tingled in my blood when that happened. Opposition, I loved. It gave some small purpose to my job, winning through to the facts I needed in the face of it.

She was taking her time. I wandered round the room, a mish-mash of junk furniture she'd tarted-up with paint and varnish, but a bright room, with paintings that were obviously hers on the walls. She went for sharp, tingling colours, splashes of indefinite flowers and bright birds in flight. There were pot plants everywhere there was a flat surface, even one on the turntable of her open record player. In one corner there leaned a Spanish guitar. I picked it up and plucked it. It was in tune – I knew enough to tell that, though all I ever did was tinkle at a piano. The smell of oil paint and turps was heavy in the air, that and a smell of onions. I located them, a string of onions hanging in the corner as decoration. A memento of a holiday in France? In Spain? A strange young woman, I thought.

There was the clattering of a tray and crockery from behind the door. I stood looking at the plant on the turntable. An azalea, I decided.

She came in behind me. I turned. She'd changed into jeans and a man's shirt, hanging loose outside. She wasn't at all plump. Shapely, rather, her hips firm, her breasts thrusting against the shirt, bra-less, another challenge.

Putting down the tray on a low table, she said:

"You must tell me what you do. All of it."

"That wasn't really why I came."

"Why *did* you come?"

"Your brother sent me."

"Good old David, he knew I'd be lonely. Help yourself to sugar and milk. Unless you like your milk in first."

"I never did understand why it matters."

She smiled, seating herself on a little stool. The smile was breathtaking. The mouth I'd thought to be small and pert suddenly became huge, and her face seemed to fold up delightfully. "Sit down, do. You're so damned big, standing up."

I sat opposite her. The chair was more comfortable than it looked. "I don't think of myself as big."

The tea was Earl Grey, no mistaking it. She economised on furnishings, but knew where her true pleasures lay. The guitar was an expensive one. She reached over and tapped my knee.

"You promised to tell me about your job."

"I did nothing of the sort. I came here merely to ask you why your brother should think that you would be able to tell me . . ."

"Has this sentence got an end?"

"It has. Had. I've lost it now."

She laughed. Her tinkly laugh; she had a whole assortment. "Then it couldn't have been important. Tell me. Your job?"

"I don't understand why you want to know."

"When I find a new friend, I like to hear whether he's got a purpose in life."

"Friend?"

"Aren't we friends, Ken?"

"I usually take a little longer."

"But you've had time to look round this room. You know me now."

"Hardly."

"I like colour, sound, a good book, and accomplishment."

"I don't know if you're bad-tempered or easy-going, if you're intense or casual, if you're happy or miserable, bored or excited, depressive or manic."

"All those," she said, bunching up her lips and staring at me with intensity.

"All I'm certain so far . . ."

"So far?"

I grinned at her. "All I'm certain is that you're playing some sort of personal game with me, and I don't think that makes you a very kind person. And that you make a fine cup of tea. Can I have another?"

"I like you, Ken Beacham." She reached for my cup. "You shall have another. And I didn't intend to be unkind . . ."

"You were mocking me."

". . . I'm just interested in people."

"Then you should have my job. It's what I like about it. Meeting people."

"There's something to *like* about it?"

"Oh yes! I meet people such as you. It's what's known as an experience, Kaye."

"Your life must be very empty of experiences, then. You didn't tell me what you *do*."

So I told her what I did. It took a little thought, and so absorbed some time. She sat watching me with her elbow on one knee and her chin clasped in her palm, grey eyes unfalteringly on me, frowning, concentrating.

"And that's it?"

"Variations on that theme."

"But it's all so empty – so pointless."

I felt a bit niggled at that. "I wouldn't say pointless. You live in a closed society. There has to be law and order to it. People up there in Westminster make the laws, so other people have to make sure they're carried out. That's what we do in the Civil Service. We administer those laws."

"So pompous!" she said with scorn. "It's all down there, down on paper, and you do what it says. *Anybody* could do it who can read. But what do you achieve? Tell me that. From what you say, the whole point of it all is that everybody has to fit into a formula, to satisfy these laws of yours. That's a nothing achievement. What's outside your paltry books of instructions gets discarded. You've ironed it all out. Is *that* achieving?"

"Ironing it all out could be."

"To a set of rules! Break one, and you're in trouble. Tcha!" She tossed her head. For some reason it really meant something to her. "When you go – when you're dead and gone – what will you leave behind that's *yours* and not *theirs*? Will they open a file and say: 'Ken Beacham cleared this case'? Will they?"

"And when you're gone, they'll walk into the 'Elephant and Castle' and not even glance up at your sign," I said, with a touch of anger.

"I have a mural in the Angel café in Brook Street. So there."

"Depicting what? Civil Servants drinking Earl Grey?"

This I snapped out, my annoyance no longer being under control. Her attack was paltry. My response held less patience than usual. I was not trying for a laugh, not even her smile. Just an end to it. But what I got was her laugh.

"Oh, you're funny, Ken! You're staying to tea, are you?"

I hadn't realised the time. Friday evening, and five already. I always liked to deposit my brief-case, with a gesture of finality, at the office every Friday. I'd be late for that now.

"I've only got a couple of questions."

"Scrambled eggs on toast do you?"

"Can I have mine poached?"

"How you like. I'm a wizard with eggs. That's what they'll say about me when I'm gone. 'She was a wizard with eggs'."

Then she flaunted off into the kitchen, leaving me wondering what I was getting out of this meeting, where I was going.

We ate in her kitchen, sitting high on stools at a narrow counter along one wall. The washing machine factory was visible through the window in front of us. I pointed a spoon at it; we were on cream and tinned peaches.

"If you think the job's easy . . ." I said.

"Did I say that?"

". . . you should've tried sorting out the case I had there. Though, come to think of it, a woman would have found it easy."

"How's that?"

"One of their ladies was blown off the toilet seat."

She spluttered. "Never!"

"And I had to go and see whether it came under the heading of an industrial accident. The degree or otherwise of incapacity was not my affair."

"Don't you love these official phrases!"

"It gets worse. Let me explain about arising out of and in the course of."

"Do, if you must. Coffee?"

I nodded. "That's the definition in law of an industrial accident. It's an accident arising out of and in the course of employment. Doesn't have to be industry, of course. Any employment. Would you like to hear the legal definitions of accident and employment?"

"I think I can live without. But this . . . arising out of . . ."

"Call it 'because of and during employment,' then."

"So why can't they say that?"

"Lawyers, you see."

"Ah! Go on."

"To come into the bracket of an industrial accident it has to arise out of the job *and* happen in the course of it. Sounds simple, doesn't it? But literally thousands of 'em don't quite fit. Imagine a factory. A chap at a machine, and he cuts off his finger. That's straightforward. He was there, and doing his job. But what say there's a chap playing around with an air-pressure hose and a few ball bearings, and finds he can fire 'em right across the shop floor. Then where are you if the chap at the next machine gets blinded? Oh, it happened! Somebody had to think how it fitted the law. It was definitely during the course of his employment, but did it arise out of it? Are you with me? What would you say?"

She showed a reluctant interest. "Well . . . it wasn't to do with the job, shooting ball bearings."

"So that'd throw it out. Right. But you see, the accident wouldn't have happened if he hadn't been there, *doing* his job! It was a kind of hazard of the job, having to work next to an idiot. So he got his decision in the end. It created what we call a precedent."

"It's all words, all juggling with things on the edge of . . ."

"That's what it is."

"And you have to make those sort of decisions?"

"No. I report the facts. I'm the very devil at ferreting-out facts."

"Facts to do with ladies on toilets?" She nodded towards the factory.

"Yes. But that took patience. Ladies are authorised to go to the toilets. But not, in that factory, to smoke there. It was known to happen, though, so it could be accepted as authorised because it hadn't been forbidden, not in the ladies, anyway. This one was sitting there and had lit a cigarette. She tossed the match down the bowl, and there was a flash of flame. An explosion."

She grimaced. "Yuk!"

"Another of their women employees had been using thinners for the glue they use on their rubber seals. It'd got a bit thick, so she was supposed to pour it into a sump. She'd short-cutted and poured it into a toilet bowl and forgotten to pull the chain. Hence the explosion. The trouble was – from my point of view – that the one I interviewed, the victim, had a whole bunch of her mates who thought it was the screaming end of humour, especially as I was a man. They got round me like a rugby scrum, saying I should view the actual toilet basin, and insisting she should show me her burns . . .!"

"And did she?"

"I ran."

She burst out laughing, her hearty laugh. It shook the coffee mugs.

"My hero! And what did you recommend, in that case?"

"I'd got the medical report. The burns were minor. She'd been hoping to get a favourable decision from us to back up a damages claim against her employers. And the burns were minor because she hadn't gone there to use the toilet for its normal facilities. She'd gone for a smoke. She was protected by her underclothes and her jeans. So she was doing some-thing not authorised, and I recommended disallowance."

"You're a hard man!"

"I report the facts."

She sat beside me again, staring out of the window. "And you think all that matters?"

"It mattered to that woman, to her employers, and to the public funds."

"You go around, pestering people for information . . ."

"Yes. For instance . . . Mrs Trent has applied for an Industrial Death Pension. She'll get it if Leonard Trent was still involved in his employment when he crashed his car."

"So . . . you've got round to it at last."

"It's been a bit of a struggle," I admitted.

"Let's take our coffee into the other room." And she was away before I could disagree.

She allowed me to sit, but moved around while we talked, not nervously, not in agitation, but simply, I felt, because she was a restless person.

"You've been clever, haven't you!" she demanded. "All that rubbish about the law of it – you were only leading up to this."

"You're the sort of person who needs to appreciate the necessity, so I'm stretching things to tell you the background."

"Stretching what?"

"Any information I find out is confidential."

Her eyes shone. "You do it all the time. Hints, suggestions. And that was to tell me that anything I say *now* will be confidential."

"If it needs to be, yes."

"Needs! Needs! I don't *care*! But I don't want Virginia Trent hurt."

"How will she be hurt?"

"Tell me what you know, first."

"It would help if you kept still for a minute," I said.

She didn't reply, but put down her mug and went to stand in front of her painting. She stood with hands

69

gripping her elbows, and I got only a profile, and wished I could paint.

"The important thing is whether Leonard Trent was going *to* his Managing Director or driving away." I paused. No reaction. "If he was leaving, then any claim by Virginia Trent's going to be disallowed. The evidence I've got up to this moment is that he'd been to Mr Lorimer's office, and had left it. But there's one fact that doesn't make sense. He was driving east, in that case, when he crashed, but his home is west of the factory."

She murmured something I didn't catch.

"In this direction," I said. "Trotter – sorry, your brother – said I should ask you, but I don't even know what I'm supposed to ask."

She turned. Her face was completely blank. "Lennie was coming to me."

"You were expecting him?"

"He was late. The snow."

"I've heard about the snow."

"And that's all you want to know?"

"If that's all you want to tell me."

She'd told me enough. It explained his hurry, even if it wasn't panic, and his direction. It looked as though I'd got a bloody murder on my hands. I waited. She came and sat on her stool again, and her smile was painful.

"He'd arranged to spend the night. He intended to phone Virginia and say the snow had delayed him, and he was staying the night in some hotel or other. But he'd stay with me." She said it to her knees. "The night."

I said nothing. She was close to tears, and I'm useless with weeping women. She lifted her head. "Is *that* enough for you?"

"Thank you, yes. Is that what you meant by hurting Virginia, that she might find out?"

"Yes."

"Not the fact that she'll lose her pension?"

"Christ, is everything money to you?" she flared.

I nearly said it might be to Virginia Trent, but caught myself. I looked round for my brief case.

"You're not leaving?"

"I'm late."

"Keeping your wife waiting?"

"My wife's in Birmingham. I'm relatively new to this area."

"I'll play you some music."

"Guitar music?"

"Bach."

"A bit heavy for me."

"Spanish music, then."

"That sounds very pleasant."

She didn't want to be left alone. The death of Leonard Trent had left a fearful gap, and at least I was a presence. To hell with the brief case, I thought.

"D'you know," she said, "you haven't even taken off your anorak."

So I took off my anorak and she played guitar for me. Spanish and flamenco. I said she was good. To prove me wrong she put on a John Williams. It's too easy to denigrate yourself by comparison with the top artistes, and I told her so. Severely. But she was fierce, and said that's what you should always do. Whatever that meant.

Around eight we went out – in the Mini – to a place she knew and had a drink where the juke box was blessedly out of order. She would not say another word about Leonard Trent, and I didn't press her. I was his stand-in. I wasn't sure I liked the feeling, but when she loosened-up and chattered away it was to me she was talking, a stranger, a new friend, pouring out to me her personality with an attitude of take it or leave it. Content, amused, intrigued, baffled – I took it.

I was uncertain how far the substitution was intended

to go. After all, Leonard Trent had intended to stay the night, but had not done so.

It transpired that neither did I. We went back to her place for a nightcap, as she called it, which turned out to be a glass of her home-made gooseberry wine, and then she made it clear that I should leave.

She said nothing about meeting again, perhaps in an old-fashioned way giving the lead to me, and I was hesitant to mention it, in case the suggestion carried an official undertone. So it was a touch of the fingertips and a goodnight, and I had to admit to a feeling of disappointment.

It was nearly eleven when I got to the office, but I was still determined to dump my brief case. Any other week-day I was prepared to take on out-of-hours visits. Week-ends were sacred, and leaving the thing at the office removed the temptation.

I had my own keys. The front door, the one that shut off the burglar alarm, and a key to the cabinet in benefits section, in case I need to consult a benefits file. I went in, switching on lights, threw the brief case on my desk, and then, on an impulse, went and opened up in benefits section, looking in the index for Lorimer. There was no claim in either the name of Philip Lorimer or Marjorie Lorimer. Well, there wouldn't be, would there! In another section, there'd be a claim for Death Grant, perhaps, but you can't class a death by suicide as an industrial accident. Suicide is not part of an MD's duties.

I wondered vaguely whether he'd been employed under a contract of service or a contract for services, and took with me a claim form for Industrial Death Benefit, just in case, paused to pop it into my brief case, and left.

There was a police car parked behind the Mini. The uniformed officer approached me. "Sir?" He'd spotted the lights on.

I explained. Once again I produced my warrant card.

He said I was a bit late, wasn't I, and I told him it was all go, and that was that.

It'd been a full day. When I let myself into Mrs Zalusky's, I realised it was going to be another one, starting early next morning.

Chapter Six

It was a 60-mile run to Acocks Green. Halfway there I had to stop and fetch out the plugs, and de-louse them, but apart from that the Mini ran well.

Our semi was in a long avenue of similar semis, the only difference being that the builder had got tired of running them in a straight line, so he'd put two curved set-backs to the houses halfway along, just to provide relief. It meant that our place, one of the centre ones in the circle, had a very long front garden but a short back one. I'm no gardener, and would happily have left a long rear garden to grow wild, but you can't do that with the front, Lena said. What'd the neighbours think? So, like it or not, I'd had to titivate the front with a lawn and borders and a rose-bed in the middle, and in spite of myself had developed a possessive interest in the damn thing. Just at that time, plants were stirring and colour was showing, which should've pleased the neighbours even if Lena never showed any interest. That garden was perhaps the one reason I'd been reluctant to leave. Between you and me, the fact that the neighbours' likes and dislikes had forced me to it was what persuaded me to go.

My Cortina was in the drive. There was room for the Mini behind it; we had a long drive. Lena saw me draw in and was at the front before I'd slammed the car door, not exactly welcoming, but, I thought, satisfied to see that her letter had forced me to visit.

"It's you," she said.

"I got your letter."

"And if you hadn't?" she asked, following me into the kitchen. I was heading for a pot of tea.

"What's that mean?"

"You'd have nothing to do in that place, over a week-end. Nothing but your blasted job."

Nobody liked my job. What was upsetting the women these days? In practice I'd have been driving out into the country, exploring.

"I've had a new idea for the bridge book . . ." I began to tell her.

"Oh . . . that."

I shrugged. Her contempt was excusable, acceptable. For seven years I'd been playing around with an idea for a book. A disaster thing. A minor disaster. But you don't want to hear about it.

My comment satisfied her, though. In the back of her mind was the conviction that with every other woman but herself I was the great lover. Maybe I would have been, with some other woman but Lena, whose ideas on sex comprised one cross on next month's calendar, and a rigid refusal to attempt any alternative that prevented her from admiring the ceiling.

Then she laughed, the laugh she used when she was conceding to my masculine weaknesses. "Your trouble, Ken – d'you know what your trouble is? – It's because you're a dreamer, a romantic. Never a do-er."

She spent most of her life without a spark of imagination lighting the gloom, then she'd surprise me with those sudden flashes of intuition. Annoyed – as one is when a remark hits the target – I deliberately refused to bring up the subject that had brought me there, and spent the next hour or so chatting away inconsequentially.

"I see the roses are coming on."

"Are they?" she asked.

"I'd have liked to see how that new one looks. Deep Secret. Supposed to be a very dark red."

"No reason you shouldn't see it, Ken," leading in to the primary subject.

I dodged round that. "I'm never home."

"Not home at all, these days."

"I'm home now." I put my arm round her waist. She smiled up at me and snuggled close. It meant nothing. It was a sociable gesture and no more, I knew. She was a mile from me, smiling emptily across the space between. "What d'you want to do?" I asked. "Have you got enough in? Shall we go shopping?"

"It depends on how long you're staying." A grimace there.

"Till tomorrow evening."

"Then I can manage."

What had she expected me to say? A week, a month? For ever?

"Then what?" I asked.

"Can't you just stay around?" she demanded. "Sit still for a bit, watch the tele. Like it used to be."

"Hoe the borders?"

"Relax, Ken. That's what you should do. I've always said. You're a bundle of nerves – you never relax!"

"I'm working hard to keep on top of the job."

"That terrible office . . ."

"The terrible manager!"

"You said your last one was bad."

"This one's worse."

"What did I tell you! Out of the frying pan . . ."

"I'll tell you about him."

Which I did. It was a warm day, so we took the tray of tea I'd made onto the patch of paved terrace we'd got out at the back, and sat in deck chairs, contemplating the progress of the docks and couchgrass. She hadn't warned me about the perils of transfer; it had been her idea to try it. Basically. The fact that I wasn't even being considered for promotion had been more galling to Lena than it had to me. I'd become reconciled to it. But to her there was a feeling of disgrace, a social stigma involved. How could she say, in the supermarket, that her husband was moving up into a higher executive sphere, when he wasn't within nodding distance of it? And it would mean a bigger house, more modern – she assumed – more responsibility, and persons of better social standing to be invited round. Whereas, in the past couple of years . . . well, we'd been invited out. Lena had always been able to wangle invitations to parties that I hated. In fact, looking back on it, the point at which our marriage began to disintegrate centred on one of those parties. The Bellinghams. I'll tell you about it, some time.

So now I told her about Harkness. The manager you get is pure luck. The office you apply for transfer to is entirely your own choice. The snag is that you have to work with lists published in a weekly bulletin we get, and most vacancies go first to people waiting for promotion, who've already got it but only need an office to go to. Once you've decided to apply for transfer, without the promotion attached, you need to apply for nearly every advertised vacancy. You can't – just can't – go and see every place you apply for. So you get the ones nobody else wants. It's a law of nature, and it had happened to me.

And you can't go back.

I told Lena about Harkness, making him sound a terrible ogre, but trying for humour in my description of our struggle over the figures. She sat watching me. I thought her face looked thinner, her nose sharper, her eyes more guarded, her hair duller – then I took a good grasp on my sensibilities when I realised I was comparing her with Kaye.

"You let people walk right over you," she said in disgust, when I drifted into discouraged silence.

"I'm holding my own."

She made a sound of disbelief, and looked away from me at the jungle of our back garden, not seeing anything, and every angle of her tense posture shouted out her disparagement.

Suddenly I felt a great tenderness for her. She tried so

hard, but life always defeated her ambitions; life and Ken Beacham. I wanted to take her in my arms and encourage her with soft words, tell her everything would be all right, but after six years of marriage I still didn't know what would be all right for her. If her ambitions had been more complex, or completely unattainable, I could have seen an aim, a target, but she undermined me by aiming so low. Simply the next step, the next move. All her intensity would be centred on a new cooker, a replacement car, a simple two-piece costume. And social advancement. All of them so low on my horizon that my radar wouldn't pick them up, and I always failed to guess, to anticipate, to surprise her with any impulsive enterprise. My fault. Something was missing in my awareness. I was too introspective.

"You're a loner," she'd said once, with one of her bits of insight. "A loner in a job where the whole idea is team working." Oh, the clever girl! If only it hadn't come in such meagre quantities, like a tap dripping wisdom and understanding, irritating rather than quelling a thirst.

"So what are you going to do about it?" she suddenly demanded, having rationed my relaxation to the exact second.

"About what?"

"You *know* what!" she burst out, her cheeks flaming.

"I can't do anything about it." It was all I could think to say. Now was the time I wished I hadn't given up smoking.

"You've got to do something," she decided emphatically. "I'm not going to live in that terrible town."

"They wouldn't allow me to transfer back. Anyway, they've probably filled my place here."

"They could fit you in, and you know it."

I sighed. I knew they could not, would not. "I did explain what it could mean, applying for a transfer."

Then strangely she replied quietly, in a defeated tone. "I just didn't understand."

"So there I am and there I've got to stay."

"Defeatist."

"Realist, Lena. You have to take what turns up, and do the best you can with it."

"Well . . ." She thumped her fists into her lap. ". . . I for one don't intend to."

I didn't ask what she intended. I waited.

"Have you stopped the house?" she asked, nodding, ticking off the points she had to clear in her mind.

"They're preparing contracts."

"You mean you've done nothing?"

"Lena . . . I'll have to pay for the solicitor's work, anyway, and nothing's settled until I sign the thing. And I can't sign until we've got a buyer here, anyway."

"You'd better cancel it all."

"What we'd better do," I said, taking it steadily, "is have a run up there in the morning. I'll drive." Knowing she hated driving. "I want you to see the place I've found."

"I don't need to."

"You haven't even *seen* it, for God's sake."

"If you're going to shout . . ."

"I'm sorry. But usually the wife's along when new houses are looked at. It's a tradition. Left to myself, I had to find a place I thought you'd like. We'll drive up. Use the Cortina. You never know, you might love it."

"The Cortina's not running right."

"So what's the matter with it?"

"It won't start."

It wouldn't start when she went shopping because she gave it full choke even when the engine was hot, and flooded it. We'd argued about it a hundred times. "It's the choke."

"I wish you'd look at it."

"It's the way you over-choke it."

"*That's* something for you to do tomorrow – see to the car. Instead of talking nonsense about driving miles to somewhere I don't want to go."

It was hopeless, and I knew it. When I got back I'd

borrow a camera – buy one, damn it, I'd always wanted a camera – and take a set of pictures of our new town and its outskirts, main square, the bungalow, the view from it. And she could look at those. I could even – delicious thought – ask Kaye to do me a painting of the valley at sunset . . .

Lena was saying: "But I'm glad you're home, Ken. I shan't have to go alone."

"Go where?"

"You see, you never listen! Do you realise how annoying it is to keep having to repeat yourself! And what were you smirking at, anyway?"

"I was smiling with pleasure at the thought of working on my Cortina tomorrow."

"Never mind tomorrow. You'd better have a bath, and I'll press your brown suit. We're going to Mrs Pearson's this evening. A little party."

"Not a party!"

"Her husband's the manager at . . ."

I didn't care where he was at. It was a party, and we'd be there, exchanging inane social comment, and all Lena wanted was not to have to think, discuss, consider. But it was just such a party that had started the rot. I think I mentioned it. The Bellinghams.

This had been about a year before. I'd been involved in the previous week – weeks, rather – with a ridiculous case involving a wages clerk who'd developed what he considered an original fiddle. He'd been working for a builder with about 40 regular bricklayers and footings men and the like on his pay-roll. The wages clerk had invented three of his own, put them in the books, and when he went out each Friday in the van, around the building sites with the wages packets, he would come back with three spares in his pocket. It always shows up, because of the difficulty with income tax and insurance, but he thought he was clever.

He'd got one original trick, though. The three men were real people, who were employed by the sub-contractors, the roofers, the carpenters, the plumbers. So each of these three

80

men had to be traced, to check whether in fact they were in on the fiddle, too, collecting two wages packets, or one and a half more like.

The trouble was that the sub-contractors were difficult to trace, the men even more difficult. When I got to the third, I found his name to be John Frederick Parkes. But he wasn't on the job any more. His given address took me to a Mrs Helena Parkes, a stoutish lady in her fifties, who very nearly passed out when I asked to see her husband. She had been drawing a Widow's Pension for him for six years, he having disappeared off a barge in the Thames, and having been declared dead.

The eventual outcome was discouraging. The man I was after was never found, but a description tied him down to a previous lodger of Mrs Parkes, whom the police decided was an escaped prisoner from Winson Green. As far as I know he's still escaped, but Mrs Parkes, who had really been pleased when her husband disappeared – in fact, would have shoved him off that barge herself if she'd been there – was going to be very relieved when she heard her pension was safe, and that he wouldn't be returning to the ample bosom of his family.

The resolution of this case came on the afternoon of the Bellinghams' party. Lena knew I liked to go round and tell people the result of the cases I'd been dealing with. They would get formal notices in writing, but when you've worried and harried them, they deserve more. I told Lena I'd drop her at the Bellinghams, trot over to see Mrs Parkes, and return. She didn't like that. "To hell with Mrs Parkes." I said I'd be only half an hour. She grumbled all the way to that wretched party. "I'll stand out like a sore thumb." Trite – but sore she was. I left her at the house and drove over to see Mrs Parkes.

The trouble was that she was right the way across the town, and I'd had the Cortina only a few weeks, and hadn't got used to that choke. The wire slipped in the middle of town. I was half an hour finding out what the hell had happened, a good hour at Mrs Parkes' – damn it all if she didn't want to hold her own celebration party! – and all in all it was a disaster.

Lena was standing in the corner of what the Bellinghams called their lounge, one glass in each hand, staring into space, and alone. Her mood of smouldering resentment would've sent anyone flying.

"I got caught."

"I hope you're pleased with yourself."

"I'm here now."

"I hope your Mrs Parkes was thrilled with the news."

"She was pleased." I took the drink from her. I was full of tea and couldn't face gin and tonic. "And I," I said, "was pleased she was pleased."

"It's not part of your job," she said, spacing out the words past a fixed, idiotic smile.

"That woman has hardly slept for a week."

"Then I'm surprised you didn't stay and sleep with her."

I stared at her. Her eyes were glassy, and I knew then that a wedge had entered between us.

So I wasn't happy to be facing another party that evening. Coming home for the week-end had been a mistake.

But we went to that dratted party, and what Pearson was manager of was a supermarket, and I had to listen to how he'd managed to cut twopence off a large packet of detergent, and why he suspected the girl on No. 3 till was doing him rotten, and when he expected to get the larger branch at Kings Heath. And a merry time was had by all.

The car wouldn't start when we went to leave.

"You see," Lena said. "Clever dick."

The points. It was the blasted points. That model Cortina was always sensitive to point setting. Ever tried re-gapping points under a streetlamp in your best suit, with your hosts still standing in their doorway and wondering whether it would be bad manners to go in with guests not actually waved on their way? I was in a savage mood when we got home. Lena was coldly, crisply silent. When I came back from washing my hands she hissed: "I could kill you . . ." and marched off to bed.

Fortunately, there was no cross on the calendar for that day, so I didn't miss anything.

In the morning I made a proper job of the points and cleaned the plugs, re-set the rich-mixture control, went round to the local garage and did the tyres, and got my Cortina running like a dream. I didn't get time to look at the Mini.

Lena was having one of her quiet days, which meant that her mind was working away, furiously and incisively. Over dinner – and I will say she was a magnificent cook – she said:

"Did you see their house? Did you take time out from talking to that brunette – and God knows who *she* was – to take a look at the place?"

"The Pearsons'?"

"Of course. What did you think I meant?"

"I couldn't remember a brunette."

"Liar." She gave me one of her sly looks. "Why can't we get a place like that?"

"Can't afford it."

"*You* could do his job, Ken. You know you could."

"Yes. I could do it."

"If Pearson gets his move . . ."

"For Christ's sake, Lena!"

"You've got no go. No enterprise."

"A supermarket? The turnover must be terrific."

"It's a busy store."

"I meant the staff."

"Tell them who you are, and they'd go down on their knees."

"Likely, I must say."

A good cook. Why did she have to spoil the meal?

"Harry Burnett's in the running for it."

83

"Good for him."

"You saw him. The tall chap with the glasses and the silky hair, and that lovely suit. Distinguished."

I stared at her. She remembered Burnett clearer than I did the brunette. "I wouldn't stand a chance against him."

"Oh . . . I don't know."

And, annoyingly, she didn't.

We said no more about it, about anything. Nothing had been achieved and nothing settled. At around six I said I'd be getting off, then. She came to the car with me, her car.

"You'll think about it, Ken?"

I got in the Mini and slid back the side window. "Think about what?"

"What you're going to do."

"I'll tell you what I'm going to do. I'm going to do nothing. That contract can sit in the solicitor's office until he tells me I've lost the place – and I'm going to wait for you to come along and at least *look* at it. And I'll expect you to come along with an open mind, not closed to every suggestion and idea, and with the same mind made up to the fact that I'm stuck there. I'm *not* going to ask for another transfer. I'm *not* going to resign and try to run a supermarket. So think of that, Lena."

I didn't usually lay things out like that. But she'd pushed and worried and pestered me to apply for the transfer, just because we were getting nowhere. It hadn't been my idea. What . . . me? Old Ken Beacham, with no push, no go, no initiative! You can't accuse me of wanting the transfer. But I'd got it. That was that. I couldn't see why she was unable to reconcile herself to it.

She stood there, a hand on the car door, her face set.

"Then I'll have to do some thinking, Ken."

"As long as we know where we stand."

She bent and pecked me on the cheek, her head through the window. Strange, that. Quite out of character.

"Oh, I love you when you're so firm and masterful."

This was said in such a cold and sardonic voice that all I could think to do was drive away, and watch our For Sale sign fade from the rear-vision mirror.

I'd forgotten to ask her whether she'd had any enquiries for the house. Probably she'd have discouraged them, anyway. All the way back, I tried to worry about it, and found I couldn't.

When I pushed open Mrs Zalusky's front door, she called out: "There's some tea made, Ken."

I was home.

Chapter Seven

Monday morning. A nice, clear week in which to dig in and impress Harkness with my ability. If that was what I wanted. I wasn't sure. My brief-case was where I'd left it on my desk, but it lay there thinner. I jerked it open. All that was left in there was my notebook and the folder of spare forms I carried around. I went over to my filing cabinet. It was unlocked, and empty of actionable files.

I knew what had happened. Harkness had decided to do a managerial check. This was part of his job, but the usual thing was for a polite request to come in: "Can you let me have your current files sometime today?" That sort of thing. It gave you time to write them up to date, and check you weren't leaving yourself wide open to criticism. But to walk in and help yourself – that was quite unprecedented, and not a little officious.

I went and brewed a cup of tea; his milk hadn't gone off. I sat at my desk and waited, my anger gradually cooling. Then he walked in.

"Ah, there you are, Ken."

The files were a fat bundle under his arm. He banged them down on my desk, then looked round for a spare chair, found a folder in the corner, and sat facing me. He did not avoid my eyes, but he managed a small apologetic smile that showed the edge of one tooth.

"Sorry about that," he said. "I should have given you warning, but I didn't know myself. Found myself at a loose end on Saturday, so I called in. About time, I thought . . ." He gestured to my pile of current files.

I could see that every file had a piece of white paper

clipped to its top corner. Any comments he'd made were not going to be permanently on display on the minute sheets. Playing safe?

"A loose end?" I asked. "Couldn't you tidy the garden, or wash the car?"

"No garden," he explained. "I'm in a flat – Horseley Palace. No car, it's in walking distance."

"My wife always objects if I work on week-ends." Me too.

"No wife, either." He shrugged.

I didn't know what to say. His whole life was the office.

"I've made a few comments," he said at last, having given it a few moments, during which I might have suggested we should have a drink together, some time. "Nothing serious. Three cases where I felt we were getting nowhere. I'll recommend closure if you'll minute them to me."

"Three less, then."

"Yes." He seemed uneasy. "Are you happy in this job, Ken?"

"It interests me."

"Yes. Yes, I got that impression. Do you think, perhaps, that you're inclined to allow yourself to become too interested?"

"Can there be such a thing?"

"I'm sure there can. This Virginia Trent case, for instance . . ."

"That one? I haven't got it all written-up. I did some more work on it, Friday afternoon."

"I'm sure I can't see why. It seems safe to recommend disallowance as it stands. He'd left the sphere of his employment."

"It's complicated."

"I see that. And Friday afternoon's work? Did it alter the picture?"

He was reaching out and drawing the file towards him. I felt possessive about that file. "It only confirmed what I suspected, that he'd seen his Managing Director, and was driving away."

"Well then."

"I'm just not happy with it."

"It's not for you to be happy. Write up your Friday visit, and let the I.O. see it. The decision's not yours."

Quite true. The Insurance Officer made the legal decisions, on what I told him. Or her, in our case.

"It could lead to an appeal," I pointed out.

"Then we'd have to examine it deeper. When that arises."

"At which time there'd be criticism from R.O. – criticism of *me* – that I hadn't gone far enough at this stage."

"There are no grounds she could appeal on."

"Not as it stands. I want to go further," I said. "That's all."

He said nothing, his hand spread on the file, middle finger tapping it rhythmically. "We're wasting time on it."

"Not a waste," I said. "Not if we get it right in the end."

It seemed a good idea, just at that time, to make it quite clear where I stood. There are two ways to look at any job. Either you learn how to cut corners and shave off edges, and make the work as effortless as possible, or you try to do a decent job to the best of your ability. It's a matter of self-esteem – not what other people think of you, but what price you put on yourself. I was never any good at cutting corners, and it was as well that he learned that as soon as possible. There were lots of ways how he could control the way I handled the job. He couldn't tell me how to do it.

I wondered what he'd say if I told him it looked like murder. He'd say murder wasn't our affair, and take the file from me right there and then. Refer it up. Somebody in a much loftier grade would decide whether to inform the police of what I suspected, and we'd leave it to them. But my last pointer had been a remark by Kaye. "He was coming to me." I hadn't even got it in writing. I didn't dare leave it there.

Harkness chewed it over in his mind. You could see it ticking over. Then he slapped his palms on the desk surface and got to his feet. "Then see that it *is* right," he said equably.

As he was folding up the chair and leaning it against the wall, he said: "Oh, by the way . . ."

I tensed. The casual, lead-in tone, that'd been. He turned.

"Jack Parsons came to see me yesterday. Parsons on contributions, that is. You'll have met him, I'm sure. He's asking for a change of duties, and suggested Inspector. What d'you think?"

I hesitated. "What are you asking me, Mr Harkness? Whether I think he'd be all right? Anybody could do it, and you know that, and anyway you'd keep an eye on him."

Parsons was one of the young live-wires, only two years in the grade and already going round the executive jobs like a firecracker. It looked good on his record, but he would only half know every job – could feel his way through, but no more.

Harkness paused at the door. "That's not what I meant. Do *you* fancy a change of duties?"

Supervisor of a section? I hated it. "I'm happy as it is."

He nodded. "All the same, I'll arrange cover for him, and you could take him round with you for a week. Show him the ropes."

"When?"

"Shall we say – when you've cleared the Trent file. Next Monday, I thought, we can start. I'll put in an application for his warrant."

That was a neat way of limiting my action on the Trent file. He closed the door behind him, leaving me staring after him and contemplating a period on contributions section, sheer bloody murder as far as I was concerned.

I set to and had a quick run through his little comments. There wasn't much in them. Surprisingly, on one of them he'd dug out a code reference I'd missed, which simplified the position considerably. For that I was grateful.

I hefted the briefcase, preparing to attack another day, when Jack Parsons came bursting in. He was in his early twenties, this chap – I could give him a dozen years of experience – slim and full of energy, earnest and brash.

"I hear I'm coming out with you next week, Ken."

"So I've been told."

"Use my car, shall we?"

Good heavens, had he already been considering what he could wangle on his mileage allowance? I smiled. "The way the Mini's running, we might have to."

"Great!" he said. "You know – I've always wanted a go at this. Get out on your own, with nobody looking over your shoulder. What d'you do? Dash round in the morning and clear 'em all, then give yourself the afternoon off?" He was grinning, tapping the side of his nose.

I stared at him seriously, looking, I hoped, shocked. "Lord, the ideas that get around! I'd leave all your evenings clear, that's all I'm saying."

He seemed shocked. "Then we claim overtime," he decided, the smile climbing back into position. "Or time off in lieu."

"That's the catch," I told him. "You take time off in lieu, and you can't get it all done, not even using every evening. And just try claiming overtime! You'll be told your work load doesn't justify it, and you ought to be able to clear everything during the day. They've got you all ends up."

"Still . . ."

"Mind you," I qualified, "there's job satisfaction."

"There's what?"

"But I can't stop now. I'll never get to bed tonight if I don't get moving."

I left him standing on the parquet pattern in the hall. I was feeling just a little better about things.

During the morning I did exactly what Parsons had suggested; I scattered round, doing a day's work in half a day. Mainly it was small factory offices, slogging over wages records. There are dozens of different methods of book-keeping, but after a few years you get to know them all, and it's easy to see your way through them. No trouble. Everything in order.

By 2.30, sustained by a cheese sandwich and half of bitter at a pub, I was out at Boraston Fields, going to interview Mrs Marjorie Lorimer, widow of Philip. A phone call to David Trotter at the factory had extracted her address.

Strictly speaking, I was going outside my area, which was against the rules. I should have passed the query to our neighbouring office for interview, but how could I possibly do that when, on the face of it, the death of Philip Lorimer had no possible connection with a benefit claim from Leonard Trent's widow? So I went myself, knowing that I wouldn't be able to record the visit.

Boraston Fields was way out to the south, in the outer suburbs of the next town. Boraston had been the owner of a large estate, who'd died and left his heir with embarrassing estate duty problems. The house – Boraston Grange – was too insignificant and featureless to attract National Trust attention, so the whole 20-acre estate had been sold to developers, for the erection of not more than ten modern luxury homes.

These were now well established, splendidly landscaped into the existing grounds so that no house was visible from any other, while at the same time enjoying a cleared space around them and the relaxing view of endless matured trees and shrubs. The Lorimers had a bungalow called Cataracts, but that must have referred to the wisteria reaching almost to the roof and spreading along one wall. A gardener was plodding over an acre or so of lawn with a motor mower, not pausing even to wipe his brow, aware that he could hardly fail to be under constant surveillance, with all that double glazing. As I must have been, parking the Mini. The front door was open before I reached the wide, pillared terrace.

Marjorie Lorimer was a woman in her early forties, slimly mature, expensively dressed, contained and confident in her appraisal of me. She was dark, hair and eyes and the cultured tan. In her eyes lurked humour, but for the moment it lay low.

"Are you Mrs Lorimer?" I asked.

"I am."

"I'm an Inspector from the Social Security Office, Mrs Lorimer. I wonder if I can have a word."

"Can you tell me more?"

"It concerns the death of your brother, Leonard."

"Oh!" She eyed my anorak and the slacks that hadn't been pressed for months, the briefcase that a dozen successive Inspectors had thrown around. "You'd better come in."

She took me through into a snug room at the back with a view of the rear, where a natural waterfall ran into a rock-surrounded pool, and out again, wandering through shrubbery and away. Hence Cataracts. She indicated a chair, beside which I set the briefcase, then she sat opposite me, helping herself to a cigarette from a silver box.

"Do you smoke?" she asked.

I shook my head. "And I'd also like to talk about the death of your husband, if you don't mind."

She did not react. She stared at me through a cloud of smoke, waiting for me to go on.

"Basically," I went on, feeling uneasy at her lack of reaction, "I'm working on a claim made by Virginia Trent."

She nodded. "I heard."

"But I find your brother's death is linked in some way with your husband's."

"They happened at around the same time. Otherwise . . ."

"Leonard was on his way to your husband's office."

"Do call him Lennie. Everybody did."

"Or on his way from it."

She leaned slightly forward. "Is there any reason to believe that?"

"Leonard . . . if you wish, Lennie, was taking a set of order forms to your husband. He seems to have got there and delivered them. That's what I mean."

"But I understand that Lennie never got there."

If we were going to continue in that formal manner, I was going to get nowhere. I'm not versatile. When talking to people I have to make it informal and chatty. Otherwise I'm lost. She was stiff and contained, a strong woman emotionally. She'd controlled it and kept it in its place. But two men in her life – perhaps the only two – had died that January night within minutes of each other, her husband and her brother. That had been three months before, but the shock was still with her, and nothing had happened to shake it free and cause her to take it out and have a good look at it.

I tried again. "The order forms were on your husband's desk. If Lennie hadn't brought them to him, there'd have been no reason for . . ." My nerve went. I couldn't say it.

"Suicide?" she asked. "Oh, don't worry, the word's commonplace to me now. Say it enough times to yourself – say any word – and it ceases to have any meaning. But really it had no meaning from the very beginning, because it was impossible. Philip and suicide? Nonsense!"

More animation had entered her voice. I leaned back and crossed my legs. "But . . . those order figures?"

Her laugh was a harsh little bark. "Figures? He'd kill himself over a few figures? Clearly, Mr—"

"Beacham."

"Clearly, then, you don't understand a thing about it."

"That's perfectly true. That's why I've come to see you."

"Does my husband's supposed suicide interest you? How strange!"

"It's linked with Lennie's death. I'm certain of that. I find I must try to understand, so if you know anything about it . . ."

"I know everything about it. At one time, in another

town, I was Philip's PA. He used to tell me everything he had in his mind, and he's continued to do it. There's nothing about that factory I don't know. Heavens, I could run the place if I had the chance."

I smiled. There'd been a crisp, confident snap in her voice. "I'm sure you could."

"Your vote of confidence is appreciated." She tilted her head. For a second the smile invaded her eyes. "That's what Philip was always saying – to me – when things were tough, and I'd support him and go along with him. He knew, anyway, that I was always behind him, but men need a constant reminder. They have to know they're the beginning, middle and end of their woman's life. Have to be certain . . ."

She stopped, turning away to scrabble for the cigarette box, a strong, loving woman whom any man would be proud to look at and assure himself she was his. I waited. Plenty of time. She lit another cigarette, her eyes challenging me to comment on her moment of weakness.

"When things were tough?" I suggested gently, wondering how tough it could be with a home like this.

"You're a Civil Servant," she said. "Oh, don't misunderstand. I'm not disparaging. It's steady and it probably has its problems, but it's reasonably safe. But out in the world of industry, in administrative positions, it's like a jungle. They work under contract, renewable depending on results . . ."

I cut in quickly. "But on a salary?"

"Of course. Payable monthly. Tax deductions made, and all the rest."

"And there's control of how he does it?"

"I *was* telling you."

"Sorry." It mattered, though.

"Control, you say. Philip was answerable to the board. They tied him hand and foot, then tossed him in. Any trouble, and he had to sort it out himself, with no support from the board, only a refusal to renew his contract if

94

he failed. That was all that ever mattered – success and failure. Let me explain . . ." I had no intention of stopping her. "They come into industry from University. Junior Managers. But there's nothing secure about it, from both sides. If the management doesn't like your performance, you're out. And always there's the man's own desire to better himself and look for advancement elsewhere. That's what life's like in industry, Mr Beacham, for the administrative staff. Nothing ever settled, nothing safe and secure. In the 15 years we've been married, we've had eight homes in eight parts of the country. This one . . . I've loved. We'd been here a year, but already I knew we were possibly going to lose it."

"You'll lose it now?"

She shook her head wearily. "They're still arguing. The house would be mine, under Philip's insurance, this and a large sum of money. But there's a suicide clause. They're still talking about it, but I know how it'll turn out. I'll have to leave here. I was a PA, and I can be a PA again."

"I didn't mean to pry into your private affairs."

"It's a relief to talk to somebody about it. Somebody who'll listen."

"It's what I'm best at – listening." I smiled. "I don't think I can offer any practical help." Playing it close to the chest, there. Practical help would be to prove that her husband was murdered – by her brother.

She seemed to shake herself, and responded with a genuine smile herself. "But I'm being very remiss. Can I get you coffee – tea?" And she was on her feet, making the refusal difficult.

"Coffee, please."

"And do take off your anorak. I can't stand formality."

Off she marched, leaving me thinking. I hoped she wasn't confusing me with the private insurance people. But no: she'd said, "they" were still arguing about it.

She came back with a tray. I was being very informal in my grubby old roll-neck sweater.

95

"That's better," she said.

"But things were tough?" I asked. "Towards the end."

"Nothing he couldn't handle, but the board were being difficult. We were already planning our lives on the assumption his contract wouldn't be renewed. It wouldn't have been the end of the world for us – help yourself to sugar – that's what I want you to understand. It'd happened before. It would mean a few months looking round, writing off for advertised vacancies, perhaps dropping down a grade or two. We'd lived through it before. You sell up and you dig in, and wait. There's a flat. We always kept this little flat going, up Manchester way, the place we lived in when we were first married. We'd always have a roof over our heads, Philip said. He called it his bolt-hole. You see what I'm trying to say to you? Whatever happened, it wouldn't be desperate for us."

"You're trying to persuade me he didn't commit suicide. I can understand that. But it's Virginia Trent's claim I'm concerned with – and Lennie's death."

"Philip did not take his own life, I'm certain of that."

I was becoming certain, too. "But – the figures. If he wasn't feeling desperate – your word – why would he wait around, and so late, to get the order from Lennie."

"The figures!" she said in disgust. "He could have had Lennie phone them through. *That* wasn't why he stayed so late. They were his excuse, that's why he didn't want Lennie to phone in too early. It would've removed his excuse."

"His excuse to what?"

"*Be* there. Simply that!"

"Does an MD need excuses?"

"For what he had in mind? Call it a cover, if you like."

She was leading me on, her remarks demanding my responses. I tried to break the pattern. "You were going to tell me about the figures."

Her eyes twinkled. She saw what I was doing, and in some way I'd done exactly what she intended. She was a clever woman. She could very well have run that factory.

"You've seen these figures?" she asked.

"A sample."

"And what did they show?"

"A steady fall-off over the next few months."

"And what did you assume from that?"

"A possibility that the product could be obtained elsewhere – in the next few months."

"Then let me explain why they mean nothing of the sort. Suppose you open a new factory requiring 2,000 items each month. Do you order 2,000 a month. No, you do not, because you know what life's like. You order 3,000 a month, knowing there'll be a fall-down on delivery. That's basic. It then settles down, until you become more confident, and *then* you order 2,000 a month. But suddenly deliveries *do* fall back. You give it three months, but by then you're 500 behind in your requirements. What do you do?"

"I'd worry."

"You're ordering six, eight months ahead. So you make your orders 2,500, 2,000, 2,000 and so on, and in the last month, 1,500, to even it out. Next month you're 700 behind on the 2,500, so you make your order 2,200, 2,200, 1,800, 1,800 and so on. There's a hint in those figures to the MD who's supplying you. The hint is that he'd better do something about it, because *he*, you see, has to order his requirements – such as basic castings – in line with the orders he's getting. And he'll see himself in trouble if he can't pull back on the arrears in his deliveries."

"It's very complicated."

"I'm simplifying it for you."

"And what point are you making?"

"That a set of eight or nine months of figures, all decreasing, does not mean that the overall order is going to collapse. The small figure at month nine will become a large figure by the time it moves up to month two or three."

"Those figures I saw meant nothing, then?"

"They meant a lot to a Managing Director. That's his

job, to see behind them. To Philip, the figures he'd been seeing simply meant that the arrears in deliveries were mounting too high. They did *not* mean the end. Nothing in what Lennie was taking to him would even suggest the thought of suicide."

I moved easily to the point she'd tried to bring me round to before. "So it was for another reason he stayed late?"

"Yes." She smiled openly. "You're a very susceptible man, Mr Beacham."

"It's the job."

"You must be good at it."

"I'm beginning to have my doubts. Tell me . . . why?"

"He suspected sabotage. As simple as that. Philip had been there a year, and he'd got the job at his fingertips. But still the arrears kept on mounting. Machine breakdowns, faults in setting-up, minor strikes over paltry matters . . . it was as though a plague had hit him. He had his suspicions *why*. There was rumour he picked up about a takeover bid in the background – not his affair, of course. He had no shares. But he was determined not to lose his position over some underhanded attempt to depreciate the value of the stock. He stayed that night, with an excuse to sit in his office over the phone, but he intended to do a little quiet detective work, and try to spot any person, authorised or not, interfering with anything."

"But surely . . . you're not saying . . .?"

"Not saying what?"

"That someone caught him at his detective work, and put a pistol to his head . . ."

"He was shot at his desk. The police were quite certain of that."

"Then what *are* you saying?"

"Only that the order figures were of no particular interest to him that evening, and that he was very far from thinking about suicide. He was fighting back. He

98

said *we* will beat them, Marjorie. He included me in the fight, you see. Always we shared. He wouldn't take his life, and leave me out of it. We'd have to share that, too."

It was a simple declaration, in no way intended to be dramatic. If I'd needed convincing – and I hadn't – I was now quite certain that Philip Lorimer had been murdered. But oh dear me, what was I to take to Harkness? What could I say to the police?

"Then," I said desperately, "he would have to have been shot immediately after your brother left him. We know that, because the order sheets were on his desk."

But she could see straight through me, and was even amused at my naïve attempt at tact. "Why do you say that? Immediately after."

"It was what occurred to me."

"You're not really enjoying this, are you?"

I always preferred to guide the interviews. "I should have come better prepared."

"You're afraid of offending me by saying what's in your mind. Which is that my brother must have killed my husband."

"You've just spent quite a while persuading me that somebody did. And if he delivered those order forms – there'd have been no time for anybody else to have done it."

"But Lennie could not. Simply that. As you said, you didn't come prepared. A long talk with Virginia would have done it. She'll be so amused when I tell her! Lennie – my little brother – oh, he was hopeless. Not a serious thought in his head. Philip was trying to help him, and knock some sense into him. But Lennie was just not a businessman. Wild when he was young ... oh, we *did* have some trouble with him! Then he got the job at Crayshaw's – that would be four years ago. He was bright, quick at picking up things, intelligent – too much for his own good, really. He could walk through his job, and that left too much of his mind free for . . . mischief, say, a bit of fun. A laugh. He was plain irresponsible, and if he hadn't been able to do his job he'd have been fired long ago."

I nodded.

She went on. "If Philip could have hammered just half a dozen serious thoughts into his head, Lennie could have gone far, right up the ladder. Believe me, Philip tried. But to tell you the truth, it worked more the other way. Lennie would have Philip laughing in five minutes, and all serious talk would melt away. Not that it did Philip any harm. It helped him to unwind. They were like brothers. That's what Lennie said to me once: it was fine having a big sister, but it didn't make up for not having a big brother. They'd do *anything* for each other, and yet they were so un alike. Utter contrasts."

She sat for a few moments, not seeing me, hands clasped on her knees and a smile of pure pleasure at the memory lighting her face. And she'd lost these two men in the same few minutes.

"It was Lennie who tipped off Philip about the vacancy for an MD coming up," she said. "We were at Nottingham, then, a poor post for Philip. So Philip became Lennie's boss, but it didn't even occur to Lennie to use the situation for a chance to move up the ladder. Nor to Philip to offer it. They ate together in the executive dining room, but it went no further. I suspect, but I'm not certain – because Philip always told me his plans, and hadn't mentioned it – I suspect Lennie was helping him uncover what was wrong at the factory. But Lennie would never take it seriously enough. Nothing deeper than fixing the timing that day."

"Timing?" I was interested in timing.

"Lennie wasn't supposed to turn up at Philip's office till just after nine. That would make everything seem logical, and not tip-off anybody who might suspect that Philip was watching out."

It all fitted together so perfectly. Lennie to arrive at "just after nine" – but he'd been close to the main gates at 9.23. There was a gap. Had Lennie filled it by shooting his brother-in-law? But it didn't matter to me or the claim whether he had or not. The important thing was still that he had reached Lorimer's office, and had been driving away. That was what would matter to the Insurance Officer.

". . . and to suggest Lennie would harm Philip," she was saying, "is ridiculous. Lennie trusted Philip completely, and Philip viewed Lennie with a protective eye, seeing that he came to no harm."

"But Lennie was driving fast. It suggests he was leaving in a panic."

"Oh dear me, don't you see! If Philip was dead when Lennie arrived, then Lennie would *not* have left him. Not for a moment. And for him to drive *away* . . . fast . . . that is beyond comprehension."

"I see."

"But to be driving *towards* the office at 9.20, and going fast – that makes perfect sense, when you consider he'd be late. And it was an arrangement he had with Philip. Just after nine, but Lennie was late. Of *course* he'd be driving fast."

"Then how do you explain the fact that the order forms were on your husband's desk?"

She raised her palms a foot from her knees. She seemed tired now. Perhaps talking for so long about the tragedies had exhausted her. "I don't explain it," she admitted. "Do you *know* they were the order sheets, these papers on the desk?"

I didn't know. There was only a small brown stain to confirm it. I picked up the brief-case and sorted through the papers. "Something you could do, if you will," I said. "Fill in and sign this form. I'll say the questions, and you supply the answers."

101

She raised her eyebrows. "What is it?"

"A claim to Industrial Death Benefit."

"I didn't think . . ."

"And you're probably right. It could lead to nothing. The situation around your husband's death is rather complicated, and I can't promise anything. But there's one thing certain – if you don't apply, you can't get anything. So you can't lose. That clear? Good! Question one. Name?"

We completed the form. She signed it, no longer the clever and knowledgeable woman, but somehow confused, even uneasy, as though a die was being cast. I thanked her for the coffee, said goodbye, and left.

That application was not for her, it was for me. Purely selfish. I needed it, because the Trent file was becoming clouded in contradictions. Clearly, my next move had to be to dig deeper into the validity of those order sheets, and their movements. But . . . it was going to absorb time. And would Harkness approve of that? He would not.

Now, though, I had a new application relating to Philip Lorimer's death. Officially, it was a new case, and Harkness could hardly object to a new lot of time being absorbed on it. Besides, something might come from it in the end. Philip Lorimer, I'd decided, had been employed under a contract of service, which brought him within the bounds of the Industrial Injuries Act. So his death could be examined to see whether that did, too. The accident had certainly arisen *in the course* of his employment, as he'd been engaged in his official duties at the time. Accident you ask? Definition of accident: an untoward incident resulting in injury. If a 2 in nail in the skull didn't fit that, then I'd resign.

But whether or not this accident arose *out of* his employment . . . ah, that was a different thing altogether. Suicide wouldn't fit that – but murder might. Did a murder really fit in as an expected hazard of his duties? Didn't

102

that all lean on the question of the motive for that murder?

I could see that Harkness was going to have difficulty prising me free of the Lorimer case. Jack Parsons could never handle it. If he got the chance, that was.

Chapter Eight

Leaving my car in the office car park, just on five, I met him coming out. Nice timing. I'd sat in the car for ten minutes, making sure. I stopped dead.

"Heh! You get off at five, do you?"

Parsons ducked his head. "I reckon to."

"That's marvellous! I can't wait." I made to push past him. He stood his ground.

"Aren't you finished, then?"

"Good heavens, no! Two chaps I want to see, but they're on a night shift. And a young woman . . . I'll never get away from *her*. The last time I saw her it was nearly midnight when I got home."

His eyes opened wide. "Bit of all right, is she?"

"Strictly business. It took me that long to get one vital sentence out of her. You really have to dig for it, sometimes."

He grimaced, glanced at his watch, and turned away. "Must rush. Got a date."

"You'd better warn her," I shouted after him. "No dates next week."

Then, well pleased with my bit of background work, I went in to my office.

There had not been one vital sentence from Kaye Trotter, there had been two. She had said, as I recalled it, that Leonard Trent had "arranged to spend the night with her."

When the building was quiet, apart from the cleaners, I went out to the local shop – only 50 yards, round the corner – and brought back fish and chips, went into the kitchen to

104

borrow somebody's plate and cutlery from the cupboard, borrowed some more of Harkness's milk – he'd bought a new bottle – and because I can't eat without reading at the same time, settled down to run through my files.

Ten minutes later, Harkness broke into this idyllic scene, putting his head round the door.

"Still here, Ken?"

"I'm going out again later. The Trent case is getting complicated."

"Will you be taking time off in lieu?"

"I considered it, but there's a lot of work in."

"Not if you closed down the Trent file. Don't let me see you till lunchtime tomorrow."

And with that he left. There'd been a strangely jaunty tone in his voice.

I continued to read through my files. Each one he'd noted inside: "Seen and approved. P. Harkness (Manager)," beneath my latest entries. Strange, that. He'd made one or two useful suggestions in his clipped-on notes, and even handed me a valuable reference, but the files would give him no credit. He was a most unusual manager.

I drove out to Crayshaw Brothers Ltd.

The same chap was on the gate. Geoff something. I told him I ought to get a written statement from him about the evening of Leonard Trent's death, but now I found him reluctant. This was not unusual. People hate to commit their comments to paper, and then sign at the bottom. Neighbours are quick enough to write to the office about people working while receiving benefit, but very rarely go further than signing themselves "Well Wisher". Now, in writing, Geoff Arblaster, as it turned out to be, refused to commit himself on the vital point, for me, that no car had driven past his gate just before the crash. I had to let it go in the end. It wasn't critical, only an impression he'd had, but I found it irritating.

However, as though to even the balance, he was eager enough when I asked if I could see Mr Peterson, the night foreman, taking me in through the side door and pointing to the far end of the shop floor, where the lights were. I made my way very carefully through the maze of silent, dark machinery.

Now it was clear to me how anybody could work their way round to the Stores at night, and make any amount of noise breaking in. The activity was as concentrated as the light. The howl and whine of no more than half a dozen machines was like a wall, through which I had to force myself. Once inside the cage of light I got the impression of isolation, as though nothing more existed in the whole world but this compressed nucleus of battering sound and hypnotising light.

I recognised the little glass-sided shed as a foreman's office, and found Peterson asleep in his chair with his feet on the table. At least, he was until I opened his door, when the influx of sound jerked him awake.

"Who the hell're you?" he demanded, bouncing to his feet.

To begin with, he was angry and aggressive at the interruption, a stocky, bow-legged man getting on for retirement, with a polished bald head and tiny metal-rimmed circular glasses, over which he glared. When the anger faded, and I mentioned the word "Inspector", he was at once suspicious. I would have bet he was moonlighting, holding down another job during the daytime, but that wasn't my interest, and it took me five minutes to persuade him so. When I finally got him round to the night of his MD's death, he became all coy. Who wants to know, and why? Then, at last, I got him into the "things that happen to me" mood, when he'd be prepared to tell me the story.

Yes, he remembered it. Would he ever forget it! The pressure on, and him working his head off, keeping the lads up to the mark, as was his habit, and Trotter hanging around into the bargain. Well – what did *he* want, sticking his nose in? What did he think he could do that he, Peterson, couldn't handle? But of course, with no Stores staff on at night, then if a tool broke or a machine failed, and no maintenance – what're you going to do? What would *you* do, he challenged.

I had to admit to a complete lack of inspiration.

But with only a dozen machines operating out of 200 it's usually easy. You just switch the job to another twin machine. Only, that night it was a copy Fischer lathe that'd gone, and already there were two out of action, and the only one left was that spooky one in Bay 7 – needed the feed lever leaning on at the right time, so it was a bit dicey. Well – you either stop the job or risk a hundred carb bodies half a thou oversize.

Big decisions, I had to agree. The pressure he had to work under! Gratefully, he plunged on.

"And Trotter had to be missing. Said he wanted to be in Lorimer's office at nine, but he wasn't back here at twenty past, and who's going to stick his neck out? Not me. So I went looking for him, while Harry had a break and a drag. Well, I got up there – through the pump shop and across the yard, you know – and it all seemed quiet to me. And then I saw Lorimer's door was open, and when I got to it, there was Trotter kind of backing away from the desk, with his hands held out in front of him. I just stood. Stood. You know."

"And this would be – what time?"

"Coming up to 9.30, I reckon."

"You'd heard nothing? No sudden noises?"

"What sort a sudden noises?"

"A crack. A bang."

He stared at me. "Not a sound, and that yard's as quiet as the grave at night. Here, you don't mean . . . nah, couldn't be."

"Couldn't be what?"

"He musta done it before. 'Cause Trotter was there till just after nine, then down at the gatehouse, then coming back. He was there just before me, and *he* heard nothing."

The timing fitted perfectly with what Trotter had told

me. It fitted, also, the time Trent could have arrived at the office to see Lorimer, some time between 9.05 and 9.20, give or take a few seconds.

"Tell me what you saw."

"Trotter backing up, his hands out."

"Saw at the desk, I mean."

"Lorimer, sitting at his chair, his head down on his arm. I don't like to think about it."

He loved it. "Go on."

"The other arm out on the desk top, and the nail gun right next to his fingers. Where he'd dropped it."

"Anything else?"

"The police came. Dunno how they did it so quick. I was sitting in a corner on a chair. You know, your legs go weak. I suppose Trotter must've phoned. I dunno. I just sat there."

"And did you see anything else on the desk?"

"Such as?"

"Papers. Documents."

"You mean the orders? Oh . . . them! Yeh, they were under Lorimer's arm – the one he'd got his head on. You know about the nail?"

"I know about that. But all you saw was papers? They could have been anything."

"Oh no." Shaking his head. He knew. Peterson risked his hand so rarely that when he had one positive item of knowledge he could dare to be emphatic. "It was the orders right enough."

"You actually *saw* they were?"

He recalled he was a foreman. He popped up his head and stared around quickly for skivers, and subsided.

"When they were shifting him – Mr Lorimer – the papers fell on the floor, and Trotter grabbed hold of 'em, waving 'em see, and shouted something about it was them as'd done it, the damned orders, and one of the coppers said he hadn't ought to've touched 'em, and he'd gotta take 'em along as evidence."

"And that was the last you saw of them?"

"Me? Oh yes. I don't normally see any orders. People tell me what to produce, and I make sure it's done."

I'd been probing an idea that the order sheets I'd seen were not the ones from Lorimer's office, in spite of the brown stain, which could well have been coffee. I thanked Mr Peterson. A signed statement, at that time, seemed unnecessary, as I was chasing shadows. In any event, it would've quite unnerved him. I said good night. He straightened, hitched his jeans, and said he'd better go out and see what the bastards were doing.

Going from that pool of light into darkness was disturbing. For a full two minutes I had to stand and allow my eyes to accommodate, and even then had the devil's own game to find the exit door.

The evening air was quiet and sweet. I took several deep breaths, and went to sit in the car.

I had only one excuse for visiting Kaye, and that a slim one. I didn't want to use it up, in case I couldn't think of another. I pondered this for a while, decided to risk it, and drove away in the direction of the Macklin Shopping Centre.

Only one shop showed a lighted window, the fish and chip shop. A dozen youths were sitting on the wall round the decorative planted arc, shouting something to somebody I couldn't see. Only one car occupied the parking patch, and that was just drawing in. A red Cavalier. As I parked beside it, David Trotter slammed and locked its door.

There was a light on in his sister's flat. The one next door was dark. He was moving with brisk anticipation. Perhaps she re-charged his batteries.

It was disappointing that Trotter should have decided to visit Kaye. I very nearly lay low, and let him get on with it, but on impulse I jumped out and intercepted him.

"Mr Trotter."

He turned, scowling. "Oh, it's you." Then he smiled.

"Fancy meeting you here." But the smile held something that was not pleasant.

"Those order forms we were talking about . . ."

He frowned. "What?" And turned away.

It was difficult, because he refused to stop, and moved across the square as we were talking.

"The order forms you showed me."

"Oh yes?"

"I understand the police took them away."

"They did."

"The same ones you showed me?"

"The very same."

We'd reached the door next to the newsagent's. It was shut now. His finger hovered over the bell-push to the flat.

"Then how did you manage? The whole factory was waiting for those orders, and the police took them away?"

He sighed. "We're not helpless, you know. In the morning I phoned Manchester, and they read out their copies. I took down the figures, and we managed till the police sent back the order sheets. Three weeks, they had 'em."

The finger moved on the bell-push again. I said quickly: "I wish I could be sure of that."

"You calling me a liar?" He said it quietly, but I saw he could be a dangerous man. Then he laughed. "Aren't you coming in?"

With him there? Was it likely? I shook my head. "*Can* I be sure?"

"They banged their bloody stamp on them. Want to see? I'm at the office at seven-thirty every morning."

"Too early for me." If I was on a half-day rest, it was. "Later, perhaps?"

He grinned, nodded, and said: "I'll tell her you called. Nearly."

By the time she opened the outer door to him I was back inside the Mini. As I drove out, a youth threw a ball of chip paper at the windscreen, and ran from under my wheels laughing.

Nine o'clock when I got to Mrs Zalusky's. Couldn't catch her out, though – she'd just brewed a pot. Mr Z said how-do, and Mrs told me the phone had been going all day.

"Who was it?"

"But you're never here."

"Did they say who it was?"

"You're working too hard, Ken."

"I've got tomorrow morning off," I told her. "Who was calling?"

"Your wife."

Lena never liked using the phone. "I can't see who I'm talking to," she'd say. I sat, lowering my face as I deposited the brief-case.

"She'll call again," I said with confidence.

But she hadn't when I went up to my room a little later, Polski sneaking up ahead. He knew he wasn't supposed to at that time, in case he hid in one of the bedrooms, but he hadn't seen me all day, and he reckoned he could pull a fast one. I could've sworn I'd shoved him out, but in the morning he woke me by sitting on my face and purring in my ear. It was nearly half past nine.

I let him out quickly before Mrs Boss found out, and was down just after ten. Things to do. There was a letter for me from Lena.

I took it out to read it in the car, but that didn't happen.

The Mini had been vandalised, door levered open, the seats slashed, instrument panel bashed in, and my little store of tools under the passenger seat stolen.

When I looked under the bonnet the battery had gone, too.

This sort of thing quite undermines you. It's like a punch in the stomach, and for a few moments I actually felt physically sick. Then I marched back into the house to phone a garage, and to tell Mrs Zalusky. The news aroused her husband to passion. "Shoot 'em all, that's

111

what I'd do." Much as I felt myself. It was not as though the Mini was worth much . . . but it was transport. The garage said they'd send round a tow, so I went and paced the pavement until it came. Just my luck – it had to be on my own time.

I rode with him in the cab to the garage, then watched as they pursed lips and shook heads, and said eventually that they'd expect the insurance people to write it off.

Which reminded me it was Lena's car, the insurance in her name, which in turn reminded me that I still hadn't read her letter, and still couldn't because there was now a question of whether they could hire me a cheap car to keep me mobile. While they sorted out a little Fiat for me I got the envelope open, and no further, because there were forms to be signed, so that in the end my morning had evaporated by the time I sat in the Fiat and read the letter.

Monday

Dear Ken,

I've been trying to get you all day on the phone, but I suppose you've been out chatting up your women clients. I'm rushing this letter to the post so that you'll get it Tuesday. I hope. I'm sure you will.

I've been thinking, Ken, and I've made up my mind. There's no question of coming to live in that wretched place. Either you come back (with or without that job you can't let go) or I can make my own arrangements.

Please yourself.

If I don't hear from you by mid-day on Tuesday I'll know. Harry Burnett had asked me to go and live with him. I think that would be best. All round.

Lena.

He of the silky hair and the spectacles, who might be taking over the supermarket from Pearson!

It was 12.17. I drove the Fiat – what a peculiar gear

change! – to the nearest phone box. There was no reply from my home number.

No leeway from Lena. As always, decisive. I could imagine her, bags packed at her feet, her eyes on the clock in the hall, and at the first stroke of twelve out and off, slamming the door firmly. And probably glad that I hadn't contacted her. Get stuffed, Ken Beacham.

I sat in the Fiat a little longer, trying to get used to the idea, then got out again and called the office, asked for Harkness, and told him what had happened to the Mini. That I'd phoned him, told him I had no intention of going in at all that day.

He was remarkably sympathetic. "Anything I can do for you on the files you've got?" he asked.

"They'll wait till tomorrow."

"Then I'll see you in the morning."

I hung up. Problems were mounting. I wondered why he was being so reasonable. If Jack Parsons' warrant had come through – and *that* would have been quick work – I wouldn't have been at all surprised if Harkness sent him out on an easy one. I threw my anorak on the back seat and drove to Crayshaw's.

David Trotter was out at lunch, so I slid into the factory's canteen and got myself sausage, bacon and chips, and nobody queried it at all. I've found you can do this in the big places. When Trotter returned I was chatting-up his secretary, getting her impression of her boss, though she didn't realise it. Worked like a steam tractor, she said. Had much the same personality, I gathered, with a weak regulator on his pressure valve.

"What kept you?" he asked.

"Trouble with my car." I hadn't even been able to remember the name of Lena's insurance firm.

"It's probably got one of our carbs," he said, and he laughed loud and long. Something had put him in a good mood. "Come on, if you want your proof. Though God knows why it's important."

113

I watched him dig out the large folder of order sheets, feeling that now, after encountering Mrs Lorimer, I could probably read more into the figures than he did.

"It's simply a matter of proving that Trent reached Lorimer's office," I explained.

He glanced round at me over his shoulder, one eyebrow cocked. "I thought we'd gone through all that. And anyway, I saw him drive past the main gate."

It wasn't what he'd said. He'd had an impression. "And," I said, "the order forms could've got shuffled around in all that confusion."

He spread the folder, fingers flicking through for January's orders. His voice was even, calmly angry. "Are you calling me a liar?" Almost the same phrase he'd used the previous evening. His reputation for veracity was precious to him.

"People make mistakes," I said easily.

He grunted, stood back, pointed. "Those are the same order sheets. The ones you've already seen. Check for yourself."

I did, feeling the strength of his presence at my shoulder. Under the pressure of it, I deliberately took my time.

I found the same brown stain. I found, on the back of each of the sheets, a round, black-ink stamp, like a Post Office cancellation, with the word "Police" in the circle. It was a well-worn metal stamp. Each impression bore a scrawled initial, and the date: 7th January. On the front of each sheet, angled in the top corner, was a blue rubber stamp: "Crayshaw – Production Control." Across its centre the date: 29 January.

There was no getting round it. These had to be the order forms taken away by the police from Lorimer's office.

I turned, grinning. "Did they take your fingerprints?" He stared. "Elimination," I explained. "Scene of crime evidence."

"You trying to be funny?" he growled.

I had been. But he had no sense of humour. People who

always tell the truth seldom have. He scowled. I said it'd been a joke.

"If you'd seen him with that nail in his head, you wouldn't think it was funny."

He was right. I felt chastened. I couldn't even find a smile for his secretary when I left.

I sat five minutes in the Fiat, trying to sort out the motivation of my present inclination. Suddenly I wanted to see Kaye again. I could tell myself that something she had said needed clarification, and there was truth in that. But behind it there was still the fresh shock of realisation that my wife had left me, and subconsciously I sought a feminine bosom, if not exactly to cry on, at least to admire. And overall – was it the first or the third in order of importance? – I simply wanted to see her.

There was no reason she should have been at home, and even as I parked I could see that the front door was shut. There was a finality about it, because she shared it with another flat, and both would need to be absent for it to be locked at that time. I tried it. But no. Rang her bell. No response. Well . . . you don't do years at my job and be so easily discouraged. I walked round into the service yard behind the shops.

There she was, struggling to insert a large, square package through the rear door of a Ford Escort. As I stood and watched, admired her cussing, and wondered how she'd got all that leg into the jeans, she turned and saw me.

"Don't just stand there," she said, her face red and hair blowing in her eyes – she hadn't got it tied back that afternoon.

"You do it through the front door," I told her.

"Then help me."

I opened the front door for her, and stood back.

"It's heavy," she told me.

"Allow me."

"About time, too."

"I have to observe respect for your independence."

"You just want to prove how clever you are, you big oaf."

This was our second meeting. We were getting along fine.

Chapter Nine

"How far is it?" I asked.

"What does it matter how far? All I ever hear is: how long will it take – how far is it – what'll it cost? Why can't you just sit and relax, Ken? I'm not even asking you to drive."

I stared ahead. A corner was coming up fast. "I rather wish you had."

She laughed, double-declutched neatly, and swept us round the corner.

It was a fine afternoon, with no more than a thin layer of cloud on the horizon. This had been her idea. "If you want to third-degree me, you'll have to come in the car." I'd thought she meant sit in it and talk. When she'd started the engine I'd asked where we were going.

"Seeing you're such a strong, male animal, you can help me put up the sign. That's it on the back seat. 'Elephant and Castle.' Two paintings for the price of one."

I was trying to remember whether I'd locked the Fiat. "I hope they pay you for two."

"There you go," she said through a mouthful of hair, having left her side window down. "Money, money, money."

"It's useful to have around."

"It saps your spirit and undermines your enterprise." That sounded like a rehearsed opinion. "Why d'you suppose artists and composers are supposed to live in garrets?"

"Because there's no money in it."

"No . . . because the money isn't important, it's the painting and the music that matter."

"They starve in those garrets."

"They're bang full of achievement."

My turn to laugh. It was a merry journey, all told, just one extended argument for the first 30 miles.

"How far now?" I asked.

"Can't you relax for a minute!"

"I hope they pay you mileage."

"Shall I turn round? Do you want to go home to your wife?"

"She's in Birmingham."

"I forgot."

No she hadn't. That young lady didn't miss a thing. She was competent and alive, bouncing with a sense of purpose, determined, wherever she went, to spread the magic word. Suddenly, bursting in on her, she'd realised the true meaning of existence, and it was all so exciting, so full of joy, that she had to strew behind her the husks of other ill-used lives and leave a trail of freed and happy converts.

We were up in the hills now, winding in forest country, with the silver birches backed by sombre firs, their new, thrusting buds like pale green sparks against the darker backcloth. She concentrated on her driving, yet I felt she missed nothing of the scene. It was her philosophy to extract the last iota of experience from every escaping moment.

"Another mile," she said. "You'd never guess there was a pub there at all."

"But the customers find it, I hope."

"I did. We were coming along here, one evening . . ." She stopped. There had been nothing to distract her.

"You and Lennie Trent?" I suggested.

"I don't want to talk about him."

"It was you mentioned him."

"There's the turn-off."

The building was not visible from the road, but a large sign ensured that nobody missed it. We drove over pine needles, looping through the trees. It was fake

Tudor outside, but inside it was probably genuine. Those hand-hewn beams could never have been faked.

There was one thing about Kaye; nobody was likely to forget her. They hadn't. Shouts of welcome and open arms. No introduction of me was made, apart from a casual: "This is my friend."

"I'll need a ladder," she said, unwrapping the painting.

The landlord approved when I held it up for him, displaying both sides. She had put a heavy frame round it and given the whole thing a couple of coats of varnish, and fastened two rings into the top edge. We were told where the ladder was, and I went round to fetch it.

They had the old sign suspended in a frame on the top of a 12 ft pole. It was my job to climb up with the sign, unhook the old one – a poor thing that I'd have been ashamed of – and replace it with the new. A tricky business. The clever girl had got the rings exactly right to fit the hooks in the support frame.

Then we sat outside in the sun, enjoying a drink on the house and a cheese sandwich, until Kaye went in for her pay-off, and returned looking so cheerful that I suspected money wasn't quite so unimportant as she'd claimed.

She came out bearing two more glasses, and we sat, she in no hurry at all, me in less. I didn't tell her that, or she'd have suspected I was relaxing.

"The trouble is," she said, "that you've got no drive. That job's destroying your soul. David was the same, stuck on a machine, and nothing in his mind but pay-day and his booze-up with his mates. I had to push him and push him, nag and bully, before he'd risk trying to get on the staff."

"And *that's* achievement?"

"To him it is. It's what he wants. What do *you* want, Ken?"

"So that you can bully me?"

"It wouldn't take, with you. You're a cynic. With David, it was a profession he wanted. You've got your profession, and it's destroying your soul. Do you know that?"

"Do *you* know it, that's the point," I said. "How do you know what I was, so how can you say it's being destroyed? I might have been just as useless from birth."

She stared at me disconcertingly with those large grey eyes, touched her lips, nodded in self-confirmation.

"Something's there, hidden away. Oh yes. You can still find a laugh, and all the while there's a smile in your eyes, but look at those lines in your face . . ." She leaned forward and traced imaginary lines from nose to mouth with her finger. "And in your forehead. The time's running out, Ken. Much more of it, and the job'll finish you off, and you'll be a sour old cynic, not the friendly one you are now." She thrust her glasses back up her nose.

I smiled, and the finger touched the corner of my mouth. "You're working hard at it, but I'm not convinced," I said. "I quite enjoy my job, meeting people. It's steady, and the pay's all right."

"There you go again. Money. Everything comes back to money."

I'd said something like that, myself. "I'm getting set in my ways, that's the trouble. I like to eat reasonably often, I like a roof over my head, a new shirt now and then."

"Paltry stuff," she declared, sitting back. "Your job! What do you achieve? What is yours that you think nobody else could do?"

"The Leonard Trent case. That. I could have dropped it long ago, but I haven't."

The animation drained from her face, all the life gone from her eyes. Without looking down, she groped for her glass – shandy, I thought – and hid behind it. She drank, then looked away.

"Is that what you wanted to talk to me about?" Her voice was lifeless.

"On what I've got, I could've recommended disallowance,

and nobody would've worried about it. Except Virginia Trent, of course."

"What do I do – cheer?"

"All I wanted to do was talk," I told her. "It's your nagging that's done it. 'What have *you* achieved, Ken Beacham?'."

"So . . . can we forget it?"

"You got me on to Lennie Trent, when all I wanted to do was talk. Do you realise that, Kaye? Have you ever thought . . . Lord, all you ever do is think of other people, and how to improve their lives with your wild ideas about freedom of the spirit. But d'you ever think what impression you make? Do you?"

Her eyes came alive. Her mouth found it difficult to express solemnity. She clasped her hands together. "Whatever it is, you're lying."

"It's just . . . receptiveness, I suppose. You give the impression of everything that's you being *there*, on view, all that emotion and happiness and everything else you've got to throw around . . . it shines out all over you. So there's nothing hidden, so I talk, and you receive it, and I *know* what it all means to you. You're like an open flower, Kaye. So I wanted to be with you today, because I've had a letter from my wife, and she's left me. As simple as that. There, you see, it's beaming out – sympathy and understanding . . ."

"And if you don't shut up I'll throw this beer in your face."

I grinned at her. There wasn't much left in the glass. I held up my hands in submission.

"I don't believe a word of it," she said, nodding. "You made that up, just to get a bit of sympathy. It's your technique. You do it all day, persuading poor women to tell you their most intimate secrets."

"It's true. I can show you her letter."

"No thanks. So why aren't you in tears?"

"I don't know. All I've got so far is a sense of failure."

Abruptly, she got up and went into the pub, presumably

to say cheerio to the landlord, because she came out and walked straight to the car. For a moment I thought she might leave me there, because I'd used that forbidden word: failure. But no, she flung open the door for me. Then she turned the car back towards her flat, and had driven a mile before she said another word.

Then she said: "I loved him, you know. Lennie. Loved him. You won't believe that, because you think everything shows on my face, and I've been . . . been happy with you. But I loved him, and it hurts, Ken. And now it's me who wants to talk."

I glanced sideways at her. Her face was stiff, expressionless. I knew, then, what she was doing. This was for me, because I had not come to her and begged for it. I'd come to her because she was what she was. She appreciated that. Perhaps she also understood – in spite of her disparagement – what success with the Trent case, and the Lorimer one, could mean to me. But I couldn't be sure of that. She was too deep for me.

I said nothing, just waited.

"There wasn't ever any chance that it'd come to anything," she went on. "To Lennie it was just another episode in his life, and he'd have moved on when the time came. But he came to me when he wanted me, and that was all I ever needed. That and his sense of fun and his independence. Nobody controlled Lennie, not ever."

"But you tried?" I murmured.

She pouted. "There're some people who're never going to change. He'd reached what he wanted to be, completely selfish, kind, fair, agreeable, and devoted to only one thing – what he could get out of life."

"Your philosophy, Kaye?"

"No!" she said violently. "What he could *take*! I don't want anything – not anything – that I haven't worked for. But Lennie took. He was generous, absolutely free with what he'd got to hand out, but behind it all he was always taking, leaving little disasters on the way, just people who were a bit reduced after he'd finished with them. But he never realised that. It'd been great at the time, but there comes an end."

"Are you telling me this affair of yours was ending?"

"No . . . no, not like it sounds. That night, he was coming to me. Like a child with a new toy – all excitement, because he could stay the night."

"Something you said . . ."

"What was that?"

"Just that. He'd arranged to spend the night, you said. How and when had he done that arranging?"

She slowed the car so that she could steal a good, long look at me. "I don't know what you mean."

"It'd started to snow, that evening. Mrs Trent told me he phoned her from Manchester saying it'd started snowing, and he might be late. All right. So maybe he intended, at that time, to wangle an hour or two at your place. If he'd already arranged to spend the whole night with you, he'd have arranged a cover-up with her then. He'd have said it was snowing and he was staying the night in Manchester. But he didn't. He drove towards his home, the factory, or your place. One of those three. But you said to me, 'he was coming to me.' And later you said, 'he'd arranged to stay the night.' So . . . *when* had he arranged to stay the night, Kaye? That's the point. It must have been after he'd phoned his wife."

"Is this an inquisition?"

"It's been worrying me."

"I blame that damned job of yours. You can't just talk, you have to analyse everything. I don't think I like talking to you."

"We can drop it right now."

"The sooner you get out of that job the better, it strikes me."

"I'm still in it. I have to ask questions. It could mean a lot to Mrs Trent, even more to Mrs Lorimer."

Then her voice was sharp, crisp. "Why to Marjorie Lorimer?"

"I don't think her husband took his own life, that's all. No proof. Nothing but impressions. But there's no reason for suicide – and it could possibly mean she'd get her Death Benefit pension. That might help her with her own insurance – our decision might. As I say, it means a lot."

"But you're saying . . . saying . . ." Abruptly, so viciously that my seat belt locked, she rammed on her brakes and we skidded to a halt, just us and a million trees and her confused anger. "You're talking about murder!" she cried, turning to me.

"I can't see any alternative."

"Who d'you think you are!" she demanded. "You're not the police. You can't go around accusing people . . ."

"Easy, easy!" I put a hand to her arm, but she shook it off. "It's not like that. I don't have to *prove* anything. Not like the police. I don't have to produce evidence that'd stand up in court. All it usually consists of is no more than my recommendation, backed up by something about believing this person or not believing that one. I'd simply have to say it's my belief he did not take his own life. Then she's in the running – Mrs Lorimer, I mean – in the running for a pension."

"Only in the running?" she asked sarcastically. "No more than that? On *your* recommendation?"

I rubbed the back of my neck. It wasn't the time to explain the niceties of "arising out of and in the course of," as it applied to murder. "I'd need to know just a little bit more, if it wasn't suicide. It would come down to the *reason* somebody took his life. Was it personal, or was it to do with his job? *Then*, I suppose, it'd mean knowing who did it. I'd need to know that. But not to go accusing anybody, not saying 'I arrest you.' Or anything like that."

"Then . . . who would?"

"Somebody, somewhere, would give our information to the police. It'd be out of my hands. I'm not allowed to hand over to the police any information that I get from our clients. It's confidential."

Her cheeks seemed puffy, her eyes blank. She was reaching for her seat-belt release, fumbling, not seeing it. Her eyes slipped away from mine as though it was taking an agony of effort, then the seat-belt was free, she had the door open, and she was running across the crisp, short grass towards the trees.

Slowly, I followed her.

She was standing with her back to me. The pine smell was strong. I came up behind her silently, my feet cushioned, and gently clasped her arms. She jerked, but she did not turn.

"I know what you're saying," she said dully.

"I don't know, myself."

"What you're thinking, then."

I put my chin on her shoulder. "What am I thinking?" I whispered.

"That Lennie killed Philip Lorimer."

"Now why should he do that? They were friends. Like brothers."

I turned her to face me. She was shaking her head, close to tears. "I wish I'd never met you," she choked. "I'm all confused. It's not fair! You take every word I say and read things into it."

"I guessed. No more than a guess. The last thing I wanted was to upset you."

She sniffed. "You guessed right. I bet you *always* guess right! Lennie came to the flat earlier. He said the motorway was clear and he'd had a good run. He was at my place at eight. Then, because of the weather, he had this grand idea. He'd phone his wife, pretending he was half way and stuck, and say he'd be home the next day. You know. Great. And then . . . well, time just disappears . . . and suddenly he said he'd forgotten, he'd got to see Philip at the factory. And he got this order thing out of his brief-case and said Philip was expecting him. 'I've got to give him this,' he said. Couldn't let good old Philip down, I suppose. So he stuck the thing in his inside pocket and ran out, shouting he'd be back, and I shouted for him to bring up his overnight bag when he did. And off he . . . he went. And I didn't see him again."

Her face seemed hollow, all the pent-up suffering of three months scoring it. I tried to smile. "And what time was this, when he went galloping away?"

"About 9.15."

I gave it a couple of seconds. "You're sure of that?"

"It was . . . was a night with him I hadn't expected. I was happy. I resented every lost minute. Of *course* I timed it. 9.15 away – I expected him back at 9.45. I watched the clock. But he didn't come back."

9.15, I thought. It fitted exactly with the time of his crash, but only if it had happened on the way *to* the factory.

"It's all right," I said gently, when of course nothing was all right. I held her close. She was shaking. She had to be lying to me.

"The brief-case," I said. "He left his brief-case. What happened to it?"

She pressed herself away from me, head back, staring at me, glasses on the tip of her nose.

"I phoned the factory. Later. Eleven or so. I couldn't stand it. I phoned and spoke to David. He told me what had happened. And I remembered watching Lennie, him taking the order and the key out of his brief-case, and I thought: the brief-case! So I took it in my car and drove there, and all was quiet, with the car still there, all entangled with the lamp-post, and those winking yellow lights round it. I sneaked up behind it and threw the brief-case inside."

She could barely control her voice now. I was holding her very tight. She was speaking against my chest, glasses dangling.

"Like a thief – like a criminal – I went sneaking in the shadows."

"But why?" I whispered. "It was so unimportant."

"Because I loved him," she wailed. "Because it would all

126

be dirty and soiled if it came out, and I wanted to protect him from that. That's why."

While she sobbed, I held her, until her knees gave way and I couldn't support her weight, and we slid down together onto the pine needles. Then, because I was Lennie's stand-in, and because she was Lena's – I suppose – I found myself kissing her and reaching for what was lost with Lena, perhaps what had never been.

After a few moments she responded urgently to Lennie's feverish hands, and she drew me into another of her wild and exciting worlds, where achievement was all that mattered, and creation dissolved in a basic, tumultuous giving that all creation must be. Her creation. If this was it, I could meet her halfway, allow her to lead me into the uproar of it that resounded back from the trees. Until she was silent, and I was spent.

A grey squirrel watched us with interest. For him, perhaps, the trees did not topple. She lay in my arms, and neither Lennie nor Lena were within reach of our minds.

Lying with her cheek against my chest, she said softly: "I want you free of this thing, this case of yours. I want you for me, with none of it hiding behind everything we say and think. Promise me that, Ken."

I mumbled something.

"And now I've told you exactly what happened, you *will* be free of it, won't you! You told me it was decided by your recommendation. But now you know he didn't reach the office."

She twisted her head and smiled up at me. I smiled back.

"You've made everything too easy, my love," I assured her.

But how could I say to Harkness that I recommended allowance because of what Kaye had told me, when there was the evidence of the order sheets refuting it? Could I convince him that I knew the truth was in her eyes, because she'd said it during the soft aftermath of our love, when all is truth.

Driving back, she chattered like a loose exhaust pipe. I could feel her beside me, vibrating with enthusiasm, and in spite of myself – smiling vacantly at the windscreen – I felt her ideas infiltrating into my mind. I told myself it was all infantile fantasy. Creation is all. To hell with comfort and warmth, we would generate our own. We? *We* would? That was what she meant.

"And it doesn't have to be any particular place, nothing fixed, foot-loose. You take what comes. Doesn't that excite you, Ken?"

"It scares the pants off me."

"Everything out of the window."

"Out of *your* window?" I challenged, trying to deflate her before she engulfed me. "But you live in a modern little flat, gas, water, electricity. How do you reconcile . . ."

"I'm on a three-month lease. Finished next month. Then I'm free."

She said that with a wild joy at the prospect, where I, staid old Ken Beacham, set in his steady ways, would have been appalled at the unpredictability.

"And then you just . . . up and off?"

"Somewhere. Anywhere."

"Haven't you got any imagination?"

A touch of the throttle, a firm control of the car, exactly as she controlled her life. She accepted life as it hurtled at her, and steered it her way.

"There're different sorts. One kind of imagination only leads to fears. I close my mind in that direction."

I marvelled, and was warm.

"Don't you do *anything*, Ken? Your own, for yourself, I mean."

"I do the garden."

"Everybody does the garden."

"I'm writing a book."

"And don't tell me your garden's the best in the street! That's pitiful. *What* did you say?"

"I started a book. To tell the truth, I've started it three times."

The car slowed appreciably. "What sort of book?" she asked with suspicion.

"A novel."

She snorted her amazement. "What's it about?"

"A bridge. An old bridge, about 1830. Built by a farmer-landowner to connect his two estates. A suspension bridge, slung between cliffs, and still standing, still taking farm wagons. And one night a chap in a stolen trailer vehicle, loaded high, takes a short cut over it to evade the police, so that it half collapses." I stopped. You tell your ideas like that, and they're empty.

"Then what happens?" The car had drawn to a halt. We were at the foot of Duxbury Hill.

"Oh." I shrugged. "It's a kind of disaster on a small scale. They can't get to the trapped driver, and he's dying. The cliffs are cracking, and threaten to block the river and cause flooding. Some of the people want to cut it free and let him go, others not. The conflict of ideas and personal gains. You know. And I've got a murderer who wants the trapped driver dead."

"Oh." She clapped her hands. "Has it got a love theme?"

"Yes."

"A strong one? Passionate?"

"It could be . . . now."

"Then why," she demanded forcefully, "haven't you finished it?"

"You know me. I spend my life chatting to people. So when I try to tell the story it comes out all chatty, and the style doesn't fit. So I tried it all serious, and it came out stiff and old-fashioned. I don't know . . . I couldn't seem to get it right."

"You must let me see it."

129

"It's back at Birmingham."

"Then fetch it."

"Ha!" I said. "Ha-blooming-ha!"

"The most important thing in your life, and you have to be cynical!"

"Shouldn't we drive on?"

She stared at me, then settled behind the wheel again. "We'd better, before I strangle you."

We made it an evening of celebration at her place. I went across the square to the off-licence for a bottle of Spanish white wine to go with the music she wanted to play for me, and she de-frosted some scampi, which we ate with chips. My life seemed to be involved completely with chips. Then she played Spanish dance music. I wasn't sure what we were celebrating.

"You like that?" she asked suddenly, stopping.

"What was it – Albeniz?"

"It was me. Kaye Trotter. I wrote that."

Clever girl. I smiled, nodded, half drunk with the heady day. "Is it down on paper?"

"Not yet."

"Then do it. I'll get you a pen. There's one in my anorak ..." And stopped. *Had* I locked the car? I remembered wondering about it earlier. I got to my feet.

"Don't be silly!" She laughed. "Not now."

"I don't think I locked the car."

She stared at me, eyes large, as I ran from the flat.

The Fiat seemed untouched. One way to prevent your car from being broken-into – leave it unlocked. The key that'd come with it was in its ignition lock, my anorak lay, still on the rear seat. My wallet! But of course, I'd slipped it into my hip pocket – hadn't I been spending from it? All the same, I picked up my anorak and patted the pockets. There was no welcoming tinkle of my personal key bunch. I frantically searched.

My keys had gone.

Chapter Ten

When I ran up to her flat she was standing in the open doorway. "Well?" Her voice was all agony, my expression probably warning her.

"My keys have gone."

"Anything important?"

Mrs Zalusky's front door, the key to my house in Acocks Green, the keys to the Cortina – the garage had the ones to the Mini – and the really important ones. "The keys to the office and my cabinets."

"Is that all you can worry about?"

"I *do*, my pet, and I've got to go. You see that, don't you?"

She reached out and touched my cheek. "Hurry, then. Phone and let me know."

I drove like a mad thing the nearest way to the office, past Crayshaw Brothers, taking Lennie Trent's fatal route over the little bridge, then past the gates, and to the town.

There were a few cars parked up and down the quiet side-turning, along which we had our office. They told me nothing. I parked in front. The light in my office window told me everything, though. How long had it been on? Why was there not a police car there? I ran up the first five steps to the front door, then abruptly steadied myself with a hand on the railings. It was just possible that Harkness had come in to do a little overtime. I took it, then, more sedately. It would not do to appear in a panic.

The front door creaked open at my touch. Three seconds later the light in my office went off.

He had the advantage. I would stand out against the soft

light in the street, but he came from black darkness, came at a run.

His shadow was on me before I could take a breath, trampling over me. There was a sharp pain on my cheek, and suddenly I was fighting for breath from a pain in my ribs. Instinctively, I reached sideways and grabbed one of the railings, so that instead of falling backwards down the steps I was slammed sideways, back into the railings, and agony shot up my spine. I think I shouted out. He was past me. His shape took the steps in one bound, then he was away up the street, and through my gasping, clawing fight for breath I heard a car start a hundred yards away.

Down on my knees, I tried to remember how I could get to a phone, and it seemed minutes before I worked out that there was one on my desk. I got myself into the hall and as far as my light switch, and leaned in the doorway.

Files were strewn all over the floor, the cabinet drawers pulled out and ransacked. My brief-case had simply been upended and poured onto my desk. The phone was untouched. I groped for it, collapsed in my chair, and dialled the police. Then I sat, and wondered how to reach Harkness. His private number would be noted somewhere, for emergencies. Then I remembered I had a directory in a desk drawer, and there he was under H. It seemed a miracle. I phoned him. Over the siren howl dying outside, I told him what had happened.

"Are you all right?"

"I think so."

"Did you call an ambulance?"

"No. No, I didn't."

"I'll be right along."

When I hung up, I realised he hadn't asked about the precious files.

The police had radioed for an ambulance. Because I could move at all, the attendant decided no ribs were broken, especially as I was now breathing normally, and the only damage to my face was a bruise on the cheekbone and an eye that was blackening. "You'll live," he decided, and he didn't take me away.

By that time, Harkness, breathing worse than me, had arrived. Two policemen were viewing the damage. Harkness and I – me groaning – collected up the files and looked through them. There had been no attempt at destruction. It had been a search. My bunch of keys was hanging from the filing cabinet lock.

"Anything missing?" asked one of the coppers.

I looked at Harkness. "The Virginia Trent file."

"No," he said. "I gave it to Parsons to take home and study. It's all right, officer. Nothing gone."

It wasn't, I supposed, breaking and entering. Nothing had been stolen. They tucked notebooks into breast pockets, declared they would put in a report, and left us alone.

"Well . . ." said Harkness.

"My fault, I'm afraid," I confessed.

"No damage done. Except to you, Ken."

I grinned at him. "Will it go down as an industrial accident? I mean, I wasn't on duty, and I wasn't even on the premises."

He looked at me solemnly. "I'll raise a file, and get the Inspector to have a look at it."

I laughed. "I'll throw it out."

Maybe he'd been joking. He wasn't now. "It will be Parsons, not you. Anyway, you'll need time off, and take it easy . . ."

"No."

"I don't like my Inspector to be assaulted."

"You've got to have an Inspector."

"Parsons wouldn't . . ."

"Wouldn't have lost the keys?" I demanded.

"I was going to say he wouldn't have allowed himself to become so involved."

"But I *am* involved. There's something that needs explanation, and I want to find that explanation."

He was inflexible, fingertips together, grey implacable

133

eyes observing me without sympathy. "Then write it up. Let Parsons worry about it."

I tapped my head. "It's all up here."

He turned to the door. "Isn't that the trouble? Someone wanted that file – or he wouldn't have needed to turn out the lot. But it's all in your head, file or not. He could realise that, and decide to do something about it." He held on to the door. "Don't forget to lock up after you."

It wasn't until I was driving away that I realised I might well have offered him a lift home.

There were always cars parked along the street outside Mrs Zalusky's house, but usually I had no difficulty finding a space. This time I did. I squeezed in behind a Chevette, and if it hadn't been for the warning Harkness had given me, I might not have noticed someone sitting in it. But already the idea was beginning to affect me. I was tense and nervous, and found myself unable to look directly into the car, afraid to have anyone realise I'd realised. That's how confused I was.

So confused, in fact, that I didn't remember, until I walked into Mrs Zalusky's hall, that I hadn't contacted Kaye and told her the news. There'd been no shout from Mrs Zalusky. I found that strange.

The phone was on the wall by the hall-stand. I dialled Kaye's number, and she answered at the second ring.

"Ken?"

"It's me. Just got home. There *was* somebody at the office, but they ran off."

I played it down. I'd have to prime Mrs Z before I could have Kaye dashing around. I said nothing had been taken and no harm done, just a bit of bruising. I reckoned I'd get to bed, and no, she couldn't come round for a bit of soothing. I laughed at something she said. I don't recall the exact words, but hung up still laughing.

When I turned, Lena was standing in the door to Mrs Zalusky's room. She spoke almost listlessly.

"I didn't want to interrupt, you were so absorbed."

"Lena."

"You didn't phone. I couldn't leave it at that." She half turned, gesturing behind her. "There's some tea – I'm supposed to tell you."

"You've been here long?"

"An hour." She shrugged. "You might not have got my letter."

"I got it, but I read it too late." Then, because something had awoken in her eyes: "Not that it would've made any difference."

I put my finger to her shoulder so that I could speak past her. She seemed to shrink from my touch. "We'll just go up for a chat," I said to Mrs Z, and then, because Polski jumped down from the sideboard: "Not you, mate." I was surprised that Lena had been able to sit in that room, with a cat there.

She dragged after me up the stairs, plodding as though she'd walked from Acocks Green. She was wearing a floppy-necked jumper that seemed too thick for the time of the year, and the bottle-green skirt with the paeony print that I hated, because it made her complexion seem sallow. Her winter garb. Did she feel the cold? Had she come prepared for an expedition into the wilds of the north?

I opened the door, put on the light, and stood aside for her.

For a moment she stood looking, her nostrils twitching in disgust and criticism – I'd seen her do it in other people's homes – and I almost spoke up in defence.

"Is *this* where you're living?"

Then I saw that she felt it to be an insult, that I might even prefer to be there, rather than with her.

"I'm not here very often." Then realised I *was* being defensive. "You'll only need to be here one night, anyway."

She made no attempt to sit. Me, I was suddenly exhausted, and sat on the end of the bed, looked up at her, and saw she was distant, even startled.

"I'm not staying, make your mind up about that, Ken. If

you think I came all this way because I couldn't do without your hot, sticky hands all over me . . ."

"For God's sake, Lena, I meant . . . I thought you'd come to see the bungalow. I can sleep in the chair."

"The bungalow? Don't be ridiculous!"

I got my shoes off. God, my feet! "Then why did you come?"

"To give you one more chance to change your mind. You could give your office one month's notice."

I was shaking my head, partly to clear it. "Lena, please . . ."

"I thought you'd be prepared to do that. Rather than throw away what we've done together, what we've scraped and saved for, and gone through together. I thought you'd think twice before you threw all that away. It seemed only fair to give you the chance. Then I could go away from here knowing where I stand. Are you listening to me, Ken? Are you?"

I was listening, but in the background. More importantly, I was watching. She had her shoulder-bag clasped in her hands, and one finger was snapping the catch on and off. Her stance was not as I usually saw it. She was angular and awkward, wanting to sit but forcing herself to stand and be dominant. But in her face there was distress, and a fear of what she was doing. For her, an indefinite future was terrifying. And her voice did not hold any of her usual confidence. One gentle word from me, I realised, provided it hinted at abdication, would have had her in tears. I was sorry for her. Had I brought her to this? One sentence from me would wipe it clear – a hint that I had actually allowed the thought of resignation to cross my mind.

But, in time, I realised that the inspiration for it had come from Kaye's enthusiasm and fire, not Lena's dread. It seemed unfair that I should present to Lena the fruits of Kaye's passion.

"What's the matter with your face?" she demanded, and the moment was gone. "You've been fighting. You've been out drinking, and got in a fight! Is *this* what you've come to? Answer me, Ken!"

"I was in the way . . ." I stopped. I owed her no answer. "It's nothing."

"I don't believe you're sober enough to understand what I've been saying."

"I understand completely."

"So you'll do what I ask?"

"I don't intend to resign and come back to Acocks Green."

"Do you realise . . ."

"I realise very clearly. You can't imagine with what clarity I'm seeing things."

"Then there's no more to be said."

I sighed. "Sit down, Lena. There's a lot to be said."

She sat down because I was in no mood for argument, and it must have come through loud and clear. I said: "You've got my Cortina, and I've got your Mini."

"We swap." There was a kind of victory there, as though she'd won a point.

"It's not so easy as that. The Mini's in a garage, and it could be a write-off. You'll need to claim . . ."

"You've crashed my car!"

"It was vandalised." I suddenly realised that somebody didn't like me, or didn't like what I was doing.

We went on from there. I forced her to go on, presenting to her the basic and gruesome practical matters involved with the breakdown of a marriage. Who was having what. How we would split the proceeds of our house in Acocks Green after everything was cleared up. Why I would not – unless she obtained a Court order – pay her maintenance while she was living with another man. When I could collect my Cortina. (Tomorrow, she said. I'll leave it in the drive. And to hell with the Mini.)

Apart from the odd outbreaks of anger, provoked by her frantic search for independence in her attitude, she sat grim-faced and unrelenting. I wanted her to realise that *she*

137

had brought us to this, and what it meant. But right to the end I don't think she fully appreciated the enormity of thus destroying six years of marriage, and nothing would have persuaded her there was any fault in her direction.

I went down with her. Calmly she said good-night to the Zaluskys. I showed her the path through the conservatory and walked with her to the gate. By then, I felt, she was confused. It was still not too late for a word from her, "I'll stay, then, and at least look at the place you've found." But no. She actually held out her hand for me to shake it, when we stopped at the gate.

The man I'd seen in the Chevette opened the door and got out. Tall and slim. Silky hair in the moonlight, a reflected glint from a streetlamp in his glasses. He stood by the car, then went round to hold open the door for her. She had actually got Harry Burnett to drive her there, to see her husband, to persuade her husband . . . what? I stared at him. He seemed to wilt. If I'd shouted, he'd have turned round and run.

She walked towards him.

"Good luck," I said, but she didn't glance back.

I thought they seemed well-suited.

Back inside, I had my hand at Mrs Zalusky's door before she managed to finish: "Ken, there's a pot . . ."

"I know, of tea," I said. I put my head in, grinning, though it must have been sickly.

"Has she left? I thought . . ."

"She's left."

We sat companiably. She made no other mention of Lena. If I'd volunteered information, she'd have been sympathetic, and might even have made suggestions. I wanted neither, just her company and that of her silent husband, while I tried to master the urge to jump into the Fiat and drive round to Kaye's.

But I didn't think I dared to go near Kaye while the anger and resentment were still rocking me. My relationship with Kaye was so delicate that I had to approach it unemotionally, and view it warily from all directions. Unemotionally, did I say? That would've been difficult.

After I'd been coaxed into telling of my adventure that evening, and in the telling realised how stiff and pained I was feeling, I went up to my room for an early night, and sat again, long into the still hours, with Polski eyeing me hopefully, believing he was going to get another night on my bed. He didn't. I saw to that. There was just a chance I'd have to rely for some considerable time on Mrs Zalusky's hospitality. She had not been her usual jolly self, though.

Wednesday, I decided, over my bacon and eggs, was going to be a day of reconstitution and rest. In any event, it was figures day, when I had to justify, in my weekly report, the time and effort of the previous week. That would absorb the entire morning, and the afternoon could be used for bringing my minutes up to date in the current files.

At the office, all was a-buzz with the news of the foray of the evening before, and my room was filled with a constant flow of well-wishers – people I didn't even think I knew. I couldn't settle to a thing. At around 9.30 a detective-sergeant called Brown came to visit and to obtain a statement. I played it down, not revealing to him that I suspected what the intruder had been looking for – the Virginia Trent file. At that stage I didn't want the police discussing my knowledge on Trent's death. I had a feeling that they, too, would prefer me to drop it all.

But it was an opportunity to establish a relationship. We chatted generally. The chap was quick and alert, not assertive but receptive. We got along fine. It was a pity I might be losing the job.

After he'd left, Jack Parsons came in, bringing back the Virginia Trent file he'd borrowed.

"Had a good read?" I asked.

"It was interesting." But he was cautious.

"It's not fully written-up. There's a bit more to add."

He unfolded himself a chair from the corner. "Mind if

I stay? I've done my figures, so I've got an hour. Harkness said I could see how you do yours." He laughed easily. "The good old swindle-sheet."

I couldn't say much about that, considering I was going to have to hide my outside-the-district visit to Marjorie Lorimer. But you can't *start* a job with his attitude. He might work into it, depending on his personal inclinations, bending his brain in order to wangle unofficial time off and hundreds of miles of imaginary journeys, but he'd trip up and get his knuckles rapped. I simply allowed him to sit and watch, not encouraging his optimism.

I took out the last minute sheet from the Trent file and wound it into the Imperial. I'd rescued the machine when they brought a new typewriter for the three-girl typing pool, and I was learning to type. Two fingers on the right hand I'd mastered, and I was now trying to interpose one on the left. Slow going, but it occurred to me that if I was ever going to submit a novel – an actually completed one – it would have to be typed, so I needed all the practice I could get.

I typed the date, then:

Information has been received, by chance, during personal contact in my own time with a witness in this case, that Leonard Trent was at Macklin Shopping Centre on the evening of his death. This is to the east of the factory, to which he was heading when he died. As the informant had reason to note the time he left Macklin, I now understand this to be 9.15. My impression was that the informant was honest and truthful. This fits with the time of the accident, 9.23, but only if Trent was driving towards the factory.

K. Beacham.
Inspector.

No more than that. No names, no statement from Kaye, no mention of the conflict of this evidence with the evidence presented by the order sheets. I re-tagged the page in the file.

Parsons read it, glanced at me, flicked it with his finger. "Bit thin, isn't it? Not even a name to your witness."

"It was on my own time."

"Then it's not very official."

I drew my weekly report sheet towards me, and said, keeping my voice steady: "I start with a list of files, mark the ones in and out, and check that the figures balance."

"Should be easy."

"It gets complicated when the file drawers are ransacked and people take files home to read."

He scratched his head. "Lucky I did."

"We don't know the chap was after a look in that file. On this job, we make a lot of enemies. Assault's all part of the job. It could've been somebody I've offended recently."

"Gerraway!"

"One case this week . . . the Inspector last year was attacked with a spade. You have to make up your mind – do you apply for a police escort?"

"And did you?"

"I risked it. Tact, diplomacy – I got a bit of seed cake."

"You're pulling my leg."

"No. Shall we get on?"

He sat with me until lunch break. He was spot on time with that. The room seemed empty when he'd left. I went out to my café, came back, sat a few minutes, and wondered whether to go out. I'd finished my weekly report quicker than I'd expected.

He put his head in again. "Harkness told me to come out with you this afternoon."

"He told *me* to take it easy."

"It'll be easy, with me along."

I'd just decided to go and see Mrs Trent again. No reason, but frankly I was groping, worried about the case. I changed my mind.

"There's a Giro fraud we could have a look at."

"Come on, then. My car?"

"Mine. Yours isn't authorised." Nor, I realised, was the Fiat. Hell! Another complication. I got the file, looked it through, and we went round the back to our car park for the Fiat.

Mr Clive Fothergill was off from work, having squashed a finger in a machine. He'd reported non-receipt of three Giro orders, and we'd got them back to show him. Each was signed C. Fothergill. What was he going to say to that?

Fothergill lived in an estate out on the north road. He was home. His wife showed us in, to where he was nursing his finger and reading the morning's paper. I showed him the three Giro's. "Not my signature," he said, as I'd anticipated, having checked his from our records. The squashed finger was on his left hand.

"Do you recognise the writing?"

He did not.

"Is there another family of Fothergills in the avenue?"

"Not as I know."

"Have you had any difficulty with your post delivery, then, Mr Fothergill?"

"Nah! Here, what're you getting at? I ain't had the money, and that's that."

That, in this instance, wasn't quite that. The next bit was difficult. You had to proceed far enough before they realised what you were aiming for. "How many people live here?"

"Me. The missus. My daughter."

"How old is your daughter?"

"Now . . . what the hell's that got to do with it?"

I didn't need to reply. A girl – young woman? She'd perhaps have been 18 – came bursting in, all spikey hair and brown lipstick and floppy boots. "Daddy, have you seen my 'Cosmopolitan'?" She stopped. "Oh!" Enquiry, and something like shock, struggled behind the mascara. "I'll come back." The door slammed behind her.

"Your post?" I asked quickly. "What time does it come?"

"Eightish. Why?"

"You're up to collect it?"

"Not when I'm off sick, mate. I get me a lie in."

"So somebody else collects it?"

"My wife. I'm not having you sayin' nothing about the missus."

"I wasn't. What does she do with it?"

He was becoming confused and agitated, floundering. I said: "No need to get upset. I'm not suggesting anything, just trying to get a picture."

"She leaves it on the hall table. 'Cepting there's somethin' for her."

I glanced at Parsons. He thought he'd got the answer already. I shook my head, got to my feet.

"That's all, is it?" Fothergill asked.

"For now, I think."

"What's gonna happen about me money?"

"Don't worry. We'll sort it out."

"'Cause things're getting tight."

I smiled. "Tight all round. And with your daughter on benefit, too – and I'll bet she lies in all morning, and you sitting here . . ."

"She's a good girl. Up to help her mother before eight. Though of course, at half past, Dennie calls for her."

"Dennie?"

"Her boy friend. Calls on his way to work. To say hello. The daft lot. These days . . . I daren't look in the hall till he's gone."

"Where does he work, then?"

"Windways Garage, on the Peak Road."

"Let's hope he keeps his job, shall we! Say good afternoon to your wife for us. We'll be in touch."

We went outside. Parsons waited until we were in the

car. He was excited. "She knew! The girl. You could see it. It was she cashed them."

I started the car, shaking my head.

"Where to now?" he asked.

"Peak Road. The garage."

The Giros had been cashed at two different Post Offices, each in Peak Road. The Windways Garage was about equidistant from each. We went in. I asked for Dennie. He was a tall, insolent-looking youth in his early twenties, with a set of protruding teeth that would've tightened your wheel nuts.

I showed him the cashed Giros, but he said he didn't recognise the signatures. I gave him a piece of paper and asked him to write "C. Fothergill" six times, then sign his own signature at the bottom.

He tried very hard to make the "C. Fothergills" different, but his own signature, done when he relaxed, gave him away. "D. Preston." I showed him how the "r" and the "e" were the same as in Fothergill on the Giros, and how the "o" was disconnected in both cases. I told him I suspected he'd cashed those Giros, gave him a formal warning, and asked if he'd like to make a statement. He told me what I could do with my statements, and his hand slid towards a spanner on his bench. Parsons backed up a little. I laughed, being chummy, hefted my brief-case.

"They were on the hall-stand, were they?"

"Get stuffed!"

"Were they?"

"They shouldn't 've been there."

I nodded. We left. I drove back to Fothergill's, parked outside, and sat back.

"Practice for you," I said. "The Giros were delivered, because they got to the inside of the letter box. You go in and you tell Fothergill *his* property was stolen, not the Department's, and it's up to him what he does about getting the money back. We can't repeat payment, because he's legally had the money, but we'll probably prosecute young Preston. The money's between him and Preston."

"Me?" said Parsons.

"Why not? You know it all. At your fingertips. You want to be an Inspector, so go and inspect."

He hesitated, got out of the car, hesitated again, then shrugged and headed for the door.

He was gone ten minutes, then he returned at speed.

"She was there," he said, slamming the door.

"Who?"

"The daughter."

"Ah yes! I should've warned you – not in front of the daughter."

"All hell broke loose."

"Yes. It does. Shall we go back?"

He left me in the car park. Half an hour to knocking-off time – he had to go and tuck away his section. I went into my office, and there was a note on my desk. Harkness.

"Will you come and see me when you get in?"

I went along to see him.

Chapter Eleven

It seemed that any leaway I'd been given because of my injuries had now had its full fling. Harkness looked serious, even disturbed. He had the Virginia Trent file on his desk.

He didn't ask me to sit down, but all the same I did. He placed his palm on the file.

"Parsons came to see me," he said. "Lunch time." This sacrifice seemed to be stressed. "As you know, I let him have the file to study. He seems to have a good grasp of things, now, and it's his opinion that we can close the file with a recommendation for disallowance."

"His opinion?"

"And I must say I agree with him."

"You do?"

"You'll remember, I was a little concerned with the time you've been spending on this case, Ken." He sighed. We'd slipped into the friendly style. He was wearied by thoughts of the time I'd spent on it. "And the effort's quite out of proportion with the results."

"Some of the effort's been on my own time."

One eyebrow shot up. There might have been a smile on its way, but he looked down quickly. "Perhaps that's the trouble."

"Trouble?" I demanded.

"You appear to be having difficulties with it, perhaps personal ones." He cleared his throat. "We feel it could have been handled . . ."

"*We* feel? You and Parsons? I object to Parsons being consulted at all."

He blinked at my anger. Perhaps he'd taken my inoffensiveness for granted. "I merely let him see the file. As an example of how cases should be handled and written-up."

"But he chose to criticise?"

"Now . . . you mustn't take that attitude."

"Oh, mustn't I? He's never even done the job. I'll have a word with Parsons . . ."

"What he said was reasonable and to the point. I had to admit that."

There was a hint of weakness. He *had* to admit that. Had been forced to admit it? I didn't know why it made me more angry; didn't know why I was angry already. My resentment at the interference of Parsons would have been just as strong the week before, but then I would have taken it to myself, smiled at it, calmed it. It wasn't as though it mattered. Kaye had half convinced me that nothing mattered unless it was solid and achieved. I should – still humming tunelessly as I was to her tune – have been able to dismiss this disagreement as paltry. Shrug it off. Say to Harkness "You're the boss, you can do what you like." And walk away from it.

I leaned forward and spoke quietly, but now the effort towards equanimity was forced. "Tell me what was reasonable about what he said."

"Quite simply . . ." Harkness visibly relaxed. ". . . we have two contrasting items of evidence. The one, the order sheets, show that Trent reached his MD's office; the other, your informant's evidence, indicates that Trent could not have done so."

"That's the difficulty."

"But it's no difficulty, Ken, can't you see that! The presence of the order forms is positive. It's solid, and it's a fact. Your evidence that Trent left Macklin Centre at 9.15 is nebulous, to say the least. It was *said* to you. You believe what was told you. No more than that. It's simply a . . . perhaps impressionable experience that you've decided to accept as truth." He licked his lips, smiled in a rather ghastly way, and repeated "Nebulous," as though the word pleased him.

So Parsons had watched me type that minute, had read it, and not put his conclusions to me. Yet he'd run into this office and told Harkness his precious opinion.

"It is," I said carefully, "an apparent anomaly that I intend to pursue." Nicely put, I thought, grimacing. "I believe the verbal evidence."

"You will not pursue it, though, that's the point. As the file stands ..." He lifted it, and allowed it to fall again on to his desk surface. "As it stands, I intend to recommend disallowance myself, on the grounds that Trent had reached the office and left it. I can do that. You realise that?"

I ploughed on, voice emotionless, I hoped. "But there's the death of Philip Lorimer."

"Suicide. We know that. He saw the figures on the orders ..."

"No."

"No? No – what? He didn't see the figures? But of course he did. They gave him reason for despair."

"Nonsense! Those figures told him nothing he didn't already know. There was absolutely no reason for suicide."

"Not nonsense," he said, bridling. "The inquest verdict ..."

"Verdict or not, it wasn't suicide."

He raised his eyes in exasperation. Then he tried to be kind. "You can't go around saying these sort of things."

"I haven't. This is private."

His mouth expressed firmness. "Official. You sit there and say Lorimer was killed ..."

"I am sitting here and saying that if you disallow that claim – now, without further investigation – you're saying that Trent reached his MD's office, and because of the timing involved, *you* will also be saying that Trent killed him."

That was stretching it a bit, but Harkness wouldn't realise it. He fell back on dignity, on protocol. "That would be a

148

question for the police. I refuse to allow you to become involved in matters unrelated to your duties."

"The truth *is* the matter related."

He puffed his lips, blew his disgust. "Let's not get too fancy."

"Very well," I said. "Straight, then. If you take that file off me and recommend disallowance, I shall go to Mrs Trent and persuade her to appeal. I'll prepare her appeal. I shall tell her how your decision falls apart unless it's assumed her husband killed his brother-in-law."

"What are you saying? You can't be serious!"

"Deadly serious, I assure you. And you'll find that Lorimer and Trent were friends, like brothers. There couldn't be anything further from possibility than finding any reason for Trent to kill Lorimer. And," I added, driven to desperation by his expression of doom and horror, "if I have to, I'll bring evidence that Trent was happy, pleased, to be going to Lorimer's office that evening. And I shall do all this myself, at the appeal hearing."

"I will . . ." Harkness flapped his palms on the table, and got up in agitation. He stared out of the window, then turned back. "I have never heard such a statement in my life! You're speaking about . . . do you realise what you said? You'd assist a member of the public to appeal against your own Department! It wouldn't be allowed. You'd be stopped, disciplined."

"Dismissed?"

"I could pick up this phone, and you'd be off the job in five minutes. Suspended."

"Would that stop me?"

Slowly, he went back to his chair and ran his hands through his hair. He was giving himself time. At last it seemed he shuddered, and had himself under control. He looked up. His eyes were bleak but his voice was calm, even kind.

"I'll tell you what I'm going to do, Ken." Friendly again,

I noted. "I'm going to hold this file until you're off the job, and let the next man finalise it."

"No."

"No? Are we starting again?"

"We've got no further, have we? I get the file back, and I handle it. You can report my attitude to Regional Office, if you like, but this is my case. It's a matter of principle."

"I'm not going to listen to this."

"I'm only asking for time."

"But I'm not inclined . . ."

"There's Lorimer's death, you see. It happened in our district, but Mrs Lorimer lives in the next area. I've got an application from her for Industrial Death Benefit. It hasn't been stamped in yet, so it's not even official, but if it was, it'd have to go to the other Manager, and *that* decision wouldn't be yours. They'd send me a file. Investigate at the factory, they'd ask. Which I'd do. Which I've done. And if it wasn't suicide, the claim could well be valid. *That* case I'd have to investigate. Or Parsons. And the facts are in *that* file, the one you're thumping with your fist."

"Say it. Go on, say it!"

"I don't have to hand in that application form. Then it wouldn't be official, and there's nothing on earth could stop me carrying on hunting for facts in my own time. Nothing."

He held out his hand. "Give me your warrant."

"Can you afford to throw Parsons into the job with no experience at all?"

He could not. You could see that in his eyes. "I will not be pressured like this."

"I'm sorry. Really – you forced my hand."

"I'll not forget this!"

"Can I have the file?"

He held it out. "When this is over . . ." He stopped.

"Maybe," I offered, "you'll be pleased."

"Pleased? My God!"

I closed the door behind me softly. The clock at the end

of the corridor showed 5.03. Not pausing, I rushed through into the main section. There was nobody at Parsons' desk. Girls were putting on their coats, chattering in the release from work.

"Parsons?" I demanded.

"He's just left." She stared in surprise.

I ran out of the back door into the car park. He had reached his car. "Parsons!" I shouted. He paused and looked back, annoyed, nervous.

I advanced on him. "How dare you interfere in my cases!"

"Take your hand off the suiting," he said, trying to be smart.

I couldn't remember ever having struck anybody. There was an overpowering desire to discover how it felt. Painful to the knuckles, no doubt. Not having realised I was even touching him, I released him quickly.

"I tried to be reasonable with you," I said. "Your pushing and shoving – I ignored it and tried to help. No more, though. Find somebody else to train you."

"I'm not a performing dog."

I couldn't help smiling. He'd realised what he was. "When the file's yours, do what you like. Until then, keep your nose out."

He raised his chin, trying to stare me down with his contempt. "You don't have to worry. I don't fancy the rotten job. I told Harkness that, half an hour ago."

I watched him get into his car, realising that Harkness had not been seriously influenced by my arguments and threats; he'd simply been aware that he had to live with me as his Inspector for longer than he'd expected. Better the devil you know, and all that rot.

Back in my own office, I found the phone hadn't been plugged through to the exchange. They were supposed to do that. An Inspector needs an outside line, and can't rely on keeping to office hours. I stormed through into the phone room, but the three typists had left, so I had to fumble around and hope I'd done it right, dash back and discover I had. And then wonder who the hell I'd intended to call.

I dialled Mrs Zalusky's number and told her I might be late. There was no point, because I had a key, but I was half hoping there'd been a message from Lena. Or dreading. There hadn't been. I then rang Kaye's flat, but there was no response, and suddenly I couldn't think what to do with the evening. I'd had some idea of visiting Mrs Trent, but now I couldn't remember why. So I went out and tried a café I hadn't ventured into before, had a surprisingly good meal, and felt better all round.

A walk round the town square only managed to confirm what Lena had said. It *was* uninspiring, even depressing. But the sun was nudging its way round towards the point where Collier's Lane suddenly seemed attractive, so I collected the car and drove there.

It wasn't the same. The bungalow, the scene, the aura of mystery; none of these was the same. Suddenly the place I'd hunted out from the hundred or so available took on a special magic. It had been a bungalow before. Now it was *my* bungalow, they were my windows to walk round and peer in, imagining the curtains hanging and the furniture filling the rooms. That corner room – so small and compact – hadn't there been a subliminal thought that I might lock myself away there and perhaps achieve some improved version of my novel?

My neighbour did not appear, but I could almost imagine him standing at my elbow, nodding and nodding. "Didn't I tell you?" Because the sunset was different, with the smoke lying lower and the slopes bloodied deeper. And in the soft silence it seemed I was the only man alive, and that this was my land, my own, had always been so had I but known it.

I stayed until complete darkness saddened me, then I drove back to Mrs Zalusky's. Strange that I'd feel so easily accepted by that room and its confines, when

152

I'd gloried so completely in the vastnesses below Collier's Lane.

In the morning, a new file had come in, one where I was asked by our Legal Branch to prepare the papers for the police. My first such case since I'd been at that office, this would be. As I hadn't handled the original enquiry, it involved a certain amount of study, and the paperwork had to be impeccable. I had it ready by lunchtime, and took it along afterwards.

There had been no reason for me to visit the police station since I'd been in that district. It was a small building, with only one man in the duty office, a constable. I asked him whether Sergeant Brown was available. He rang through and discovered he was.

Brown walked towards me along a corridor. "Hello again. Thought of something you forgot?" He was obviously thinking about our upset at the office.

"It isn't that."

"They often do."

"I've got an Order Book fraud for you."

His eyes went blank. More important matters occupied him. "You'd better come through."

I followed him into the CID office, which could well have been any three-man office in the Civil Service. Desks askew, two battered typewriters, ancient and chipped cabinets. The only marked difference was that each desk had two phones. He sat at one of the desks, where half a cigarette smouldered in an ashtray, and gestured.

"Pull up a seat."

I did, and sat quietly while he had a quick look through the file. He looked up.

"Seems okay. We'll get on it, but I reckon he'll have skipped." He half levered himself to his feet. That was the end of it.

"There's something else," I said, having made up my

mind. I felt uneasy. I was venturing into realms that were beyond my duties, and felt that if I revealed too much the whole thing could be snatched from me. There was also the restraint imposed on me by the Official Secrets Act.

He lit another cigarette, and perched it to smoulder away in the ashtray, and spoke easily.

"This is nothing to do with that business at your office?"

"If it is, I can't possibly connect it."

"Some information you've got for us?"

"Say – rather – some information I'm fishing for."

"Ask away," he said cautiously.

"When you have evidence – something you take away from a scene, say – paper evidence, do you use an official stamp?"

"Depending on what it is. We might put it all in a bag, seal it, and put a tag on it."

"Sheets of paper, I was thinking about."

"They'd bang their stamp on the back, most likely. In the office. Initial each stamp. If it was likely to be used in evidence. What are you getting at?"

"This stamp . . . would it be available to a member of the public, by any possible chance?"

"Not on your life. What'd be the point, if anybody could get their hands on it?"

"I did rather think that."

There was a pause, then he said: "You sound disappointed."

"I'm faced with a blank fact, and I can't get round it."

"Do you have to?"

"Something like that." If I was to sustain my faith in Kaye, with all the world battering at it, yes.

"Can you tell me?"

I looked at him, and grinned. "Anything I say will be taken down and may be used in evidence? I know the Judges Rules."

He raised his eyebrows, then leaned forward and tapped

my knuckles with his pencil. "I thought this was just a chat."

I moved in the chair. "It's about Philip Lorimer's death."

"Oh? You involved in that, are you? But it was suicide. Doesn't that throw everything out of the window for you people?"

"Not everything. And it's Leonard Trent's death I'm involved with. Not Lorimer's. Not yet."

"Suicide or not, you might get involved?"

"Or not, you say? Why'd you put it like that. It *was* suicide, wasn't it? That was the inquest verdict."

He was tapping-out another cigarette from his pack. The air was already foul with smoke. "Don't be clever with me, Mr Beacham, please. Not if we're going to get along."

"I wasn't feeling particularly clever."

"You're involved with the death of Leonard Trent – you said. But the first person you mentioned was Philip Lorimer. Would there be a reason? I'm being honest with you – let's have a bit of the same."

"You'll be more upset if I tell you what's in my mind."

"Try me."

"I'm beginning to wonder whether Lorimer killed himself . . . or not."

He smiled, then, one of those smiles that are all relief and gratification. "And there I was, thinking you were breaking fresh ground! Don't you imagine we thought of that? That nail gun! Hell, it was the most fantastic suicide weapon I've ever come across. And to imagine him taking all that trouble to get hold of it – that was a bit much. But we didn't get anywhere along those lines, and there *were* reasons for suicide."

Perhaps he hadn't interviewed Mrs Lorimer. But of course he would. "The figures on those order sheets, you mean? But they were nothing – not strong enough for suicide."

"I'm aware of that. We've got experts, you know. Why

155

d'you think we took them away for examination? The things were under his arm. The set-up shouted out the connection. He'd read the orders, then shot himself. That's what it looked like."

"I understand they were folded up, as though he hadn't even looked at them."

"Do you? Do you, indeed? They were folded, yes. It didn't mean they weren't spread out under his eyes five minutes before he died. Folded and under his arm, yes. Then, when they moved the body that stupid goon – Trotter, I think his name was – he grabbed hold of 'em and waved them around. I took 'em off him . . ."

"You were there?"

"Didn't it sound like that? Yes, me. Took 'em off him and brought them back here, and our financial geniuses – genii? I dunno – they said it wasn't anything like a motive for suicide."

I stared at him with despair. I had been hoping that I could discover something broken in the chain of movement of those order sheets, but Sergeant Brown had destroyed all that. He himself had been a link in the chain. Lennie Trent had put the sheets in his pocket and set off for Lorimer's office. The same order sheets – and how could any others have been involved? – were discovered under Lorimer's arm on his desk, were impounded by the police and stamped, and later returned to the factory. Trent must have reached Lorimer. There had been time uncovered between nine, when Trotter left Lorimer, and 9.23, when Trent crashed his car. That left only one thing wrong: Kaye's statement that he had left her at 9.15.

If he'd been there, Harkness would have managed a hollow laugh.

I managed to speak. "But you still decided it was suicide?"

He shrugged. "The pistol had Lorimer's fingerprints on it. And there was other evidence. The Coroner was tipped-off, and it didn't have to be bandied around the court. Contrary to general opinion, we don't cause distress when it can be avoided."

"If only," I murmured, "to save yourselves trouble."

"Precisely."

"And can you tell me what would have caused distress, and where?"

"I can tell you, just as long as you don't go shooting off your mouth, and don't write it up in one of your files."

My hands – my tongue – would be tied. I nodded agreement.

"Lorimer, it seemed, was a womaniser. You know these top executive types, they're all drive and energy and self-confidence. It exactly fits the personality for sexual activity, so they're all a bit warm, usually getting it on the side."

"I don't think it's rampant in the Civil Service. Our top execs, I mean."

"No? Oh well, it's just a theory. But Lorimer was certainly like that – a woman in every town. These managers move around. He picked 'em up and dropped 'em, playing a dangerous game."

"There could be something in this theory of yours. Their life's like that, erratic and dangerous."

"She knew, you know. Lorimer's wife. We believe she knew, but nobody ever asked her outright. That's why the Coroner got the tip. But she was everything to Lorimer, we found out that much. However many women he was juggling with, Marjorie Lorimer was all the world to him. You understand, we didn't get down to proof. It was all hearsay and rumours. But there was the latest woman – so the whisper went – and this time he'd played too close to the danger line and it'd gone wrong. This one he couldn't shake off, and he was going to have to face his wife with it, and he thought that'd wreck everything he'd built up with their marriage. That was what was worrying him, that and another side issue – the sabotage that was going on at the factory."

It was a fresh light on Lorimer. There'd been not a breath of this from his wife; but there wouldn't have been, anyway. Even if she'd known. If Brown was to be believed, Lorimer had taken his own life rather than have to break up his relationship with his wife. Had Lorimer realised it meant he was leaving her not simply bereft, but close to destitute, too? He was a practical man, a businessman. He would have realised the consequences of suicide.

I gave the sergeant a twist of a smile. "I never heard such twaddle. What a romantic lot you are in the police. Killed himself because of a woman! Codswallop!"

He stared at his fingernails, turned his hands over and stared at his palms. "It's the Coroner who's romantic. It convinced *him*."

"You mean . . ."

"The case isn't closed. We've got our ideas. The inquest verdict didn't tie our hands."

"It suited you?"

"The evidence leaned towards suicide." Then his eyes were on me, and I was suddenly aware that I would not like to meet him in an interrogation room. "So . . . would you mind telling me just what you've got in mind, Mr Beacham?"

The choice had been mine. I'd walked into that station of my own free will, and with the intention of bringing this up.

"Mr Beacham?" he prompted.

"You've had your bit of fun, Sergeant, playing around with Lorimer's sex life."

"It was true."

"Sure it was. But did you find a motive for murder in it?"

"Have you?" he asked quietly.

"This sabotage rumour. Lorimer could have come too close."

"We haven't forgotten it. Do you know how little it takes to ruin a run of jobs? A nudge on a setting lever

158

as you pass a lathe, say, that's all. Or to ruin a machine itself? A sprinkle of carborundum powder on a bearing. A second or two in both cases. We've got a man in there – I'm saying too much, though."

I laughed. "And *you* don't know about factories, Sergeant. They keep the same men for years. The machine operators grow old with their machines. Slip a man in . . ."

"Did I say that?"

"A regular? You're paying him?"

"What the hell're we talking about?" he demanded. "There's been nothing turned up, that's all."

I was surprised at his anger. I'd touched a sore spot. "Let you down, has he?"

But his anger was that he'd allowed himself to be drawn too far, when it was he who was supposed to be drawing me. Then he grinned and reached up to ruffle his hair.

"I'm getting too tired, that's the trouble. All right. It's why we're sure it's not suicide. Our man was going to report to Lorimer at 9.30. Lorimer would've been waiting for him, so why in hell would he kill himself?"

I nodded. Sounded reasonable.

"It gets worse," Brown grumbled. I guessed he might even be pleased, though, to share it with a stranger. "Our man was actually in the yard by the pumps factory when Trotter – yes? – when Trotter came slipping and sliding up the driveway beside the building, on his way to tell Lorimer about Trent's crash. He followed Trotter into Lorimer's office. Lorimer was dead at that time. The order sheets were there, so Trent had been there and handed 'em over. Trent drove away at 9.20, say, which, if Trent left him alive, leaves 9.20 to 9.30 open. As tight as *that*. And everybody, just everybody on duty that evening, is covered for that time. Trotter with the gatekeeper, the night foreman worrying over a breakdown, and all his men round him, four men on maintenance in the pumps building, but accounting for each other. It leaves only one possibility."

He stopped, stared at me, and cocked his head.

"Leonard Trent," I said.

He nodded. I thought about it. I'd reached a dead end.

"Your man at the factory," I said. "That's Peterson? The night foreman."

"That's him."

"But he's hopeless."

He shook his head. "Subtle. That's what he is. Clever. And he's seen nothing."

I sat and thought some more. Between us there hung a thought, and it was touch and go who expressed it first. I decided he was not going to volunteer any more, so I tried it.

"So why, if you think Trent killed him, did you let the Coroner bring in a suicide verdict?"

"We could've asked for an open one, or had it adjourned – yes. But that'd force our hands. The motive for suicide was thin, I agree. But you know what they say: while the balance of the mind was disturbed. That's how it is with most suicides, and if their minds are disturbed then their reasons are bound to be thin when considered by people whose minds aren't. But murder – well, you need a damn good motive. For this sort of thing, anyway. And we didn't get a sniff. Trent and Lorimer, as close as any two men could be – and don't you go looking at me like that, mate. These two men were *not* homos. Far from it. Lorimer looked after Trent's interests like a brother or a father. Trent would've done anything for Lorimer. Thought the world of him."

"My impression," I agreed.

"So what do we do? Trent's dead. Do we do any good by digging into it?"

I was furious. "Damn it all – the truth!"

"Ha!" he said.

"And you can't leave Mrs Lorimer with a suicided husband. A husband who's . . ."

"Suicided's good. I like that."

"Can you?"

160

"We can wait. Sniff around. Why, d'you imagine, is the insurance company playing coy – because we tipped 'em off. Perhaps somebody's going to come along with just a bit of evidence that gives us a motive. Then we get our answer. No trial. No verdict. Just your precious truth."

"Somebody?"

"Such as you, friend. If you tread on people's toes – well, it's your job. But anything you get . . ."

"Now you just hold on. I'm not going to do your job for you. I'm not intending to pressure anybody, bully them, blackmail them . . ."

"Is that what you think we do?"

I was not going to set out to prove that Kaye had lied to me, that was what it came down to. The anger still rumbled. I couldn't meet his eyes in case they expressed contempt.

"You'd have to tell us, anyway," he said reasonably, "if you came across anything."

I nodded. It was a let-out, really. I'd go on – had to go on – probing for the truth, for my own sake. Now I could tell myself I was doing it to assist the course of justice. But I didn't have to believe it.

I got to my feet. "I'd have to tell you," I agreed. "It'd come through official channels. Well . . . it's been very helpful, our chat. I'll see you again, Sergeant."

"Sure to."

He didn't see me out. I walked past the desk man without a cheerio, then drove until I saw a phone box. I dialled Kaye's number. There was no reply.

It was too late to go back to the office and try to look occupied, and too early to return to my room at Mrs K's and sulk, and I still couldn't remember why I'd wanted a word with Mrs Trent, so I just drove away and allowed the Fiat to take me where it wished. This, eventually, turned out to be Boraston Fields, where I parked outside the gate, unable to think of anything I wanted from Marjorie Lorimer, either.

At one point, I saw her at a window. Maybe she didn't

161

realise it was me, the car having changed, but in any event she didn't come and ask me in for a cup of tea.

Which reminded me I was hungry, which prompted me to drive back into town, which, because I found myself progressing in the general direction of the Macklin Shopping Centre, eventually led me to park outside Kaye's flat. It was empty and dark. Gone out with somebody, I thought. A man, I decided. I parked between two other cars. Kids were wheeling round on pedal cycles, and the fish and chip shop was busy. I got out of the Fiat, restless, wondering whether to walk round to the back and try there.

It's always movement that catches the eye. The person sitting in the car to the left of mine would have been no more than a shadow, but she moved quickly, ducking her head. I paused, and looked back, bent and peered through the windscreen.

"Mrs Trent?"

She was the opposite side of town from her home. My surprise must have prompted her, because she reached across and unlatched the passenger's door, throwing it open.

"Will you come and sit with me for a minute," she said. "Please, Mr Beacham."

Then I realised she was distressed, and quickly got in beside her, slamming the door.

"Whatever are you doing here?" I asked.

Chapter Twelve

Sitting in a car in that situation, there isn't much light around and you can't read expressions. But because the car isn't moving, you can swivel in the seat to make the most of it. I did that. She didn't take the same opportunity, but sat there with her hands on the wheel as though driving, and stared fixedly ahead.

"Have you been here long?" I asked quietly.

Two fingers lifted from the wheel in a gesture of indifference. "An hour. Perhaps. I don't know."

"It'd be a coincidence," I said, "if we weren't both waiting for the same person."

"How very observant of you," she said faintly. "Tell me – did you have an . . . appointment?"

"You were hoping it meant she's due back, and the waiting's over?" I asked. "I'm sorry, no. I came on spec. Her window's dark."

"You know which it is, then? I know no more than a name and the number."

"I know which it is. I don't know when she'll be back."

"Never mind. The waiting's over, anyway. For me. How could I meet her, if I'm not alone?"

I wasn't sure what she meant, there. Then I got it. She'd intended a personal confrontation. But Virginia Trent was not a person for confrontations, not, perhaps, because she feared them, but more likely because she would not consider them of practical use. Leonard was dead, after all.

She confirmed what I was thinking. "I don't know why I came. Clearing up the odd ends and pieces I suppose.

When your husband dies, so much suddenly seems to be there, waiting to be done. What does one do with his clothes? Send them to a charity, I suppose. Which I did. It was very painful. His car? It wasn't paid for, but they took it back. Any number of little things. And just one left, now. It seemed so untidy not to clear that away, and simply lifting the dustbin lid was too casual and too easy. Do you know what I'm talking about?"

"I think so. It must all be very distressing."

"His death?"

"Well . . . yes."

"I don't think I was talking about that. Not really. It'd all been destroyed before then. You can't imagine what it's like . . . to know that he turns to somebody else for comfort and peace and . . . and excitement. You feel so . . ." She glanced at me, and a spark of anger sharpened her voice. "You feel so damned inadequate. You just have to realise you're not good enough, that you've fallen short in some way, and you torture yourself trying to decide what your shortcomings are, and wonder how you can make them good. You can't imagine."

"I think perhaps I can," I said softly. I had the advantage – I'd been told what mine were, and what I could do about them.

"A woman knows, you see," she went on, not having heard me. What she had to say could have been bounced against anybody's calm receptiveness. My advantage, for her, was that it was professional. "And men are so naive. Especially Leonard. Deception wasn't his strong point, and when a person like him changes . . ." Her little laugh was bitter, with an undercurrent of tenderness. "I think Leonard's character was settled in his teens. That was when he decided what he wanted from life. No aggro – as they call it these days – a steady stream of exciting incidents to enliven the day. Nothing serious. All just clean fun. That was Leonard. It made my life so . . . well, placid, I suppose. He was amusing, and I could anticipate his every reaction.

It took no effort at all, so I suppose I relaxed, making no effort to please him or interest him, and life just drifted along."

"It's possible you've got that wrong, you know. Perhaps that was what he wanted from life – from his wife – acceptance of what he was."

"But obviously not from his lover," she said bitterly. "How long since I ceased to be his lover, Mr Beacham?"

I was embarrassed, and said nothing, hoping this wasn't going to become too personal. And this from a man who'd had to probe the details of widows living, possibly, as wives with "friends", which is naughty when you're drawing a widow's pension! I grinned to myself, but it must've escaped, and she must have been observing me closer then I realised.

"But if you're finding this amusing . . .!" she flared.

"Oh no! I'm sorry. It was a personal thought."

She was silent. I kicked myself mentally. I waited. To have prompted her would've been insulting.

"He changed, you see," she said at last. "He would come out with these absurd ideas. That he was doing nothing with his life. How wonderful it would be to throw everything aside and just live! Oh! Nonsense of that sort. Poor Leonard – he couldn't possibly have had thoughts like that, all on his own. He never had an original idea in his life. But he was always so impressionable. I thought, you see, that I ought to meet the person who'd infested him with those wild ramblings – just meet. Not argue with. I wouldn't want that. Leonard's dead. He's gone from both of us. But I would have liked to meet her, and hand back the key to her flat. Better than just throwing it away. That would be rather like discarding part of Leonard's life. So . . . there was one thing left that I hadn't tidied away. . . . I thought: come here and see her, meet her . . . but I've said all this before, haven't I, and you haven't stopped me . . . when it was you coming to the house that reminded me it hadn't finished . . ."

She stopped, biting her lip. She'd been talking just to persuade herself how good an idea it had been, but in fact it could have been disastrous to her. She was perhaps something of a romantic herself, and might well have gone along with Leonard in his enterprising ideas, given the chance. She had imagined a calm and dignified scene with Kaye, when in fact it would have disintegrated into tears and ignominy.

She was burrowing frantically into her handbag, suddenly afraid that Kaye might appear at any second, and remove her opportunity for choice. What she produced was an ordinary key to a cylinder lock, with a little yellow tag on it. She thrust it in my hand.

"There. You can give it to her." She stared at me, crimping up her face in an attempt at macabre humour. "But I suppose you've got one of your own, just the same as this."

"I'll give it to her," I promised.

"I found it in his things."

"Yes. I'll hand it over."

"And it's not one I know, so I guessed."

"I understand."

She was fluttering, breaking up rapidly. It was like the end of an affair to her, vicarious agony, suffering for Leonard as she'd probably done so often.

I backed out of the car door and closed it behind me, but she reached over and wound down the window.

"Tell her," she said, "that I can't feel any hatred for her."

"I'll do that."

Then at last she drove away. I stood by my Fiat and watched her away into the night. It was rather like my work – I'd complete an interview and drive away, and only then realise I'd forgotten to clear a point or two. Now I felt the same. There was something I should have asked.

Several lads were bouncing their bikes up the kerb, lifting the front wheels high. Wheelies, they called it. I weaved my way between them. The smell from the fish and chip shop was strong. A young couple were tightly clasped in the doorway to the newsagents' shop. To my own knowledge that kiss had been going on for five minutes. Or whatever it was. The door next to them was locked and the key didn't fit.

But of course, that door served two flats, and would possibly be left open, for convenience, only during daylight. The separate flats would have different locks, so that Leonard Trent should actually have had two keys, not one.

I went back to the Fiat and sat awhile. I'd promised to deliver the key. I sat, getting colder. And then the smell won, and I felt hungry. So I fetched myself a plaice and chips and ate them sitting on the wall with a row of teenagers, who spoke a language new to me.

You get greasy fingers, and I had nowhere to wash. My handkerchief helped, but I was nowhere near perfect when Kaye's car swept past and turned in to the service yard behind the shops. There'd been a row of lock-up garages back there. I wasn't sure whether she had a rear entrance to the flat, though it seemed unlikely. I began to walk towards the turn-in.

I was opposite the lighted fish and chip window when she came bouncing round the corner. It wasn't a shock for her; she must have seen me from the car. So she'd had time to plan a sedate meeting. In practice, she ran into my arms, me holding my hands away from her back, and flung herself round my neck.

"Ken!"

Then she planted her lips on mine and plastered her young and vigorous body against my stolid bulk, and the whistles and cat-calls that arose only encouraged her. She took my head between her two hands and leaned back to get a good look, the glasses skidding, and I sneaked a glance around. The couple in the doorway had stopped, to admire a more-mature technique.

"I've got so much to tell you!" she cried. "And you're

167

here! How long've you been waiting? Oh, you poor dear, you must be starving. I'll let you have a key, then next time . . ." She laughed at my expression. Possibly only laughter would have dammed the stream.

"Can I wash my hands?" I asked. And be free to do some holding myself.

She opened the outer door, and had to slam it against enthusiastic advice, then ran ahead of me up the stairs. "You'll never guess!" she cried. I mounted more slowly. She was just a little exhausting when excited. Which was most of the time, I had to admit. I wondered whether I could ever hope to keep up with her, even if I managed, just once, to catch her up.

In the flat she whirled round, almost as though she might be wearing a skirt, whereas it was now tailored slacks and a white, frilled blouse, with a little jacket over it.

"Guess where I've been all day," she challenged.

"I've been trying to phone you."

"Go on. Guess!"

"A café somewhere, to look at a wall – a pub to look at a sign."

"No! Miles away." Her laugh tinkled. "That's where I've been – miles away. Mid-Wales, if you want to know."

I didn't want to know where, but was interested in with whom.

"Which was quite a run," I agreed. "Drive all the way yourself, did you?"

She was quick, turning on me, that grin almost involving her ears. "Jealous, Ken?"

"Have I got any reason?"

"Don't be silly. I'll put on some coffee, then I'll cook up something."

That reminded me. "I've just had a meal out of newspaper, Kaye. Could I just wash my hands?"

She indicated the door. She had a cubby-hole with a washbasin and a toilet bowl. When I came out she was in her tight little kitchen, with barely room for two, because of the counter and the stools, unless they were close. Even touching. I came up behind her, hands round her waist, my head on her shoulder. Her hair smelt sweet, my hands lifted her breasts. She smiled sideways at me.

"It's there, under your nose."

I was kissing her neck, which was where she said.

"The letter, Ken. On the counter. Do pay attention."

I released her and picked up the letter. A London Gallery. I scanned it. Speed-read. The essentials.

Dear Miss Trotter,

I have been considering your recent work ... interest ... small exhibition ... twenty-five to thirty ... discuss terms at your convenience ... hearing from you in due course ...

Sincerely,

Scribble-scribble.

She moved – danced – into the living room, and now stood with demure patience, almost bursting with the effort, hands clasped low, her eyes wide.

"Kaye!" I said. "Oh Kaye, I'm so pleased! It's marvellous, just bloody marvellous."

Then she screamed, the pressure mounting too high, and threw herself at me. I picked her up, arms round her, and whirled her about, she laughing at me and me trying to trap her lips, her hair in my eyes and my mouth, and for a few seconds I felt, in undiluted empathy, her delight and excitement.

Then at last I put her down, both of us panting.

"It isn't all pub signs, you know," she declared.

"Obviously."

"There are things you do just for yourself, but when they please somebody else ... Ken, you know then that you're communicating. Can you imagine what a wonderful thing that is! Something that's entirely your own – and people will stand in front of it – in front of *my* paintings, and perhaps just one tiny portion of what I felt will please them, or move them, or give them some feeling. Oh, I don't know. I just can't tell you how it feels!"

You take a complicated case and you work very hard on it to bring it to a satisfactory conclusion. Then there's a feeling of something well done, and of pleasure. Take that feeling and multiply it a thousand times – and yes, I could imagine something of what she felt. And envy her just a little.

"And I had this marvellous idea," she told me.

"The coffee?"

"Which is why I went to Wales."

"What about the . . ."

". . . coffee!" she screamed.

We were, I thought, in for an evening of her screams.

By the time she'd come back with the tray, I'd found myself completely absorbed by the atmosphere. She lived in a world of disorder. The flat was scattered with magazines, with bits of clothing, shoes on chairs and library books open on spare surfaces. It was strangely relaxing to be in the centre of it, like the calm at the eye of a storm. I felt I could trust her to whirl around me to her heart's content, destroying order in all directions, and leave me unblemished but enriched in the middle.

"There's this cottage," she said. "House, or whatever you'd call it. Used to be an inn 200 years ago. Well – the first thing I thought . . . I haven't *got* 20 or 30 decent canvases. And I know what they want – my landscapes with the little men all doing something. I haven't shown you those yet. It's a secret. But where can I *do* all those paintings? That's what I thought. Panic stations. I ran around weeping. Now don't you laugh at me, Ken Beacham!"

I was smiling. Every emotion pressed to the extreme, that was Kaye. I knew where she could do the paintings – here. This flat. Where I could reach her easily.

"And of course, I couldn't work *here*," she declared vehemently, "and certainly not on *that* scale. And it's not very inspiring, is it?" A lot she'd need from inspiration! She carried it with her. "Then I remembered Ewr Felen. That's what it's called. Yellow acre, that means, though I don't suppose there's an acre and it certainly isn't yellow, with all those rhododendrons round it. Have you ever seen them, Ken? They cover the hillsides, one mass of purple, and they'll be out soon. Oh, I can't wait . . ."

"Could we have it in some sort of sequence, Kaye. There's a good girl."

"Sorry." She flicked hair out of her eyes, plunged her nose into her mug, took a deep breath, then went on: "I used to go there when I was a little girl and stay with my gran. I loved it then, but I haven't seen it for years. But it was hers, and she left it to me in her will, and . . . well, I just haven't *been* there. Thinking of it, I feel awful. But it's mine, and the solicitor tries to rent it out for holidays. Not many people go for it, though. No electricity, and you have to get up to it through a farmer's yard and up halfway to the top of the mountain. You can barely get a car there. But it's mine, and I could work there, so I went to see it today . . ." She stopped, considering me with her head on one side. "You're not listening."

"I'm listening. You're talking about going away. You can't expect me to cheer."

"But you'll be *there*."

"Now Kaye, let's not take it too far. There's my job."

"You call that a job?"

"Kaye – my love – you'll be happy there. Not with me . . ."

She was not in a mood to consider paltry distractions. She swept on. "But you'll love it. From the front window you can see the Severn, and it's just possible to find the old coaching route round the mountain . . ."

"You're not very practical, are you? You'll need to live, Kaye. Money. Remember it? That crinkly stuff you swap for food and stuff like paints and canvases. What d'you intend to do? There can't be too many pubs around

171

there, and you couldn't even spell 'Elephant and Castle' in Welsh."

She stuck out her tongue at me. "I can, then! It's 'Ellifant Ac Castell.' You're as encouraging as a wet week-end, Ken."

"They get a lot of those in Wales, I hear."

"I shall live, live!" she cried wildly, dismissing my despondancy and gloom. "You'll see. You'll be the jealous one. Oh Ken, you've got no life in you. You're like a lump of jelly perched on that chair."

"I'm very happy for you, Kaye, and you know that." But she was bouncing herself farther and farther away from me.

"I know what *you* need," she decided.

"Kaye," I plunged in, "my wife has left me. She's gone to live with another man. My house in Acocks Green is up for sale, and the one I was buying here I'll have to forget about. There's nothing holding me here – except my job."

She was on her feet, no manic delight now in her eyes, just warm invitation. She pouted, and whispered: "Your job. Your paltry, silly, monotonous job!"

"It's all very well laughing at money, but *something* has to come in, or the larder goes empty."

"Can we," she suggested, "continue this discussion in bed?"

I held out my hands. She took them and tried to haul me to my feet, but I was heavy with worry and she came down to me, falling all over me until she was comfortable on my lap. She put a finger on my chin.

"I know why you're upset. You were waiting out there so long. But I went out in such a rush . . . you must have a key, and wait in comfort . . ."

"I've got a key." The words tumbled out, a background concern, to be discarded before I could relax fully.

"A key? To this flat?"

"One of them, anyway." I struggled, heaving to get a hand to my pocket. "Here." I dangled the key.

"But that's not mine. Where did you get it?"

"Virginia Trent gave it me, to hand over to you. When I got here, she was waiting outside in her car. She wanted to give it to you herself. Said to tell you she didn't hate you. But there was some idea of wanting to see you."

"Oh Lord, no!"

"It was with Lennie's stuff in the car. I suppose it all got back to her in the end. I don't know how these things are done. Anyway, she had it, and she wanted you to have it back. Lennie's key."

She was strangely drawn, stiff in my arms. The light had died from her eyes. "That poor woman! But how did she know about us? It was a secret. Lennie's and mine. We didn't want . . . it was never a question of breaking up their marriage. I knew that. Lennie wasn't the type. There have to be *some* serious thoughts, if a man's going to leave his wife, and Lennie hadn't got a serious bone in his body. We both knew it was temporary. But me . . . oh hell, I had to go and fall in love with all that fun in him, when I knew it was selfish as hell. Damn you, Ken, why did you have to spoil things!"

"Have I spoiled something?"

"You're so *thick*, sometimes." She glared at me, raised her chin. "But how could she have known?"

"Apparently wives know about this sort of thing. Defecting husbands show winking lights or something."

"And if you're going to be facetious, I'll hit you!"

"You hate me serious, you hit me when I try to be funny. It's not fair."

"You're a darling, but you're clumsy. It'll come with practice. But how could she know my name – *did* she know my name?"

"She said she did."

"And she came to the right address. But how?"

"I don't know, Kaye. Would Lennie have told her?"

"That's likely, I must say!"

"Well, she knew. And she thought the key was yours. If it's not, I'll take it back."

She was shaking her head. "I know which door the key fits."

"Then don't you think you ought to tell me, and I'll take it there? Another woman, Lennie had?" I caught her wrist. "One of my funnies, love."

"You can't take it there, clever! You'd have to go to Manchester. Oh dear, I suppose you'd better know, but if you ever whisper a word of this to Marjorie Lorimer . . . Lennie was a buyer, Ken. Not a salesman. But he came back from Manchester with order forms. That's a salesman's job. You haven't heard of any buying he was doing . . ."

"A mention."

"A cover. That's what it was. If you checked back, you'd find that in the three months before he died he'd been to Manchester half a dozen times. For Philip Lorimer, that was. Personally. And d'you know why? It was to do with that flat of theirs, the Lorimers", in Manchester. Have you heard – or do things go right past you – Phil Lorimer's job was rocky. His contract ran out at the end of January, and things had gone from bad to worse since he'd been there, so it was a good guess he'd be out of a job by February."

"I'd heard. I'm not too thick. Mrs Lorimer told me they kept the flat for somewhere to go, in between jobs, because of course they'd never be able to keep that big house going. Have you seen it?"

"No. I haven't seen it. Material possessions are a big nothing." She took a breath. "Well, Phil Lorimer had been stupid, and set up a woman in that flat, and when things went wrong – well, how often could he get there to see her? – she wouldn't move out. Oh I know, he could've got a court order. Lennie told me about it. But not without Marjie getting to know, and that would've been the end. Marjie's always thought the sun shone just to light Phil's way. So *that* was what Lennie was doing. He was going there and

174

trying to prise that woman loose. Threats, persuasions – I expect money did it in the end. But anyway, on the evening of his accident, that was all he could talk about. He'd got her out of the flat at last, got her key off her – he ferreted down into his brief-case and showed me the key, that one with the yellow tab. And he'd locked her out. Then he came here, so excited you'd think he'd won the Nobel Peace Prize. He'd done it all himself.

"Achievement!" I murmured.

". . . and he's such a . . . oh dear, he was such a stupid, loveable idiot that he couldn't wait to get to Phil Lorimer and tell him he was in the clear."

"He could've phoned."

"Face to face, he wanted."

"If he was sneaking time off with you, Kaye . . . hell, I wouldn't want to waste any of it."

"Face to face was how he put it. He was in a strange mood, Ken. I mean, I knew how much he enjoyed doing things for Phil. But this was unnatural. Like you want to watch a child's face when it opens a present. Like that. He looked at me with a kind of . . . sort of fierce joy. 'No, Kaye,' he said to me, 'not over the phone. I've got to watch his face when I tell him what I want to tell him.' Funny thing to say, wasn't it?"

"It doesn't quite fit the circumstances."

"But off he went. To tell you the truth, I think *that* was why Phil Lorimer was waiting there that night. Nothing to do with the factory at all. And Lennie could've phoned him from Manchester, as you said, and put him out of his misery. But Lennie had a cruel streak. I'm not sure I liked that. He *could* have phoned."

"I suppose he could." I didn't want to make a big issue of the next point. "But even then – Lorimer was expecting him at nine, but Lennie wasn't in any hurry to get there, it seems. He was with you till 9.15."

"Perhaps I distracted him," she said, smiling.

"As you're distracting me now?"

"Something like that. Or like this."

"It seems I was being too serious for you."

"We're talking about Lennie, and about Lorimer. There's just the two of us here. What're we doing, talking about other people?"

"Actions," I said, "speak louder than words."

I acted.

I didn't get back to Mrs Zalusky's at all that night.

Chapter Thirteen

I shall always remember Friday. Driving round to the office, I was trying to concentrate on what I was intending to do that day, which cases I'd tackle, and how I could justify a visit to Mrs Lorimer. And what I'd say to her if I did. But I'd barely reached my desk when the phone rang. It was Harkness.

"Will you come in and see me, Ken?" he asked. "Before you do anything else, please."

Oh oh! I thought. There had been no emotion in his voice. I went in. He had his best suit on, was freshly shaved, smelt of cologne. His ceremonial personage. I took a seat and crossed my legs. But I could see that something unrelaxing was coming.

"There's not much time," he said. He cleared his throat. "You'll need to catch the 9.30 train, unless you want to drive in, of course. It's up to you."

"In where?"

"They want to see you at Regional Office. Mr Ansell."

The Assistant Regional Controller, that was. He'd never spoken to me, no more than a nod in passing, and that had been at a Regional Christmas Party. My top-but-one boss; *nobody* saw the Regional Controller.

I allowed a small pause to build up. Harkness fidgetted with his ball-point. "I'll drive, I think. What time?" I asked.

"Eleven, he said. His office."

"My files . . ."

"Leave them. They can wait."

"I just didn't want Parsons digging his nose in. Can you tell me what it's about, Mr Harkness?"

"I'd better leave it to him."

He was afraid to tell me. I glanced away. "Then I'd better be moving. Parking, you know."

"They've got a decent car park."

"Not when I was there last. That was a training course."

"Oh, they've enlarged it. Didn't you know? And a new entrance. coming in from this direction, you drive past the building and turn right."

He was being effusively helpful. I nodded. "Thanks."

"And I'd like—" He put his fingertips together. "– like you to come in when you get back. I'd like to hear . . ." His throat seemed to be troubling him. He coughed, put his hand to his mouth, and let it lie.

I got to my feet. "Well . . ." And made for the door.

"Ken," he said, as my hand touched the knob. I turned. "I'm sorry. I didn't mean . . ." And again he had to use a gesture to end it.

"It's all right."

I closed the door gently behind me. Now I understood him. He'd phoned Regional Office for advice, following my blank attack of insubordination, and the whole thing had been whisked from his hands. Harkness, purely and simply, was inadequate for the job. He was nervous and uncertain, otherwise he'd never have asked his seniors for advice; it would reflect on his ability. And he desperately feared antagonism. I was willing to bet he'd done a management course, and taken it too much to heart. Quite simply, it wasn't working.

I drove to Regional Office, thinking about those management courses. You know what I mean.

They get lectures on personnel management and on administration, on office organisation, on how to keep the little book. They're encouraged to keep a diary and note in it the names of their staff against their birth dates.

Then it's possible to go round on the correct morning and say: "Many happy returns, Peggy." On these days a christian name is essential. Also to be recorded are details of family, children involved, husband's jobs, boy-friends. "And how's little Mary?" Hobbies and interests. "The rhubarb wine fermenting well, Gladys?" And so on. But this should not be overdone, the instructions tell you. "Two such pleasantries per day per 50 members of the staff are recommended. To exceed this figure leads to familiarity." On such facets of the humanities are people like Harkness bred. Unless they can rise above it, they're condemned to gradual extinction.

Harkness, shut away in his office, was desperately lonely and miserably afraid of failure. He would inevitably move up the ladder of promotion, his loneliness growing with the size of his permitted carpet, until he retired – to greater loneliness.

Ansell was not like this. He'd moved directly from University to Administration. He was not lonely, because there had never been anybody within reach of him. He had no fear of failure, no self-doubts, because his degree proved to him his exact level of ability. He could therefore relax. He was Assistant Regional Controller, and therefore couldn't make mistakes. He could do what he liked without criticism. So he could afford to be kind.

"Ah . . . Beacham." He held out his hand, rising behind his desk. "We haven't met. Would you like to take a seat?" He smiled. This was a great pleasure for him.

Outside his door I'd felt confident. What the hell could they do to me, anyway? That sort of attitude. But he had undermined me. I couldn't sit comfortably beneath his benign eye.

"I thought we'd have a chat," he said easily. "Always, I think, these difficulties seem to disappear with a few unofficial words."

179

I noted that. Unofficial. I nodded, not sure which of my difficulties he had in mind.

"Don't you think so?" he asked, forcing me to say something.

"I spend all day talking over difficulties, sir," I said cheerfully. "If there's no difficulty, it doesn't come to the Inspector."

"You like that thought, do you?"

"It helps to feel you're doing something useful."

"Yes. Yes, I see." He looked down at a folder and flicked a page. My personal file, the annual reports on me, every comment since I'd joined the service. "I see you've done some considerable time as an Inspector, but there are one or two facets of local office work you've hardly touched. Finance, not at all." He looked up.

I hadn't really been aware of his eyes. He had the bushy eyebrows that many bald men have, and hidden in the shadows beneath them were a pair of keen, brown eyes. But he'd be intelligent – probably got a double first in psychology or something like that. Must be bright. I decided that frankness wouldn't displease him.

"Figures," I said, "aren't alive. I like to meet people."

"Why did you apply for transfer?" he asked, apparently changing the subject.

"Experience. Change. If you look, you'll see I've never even been recommended for a promotions board, sir."

"And it's never occurred to you that it could be because of your lack of overall experience?"

"I like to work . . ."

"I know, with people. You said that. But if you'd used your obvious abilities in Inspectorate duties on one or two other sections, you'd perhaps now be a Manager of your own small office."

Obvious abilities! Clever, that. He'd slipped it into the middle of a criticism.

"Don't you think?" he asked. "You'd be dealing with people still. Staff."

"If you say so, sir."

"I do, indeed. And now – you seem to feel opposition to any change – refusing to transfer to another section."

"That isn't quite the point at issue. I have an interesting case."

He put his fingertips together and gazed at me above them. Nodded. Pushed my personal file away. "Then you'd resist any change of duties at a time when you had an interesting case? Is that it? Interesting to you, that is. But I haven't heard that the Civil Service is supposed to be interesting." He smiled. I was being treated to one of his pleasantries. It made me something special. "But when is the time when you haven't got an interesting case? Aren't they all interesting? Is Your Manager to pounce in at a specific moment when all you have on hand is boring work? You're making his life very difficult, Mr Beacham."

I'd been correct, he was very clever. "You have a point," I said.

"You know," he went on, "when we get these little upsets – and I can assure you, we get a lot of them – we find that usually, behind it all, there's something personal. Perhaps, in your case, it's the same?" He waited.

"Perhaps."

"Something we might discuss? You transferred without promotion. Were there troubles that made it necessary?"

"Oh no! Nothing like that. Just the chance of experience, a board . . ."

"And now you've found you've made a mistake?"

"Not really. Mr Harkness and I are beginning to understand each other."

"Hmm!" Clearly, it was not what Harkness had said. "Then it's domestic? You're married, I see. Any children?"

"Married, yes. No children, sir."

"Would you care to tell me," he asked, "what is wrong?"

He was staring at me with patience and kindliness. It was

181

his job to keep the Region moving smoothly. He knew how to do it. So I told him.

"My wife took one look at what was to be her new town, and now refuses to come near it. I've hunted out a bungalow, and she won't look at it. She refuses to budge."

"Oh dear!" he said. "Then why didn't you say something? You're not unique, you know. Something could be done. Indeed. Not your previous office, of course. Your old post would be filled, I'm sure, and you wouldn't want that, anyway."

"I wouldn't want that."

"But some other Birmingham office, not too far from where you were. Do you think that might ease your difficulties?"

"A long way towards it."

"So . . . you just leave it to me." He was the sort of man to whom it was always being left, and with confidence.

"I'd like some time to consider it, sir."

The eyebrows swept up. A shade drifted behind his eyes. "You would?"

"There are complications I haven't mentioned."

He seemed disappointed. "Then think about it, if you must. But not for too long, please. Shall we say . . . a week? Ask for me. Phone and tell me what you want to do."

I got to my feet. "It's been very good of you, sir."

"Nonsense." He came round the desk, one hand on my shoulder, the other reaching for the door knob. "We like to keep people happy."

Only in that last second did he strike a false note. It's in that little book I told you about. "Effort should be made to ensure a happy work force. A contented employee is a willing one." The door closed on his smile.

I had lunch in their canteen, taking my time. An official visit to Regional Office . . . Harkness could consider himself lucky if he saw me at all that day. Apart from the Trent file,

I was not anxious to be back. There'd be no progress on the Trent file.

Over Shepherd's Pie and sprouts I found myself wondering about Lennie Trent, instead of the wonderful gift that had been dangled under my nose – transfer back. I should have been wondering how to break the news to Lena, where, in fact, to contact her in order to tell her. But I was unable to find any excitement in the thought, and my mind drifted to Lennie Trent, finding no pleasure there, either.

Kaye had still said he left her at 9.15. That would have allowed Trent to do nothing, not even to reach the factory. But now I had a hint of something personal between Trent and Lorimer, nothing acrimonious, to be sure, but something that at least joined them deeper than mere friendship. The thought made me uneasy. My trust in Kaye – which was beginning to mean so much to me – depended on my being able to prove that Trent hadn't reached Lorimer. Any motive for murder involving Trent would completely undermine me.

Murder motive? But Trent had been taking grand news to his brother-in-law. The woman had abandoned the flat. What motive was there in that? None, I assured myself. But there was just visible the edge of something dark and secretive, and I hated it.

Disturbed, now unable to keep away from the Trent file in case Parsons or somebody else got their hands on it, I drove back rather earlier than I'd intended. I had thought to explore the city shops, having the vague idea that I might find a small present for Kaye. It would perhaps be a greater one if I cleared the Trent file.

On my desk was a message from the girl at the phone console. "Your wife called. Will you call her back? 629879. Tonight. At eight sharp."

Eight sharp. Dead on, that meant.

I went through to see Harkness.

No doubt Ansell had called him to tell him what had

happened. He smiled at me as I came in, glad, I supposed, to be seeing the back of me.

"And how did you get on?"

I slumped into a chair. "Fair enough, I suppose."

"I didn't realise you had domestic difficulties, Ken."

"I didn't think you'd be interested."

"Of course I would."

Lecture seven in the course. How to make yourself interested in the staff's domestic problems.

"Or be able to do anything," I said.

"I could have!" Then he laughed. Actually laughed. It appeared as a shishing noise in the corners of his mouth, reluctant to get out into the open, but it was his laugh. "I was about to say I could have helped you transfer back, but that wouldn't have done, would it! Not from me. It would've appeared that I was too eager. You get my point?"

I grinned at him. "Clearly."

"So we're going to lose you?"

"I told him I'd think about it."

"I'd be sorry to see you go."

I leaned forward. "Did I hear you right?"

"You did. Are you surprised? Ken, hadn't you realised – Fishlock on Dis Ben section's retiring at the end of June. That'd make you senior in your grade, and officially Assistant Manager. I've tried to work with Fishlock, but he's . . . do you know him?"

"Only to speak to, on the section."

"Ah, well, he's rather too complaisant. Ask his opinion and he asks back. No opinions, no imagination. I'd not accuse you of that, Ken. I think we might have got along."

"You do?"

"Given time. And you'd find it interesting. Management."

"I'd need to learn all their birthdays."

"What?"

"Sorry. A private joke." And not, at that time, in very

good taste. "But I'd have to come indoors. You couldn't have an assistant who's always missing."

"There's that, of course. You'd be sorry?"

"I'm beginning to think I've had enough of outside work, to tell you the truth."

"You see. It'd work out."

I looked at him, my head on one side. "You're trying to persuade me to stay?"

He shrugged, lifting his palms. "I shouldn't interfere. Domestic problems, they're the very devil."

"You wouldn't believe!"

"Wouldn't I? I'm divorced, you know. Adultery. Mine. One hell of a time, that was."

He meant the consequences, not the actual act of adultery.

"Yes," I agreed. "One hell of a time." I meant the act.

And he knew it. He went with me to the door, his hand at my elbow. "Those domestic difficulties . . . deeper than I thought, eh?" And he winked.

"I could well sort them all out tonight," I assured him.

It was now as close to five as made no matter. In a desultory fashion, too many distractions dulling the interest, I hunted through a few files I might tackle first thing in the morning, completely forgetting it would be Saturday, and flung them into my brief-case, along with the Trent file. It appeared I couldn't move without that file close to me.

David Trotter was waiting beside my car, moving restlessly backwards and forwards.

"There you are," he said ungraciously.

"Yes, here I am." I was wondering why his office did not claim him.

"I wanted a word with you."

"Here?"

"As good as any place. It's about Kaye."

I felt my back stiffen, and I looked at him more intently. His face was set, his shoulders firm. "I don't want to hear."

His hand was on my arm. "You ought to know about Kaye. Now don't be a fool. Listen – for your own good. I just want to tell you . . . you can't rely on what she says. She's full of wild enthusiasms . . ."

"Look," I interrupted. "I'm not going to discuss her with you."

"You seem to be getting ideas from her. Maybe that's how you do your job." His lip curled. "How you get your information. But I can tell you . . ."

"Will you please take your hand off my arm!"

"Trent found out. But not before it buggered his married life."

I couldn't feel anything but distaste for him. This was his sister he was talking about. Big brother, being over-protective? But he seemed to think it was me he was protecting.

"I suppose," I said, "he found out from you. She's of age. You can't come along here dictating and interfering."

Then he smiled thinly. "Thought you ought to know. She lives in a fantasy world. Just don't accept all you hear."

Then he turned away, leaving me angry and, strangely, with an urge to drive straight to her flat. Instead, I drove straight home.

From Mrs Zalusky's I phoned Kaye. "So much to tell you, but I've got to stay by the phone. Must ring my wife at eight." I had decided not to mention her brother's intervention.

"You could call her from here."

Why did I baulk at the deceit involved in that? Perhaps, I realised, because I feared to have Kaye observe my weakness in dealing with Lena.

"I'd rather do it from here."

A pause. She probably sensed the reason for my reluctance. Lennie had phoned *his* wife from her flat. She understood the embarrassment.

"I did want you to come," she said. "I've done some sketches."

"Later?" I suggested. "Around 8.30?" By then there would be a settlement made. I hoped.

I could almost hear her pout. "I wanted to give you a surprise."

"Nothing about you would surprise me now."

"Idiot! *Sole Mimi*. I've spent all day getting the stuff together."

"Except for the time on sketching?"

"I hate you, Ken Beacham. For that, I'll eat it all myself."

"Even if it makes you sick?"

"*You* make me sick!"

"I love you and you're wonderful, and your *Sole Mimi* will no doubt be a dream. Why can't it wait until 8.30?"

"It's me who can't wait, you fool."

"Kaye . . . love . . ."

"Why can't *she* wait?" she demanded.

Why couldn't Lena wait? Because Lena never waited. And how could I talk about possible transfers home, with Kaye beside me, possibly as near naked as damn it, and me . . .

"Trust me?" I asked desperately.

That hit the right note. "Of course I do, so 8.30. Not a minute later. And Ken?"

"Yes."

"Love me?"

"To distraction."

She kissed the phone and I hung up, not feeling too good.

Mrs Zalusky had not made her usual call to me regarding tea. I thought I'd perhaps scandalised her a little, coming home early in the morning, but I couldn't just walk up to my room without so much as a cheerful word. I tapped on her door, put my head in.

"I'm in, Mrs Z," I told her unnecessarily.

"I didn't call you," she said. "You pounced on the phone. There's tea."

187

So all was normal. I would be sorry to leave. I sat at her table, Polski at once round my shoulders, and Mr Z said he thought it might rain, as though it could possibly affect him. He sat in a calm and protected world. Nothing happened around him, nothing occurred to disturb his equanimity. And no discoveries burst like fireworks around him. Poor devil.

Mrs Zalusky said: "Your wife phoned and left a message."

"She left one at the office," I told her. "Phone her at eight."

She nodded. "That was it."

I sat quietly, but my mind was whirling and swooping, reaching to seize on ideas as they flew past. The images refused to coalesce long enough to be examined closely. In the centre of the chaos I could only wait, and hope that something pleasant would brush against me, and I could capture it.

There was one circumstance I could regularise, at that moment.

"I'm afraid," I said, "that it doesn't seem I'll be staying here much longer."

"Oh . . . I'm sorry." She had the grace to look sorry.

"And I don't want to leave your room empty, with no notice. So I'd like to pay you a month's rent in advance."

"No, no! Certainly not. I'm sure you'll be able to warn me."

I wasn't so sure. I got out my wallet and reached out the correct notes. "I'll feel happier . . ."

"I wouldn't dream of it."

I smiled. Polski purred. I placed the notes on the table. "Bear with me, Mrs Z," I asked her. "And after all, I could well be here in a month's time, anyway."

Then, with my friend jumping down to show me the way, I went up to my room. Heaven. Secure and serene. Why the hell was I looking round me with such pleasure? It was a bare room, without glamour. I sat down and waited for eight o'clock.

At 7.25 I heard the phone ringing in the hall. I had the door open before it cut off, and Mrs Z called: "It's for you, Ken."

I galloped down the stairs, Polski complaining bitterly that he hadn't had time to cadge his usual ride. She was holding out the phone.

"It's a woman." I didn't know why she was so disapproving; perhaps at that time she was disapproving of all women.

"Hello!"

"Mr Beacham? Is that Mr Beacham?"

"Yes. Who's this, please?" Disappointment clouded my voice. Either because it was not Lena, so that I'd have had time to get to Kaye earlier, or because it was not Kaye, and I'd have been hearing her voice again.

"I've been trying to reach you all day. They gave me this number."

I received messages. Ones I didn't want. But not those I might. "Who is this?" I repeated.

"It's Marjorie Lorimer. I *told* them it was urgent."

"And how can I help you, Mrs Lorimer?"

"I must see you. It's very important."

"I'll be at the office . . ."

"It couldn't possibly wait until Monday, Could you . . . would you come round to see me?"

"Well . . . really."

"Please!"

"I have to make a phone call of my own at eight o'clock. That's why I'm waiting by this phone."

"But it's only 7.30. You could make your call from here."

It would be well-nigh as embarrassing as phoning from Kaye's. "I'd really prefer to do it from here."

"You're not being very co-operative," she said severely.

"Mrs Lorimer, at this time on a Friday evening, and

189

you not even in my official area, I'd find it a little difficult."

There was a pause. Then her voice came through very thin and strained. "Can't you come . . . as a friend?"

Damn it, what can you say? I glanced at my watch. I could do it to her place in 15 minutes. If I moved fast. Ten to eight, if I was lucky.

"I'll be there."

"Thank you," she breathed.

I called out to Mrs Zalusky that I had to go out. Official, I put it, just to allay her concern. "Expect me when you see me."

Then I ran out to the Fiat.

She was waiting in the splendid porch, diminished by its size, or by something else. The night was still. I guessed Mr Z might be right about the rain. The cascade was faintly detectable. She held out her hand, palm down, a gesture purely of relief, because it was withdrawn before I could take it. I followed her into the hall.

"You can make your call from here," she told me, as we passed the phone table. "If it's so important."

"Thank you." She'd offered me a measure of privacy.

"In here," she said, and we were in a smaller room I hadn't seen, a resting or relaxing room, with magazines and books scattered about, a large TV set, and a huge hi-fi system. She had the TV tuned to a flickering, unadjusted programme with the sound down, and walked over to switch it off. She didn't ask me to sit; she herself was far too restless for that.

Ten to eight. I hadn't been far out.

"I've been thinking of what you said." She came right out with it.

"About what?"

"The suggestion that Philip might not have committed suicide."

I smiled. She'd used a tone of attack. "As I remember it – wasn't it you who went to some lengths to prove he

190

hadn't? You persuaded me. There have to be pretty strong reasons for suicide, and they weren't there."

She'd been lighting a cigarette, gesturing before I'd got it all out, impatient with me. "I hadn't realised what it might mean."

"It's fairly obvious, surely. If it's not suicide, then it can't be anything but murder."

She flinched. "And now I know what you're doing – or what you were trying to do."

I sat anyway. I'd have a hysterical woman on my hands if I produced a wrong word. My own relaxation might invade her, I thought, relaxing. It was 7.55.

"And what do you think I'm trying to do, Mrs Lorimer?"

She became agitated, turning her head away, fidgetting her lower lip between her teeth. This woman spent too much time alone, I thought. Eventually, she jerked out: "You're trying to prove that it was not only murder, but that Lennie killed him."

"There happens ... this is on evidence that I've put together so far ... but really, there doesn't appear to be anyone else who *could* have done it."

"And Lennie was my own brother," she threw at me.

She had mentioned this herself already, but perhaps as a venture into fantasy; saying it, but not listening to herself. I shook my head. I wanted to be somewhere else, preferably in the hall with that phone.

"So I have two alternatives," she said bitterly. "Either my husband shot himself, or my brother shot my husband! Do you imagine that's a pleasant choice, Mr Beacham? Do I toss a coin? Heads or tails!" Her voice was breaking.

"My phone call," I whispered.

"But I've had three months to come to terms with Philip's suicide," she said in desperation. "I thought I'd managed it. I found myself looking out of the window the other day and actually seeing what was the other side. Now you propose to offer me another ghastly possibility. You're trying to *prove* it, damn you."

"My call?"

". . . suppose I'm expected to go through all that agony again, and come to face the knowledge that Lennie killed Philip! I can't face it. I'm not going to *have* it."

"I'm not trying to prove that," I assured her. "Give me five minutes, and I'll explain."

"As though he could! As though Lennie *could*. He loved Philip. That's no more nor less than the truth."

"But I'm trying to prove the opposite, Mrs Lorimer. Will you please let me explain!"

"You came here with some idea of your own, I'm sure. You probably get good-conduct marks for every new claim . . . you got me to sign a form. Forced me to."

"A simple application." I was on my feet, arm outstretched in entreaty towards the hall. "If I could just . . ."

She shouted me down. "Do you realise what you made me do? Do you? That piece of paper says that I believe my brother killed my husband. I put my name to it. I *said* that was what I thought."

"It's not like that. You're using inverted logic."

"To hell with your logic."

"Mrs Lorimer . . ."

"I want it back. And I want it now."

Her application for benefit was in some ways my only justification for going on with it. How could I investigate Lorimer's death without it? "You must think about it," I pleaded.

"I want that form back."

Any other Friday evening I would not have had it available. Sheer chance had it in my brief-case, on the back seat of the Fiat.

"I suppose you've got it with you?" A doubt had entered her voice.

"It's in the car."

"Then get it for me. I've got a right."

"You can withdraw your application, yes."

"I would like to have it." She stared at me. "Please."

With one last look of exasperation at her I hurried out into the hall and past the phone, pausing. But she stood by it, between me and the phone table, almost as though one necessity was offered in exchange for the other. Cursing, I ran out to the car and fumbled in my brief-case, found the form, and ran back to her with it. She snatched it out of my hands, turned it over to verify that it was in fact the form with her signature on, then she tore it up, not neatly, but with those furious snatching gestures that women make to demonstrate their strength. Then she looked at me, her eyes shining, and spoke in a quite reasonable voice.

"I think you wanted to make a phone call."

It was 8.13 when she walked away from me with a fair show of triumph. I reached for the phone.

Chapter Fourteen

"Trust you to be late," Lena said.

"Better late than never."

"You never could keep a promise," she declared.

I'd promised nothing. Behind me, Mrs Lorimer expressed her restlessness by switching on her radio and prodding from one station to the other. I put a finger in my ear.

"I would have rung you anyway," I told Lena.

"I'm sure you would. To ask me how I am, no doubt. To ask about my health and am I happy. A lot you ever cared about that, Ken. Don't try to pretend."

"Some news . . ."

The two words had given her time to take a breath. "But I know you, Ken. No decision, that's your trouble. All the same, I didn't want to be unfair to you. I hope you realise that."

"Oh, I do, I do!"

"So I've decided to give you another chance."

"I don't need any chances."

"Do listen, please. If you will promise me – and I do mean promise, not one of your airy-fairy 'I'll tries' – if you'll promise me to apply for a transfer back, then we'll say no more about it."

Perhaps I'd like the chance of her saying no more. "There's no point in going on like this, Lena."

"What's that music?"

"There's no point in all this fandango to get me to ring you. There's something happened."

Her voice sharpened. "Oh, I bet there has. I can hear music. Where are you calling from, Ken?"

With one neurotic woman at the other end of the phone, another in the room behind me, I felt trapped and confused.

"Shall I give you the number?" I demanded. "Then you can call back, and be certain I'm me."

"Don't be stupid, please."

Mrs Lorimer pressed another button, jumping from Radio 1 to Radio 3. Pop to Prokofiev.

"You're not alone, are you?" she challenged, her voice crisp.

"I'm in somebody's house. Lena, I've got to say something to you."

"You're with a woman!" she decided. Her voice was brittle as ice.

"Yes," I said tersely. "I'm with a woman, if you damn-well want to know. And I'm ashamed of myself for trying to hide it! I'm with a woman, Lena, and I haven't got the slightest intention of telling you who or why."

She gasped. "And you've got the nerve to criticise me!"

"I am not bloody-well criticising anybody. I'm stating a fact. And it doesn't matter."

"Now you listen to me . . ."

"I'm finished with listening, Lena. I'm going to *tell* you something. You don't have to worry about me and other women, because all that could come to an end . . ."

"All of it!" she screamed.

". . . if you'd only be reasonable for one minute. Are you listening, Lena? Will you listen quietly to what I want to say, just for once?"

Ten seconds of silence. I counted them. Then she said:

"That's *it*! That just about tops it all off. With your woman there . . . is she at your elbow, Ken, leaning over your shoulder." Then her voice almost broke my ear-drum. "Well she can hear what I've got to say. I've finished with you, Ken. Finished. You can do what you God-damn like, rot for all I care. But don't come near me. Not ever again!"

She stopped. I could hear her panting, the breath breaking

up. She was sobbing, but sobbing with the phone still at her ear, making sure I heard.

"Lena?"

"Don't," she whispered, "say you're sorry."

"You're crying."

"And so would you."

"Let me explain about the woman, and where I am." I hated the weakness, but less than I hated the tears.

There was a little, very dry, laugh. "Oh, don't trouble. I'm not crying for you."

"Don't ever cry for me," I asked her.

"You forced me into going to Harry Burnett. You ought to be laughing."

Mrs Lorimer now had the TV off. She'd come to the open door to watch me. I lowered my voice.

"Laugh at you? Never."

"You knew what he was like. That's why you let me do it. I bet you killed yourself laughing."

I felt cold. "What *is* he like?"

She made a brave effort. "He's kind and gentle, that's more than you ever were. But he's just hopeless. Spineless. And just as useless as you, Ken. Manager, he said! It's a wonder they let him load the shelves."

"I can understand your predicament."

"You? You never understood anything."

"But – if I came home?"

"Oh, you won't find us there. I'm at his place." As I'd known from the phone number. "And a better place than you ever provided, I must say that."

"Then that's fine."

"What's fine about it?" she flared.

"If I come home you won't be there."

"If you come home?" She sounded bemused.

"I'd have to fetch you from his place," I explained.

"Don't you dare come here!" she shouted.

So it wasn't as acceptable as she said. "I won't come there, then. But the house . . . our house?"

196

"Oh, don't worry, I've taken nothing."

"I meant – if I transferred back." I'd got the words in at last, but the timing was wrong.

"If!" she cried. "If, if, if! It's nothing else but ifs with you. I've just lost all patience. Nothing ever goes right with you, Ken Beacham. So don't try your tricks on me. You haven't got the slightest intention . . ."

And then all her control went and she was screaming at me through her sobs, with me putting words in uselessly because she wasn't listening, wasn't even intending to. I could speak only quietly, and the agony was that I wanted to shout. Shut up! Let me speak! But the screams continued the other end, the accusations, the sobbed fury of her wasted years with me, her derision and her hatred. It was all in her tone; the words were no more than waves of sound beating at me.

Then it stopped. Suddenly. In the abrupt silence I heard a door slam the other end. In a calm, flat voice she said: "He's back." Then she cut me off.

I slowly replaced the phone on its cradle. My heart was beating and my hands unsteady. Mrs Lorimer, when I turned, was still watching. I walked towards her, my legs stiff. Her eyes were grave and she seemed shocked.

"Who on earth was that?"

"My wife." I tried to bring my mind round to her. What had we been talking about? Had we finished? "But we were discussing . . ."

"It was all I had to say."

I remembered. "But there was something I hadn't made clear."

I advanced until she backed off. Something, at least, I might recover. I went and sat where I'd been before, leaning forward, rubbing my face because it felt cold. I raised my eyes to hers.

"All right. Now we're all quiet and relaxed . . . why don't you sit down, Mrs Lorimer?"

She sat, but persisted. "There's no more to say."

"Much more. We agreed, when I was here last, that

there was no reason for your husband's suicide. Right? Is that right?"

"What? Oh yes."

"So you filled in a form, because the alternative was murder, and there was just a chance you'd get benefit. But I'd have to prove it was murder, and that doesn't come under my normal duties. I'm not a policeman. I haven't got a policeman's facilities and experience. But I had to try. And all I've got so far is nowhere. There's evidence that your brother reached your husband – those order sheets – and I can't break that. And that makes your brother about the only person who could have done it. Now please let me finish. I don't like that idea any more than you do, though for a different reason. But there's no motive for your brother to have killed him. In fact, the last time Leonard was seen he was anxious and eager to see your husband. Excited. There just is no motive for *anybody* to have killed him."

"If that's your difficulty . . ."

"Unless the saboteur he was after decided he was getting too close."

"*I* could have killed him," she said calmly.

I'd been fighting off a lethargy that was the aftermath of the hatred Lena had poured over that phone. But now I came awake.

"You? Are you offering yourself as an alternative to your brother? That won't do, you know." And my ridiculous, trained and programmed mind went chasing away into the law involved. If she'd killed him, could she claim widow's benefit? Could she draw it in prison? Would the benefit mount up, a fortune when she came out? I shook my head. Sheer mental exhaustion.

"I'm not," she said, "claiming I did it. I said I could have. I've got a very good motive."

"Try to surprise me," I said wearily.

"Purely and simply, I hated him. Loved him, and couldn't bear not to have him with me, and hated him because he

198

withdrew himself. So often. Every time it happened, I thought I could live through it. I'd wait, and it would end. But always there was another. It was not as though he had a settled mistress. If he'd loved some other woman, and had told me, then maybe I could have faced it. Divorce, yes. I could even face that. But I hated him because he didn't *tell* me. He was ashamed . . . no, not ashamed . . . he just didn't think them important enough. With him, they were simply vehicles for sex. I knew of every one, and I could wait. He was still mine. I had something they hadn't got from him. His love. That never wavered. But I couldn't go on loving him. Oh, I put on an act, but he must have realised. Sometimes I saw it in his eyes, the awareness that I hated him. But even then, he went on loving me. I don't know why. I just don't."

I thought, from a man's point of view, that I did. Lorimer would have realised what he was doing to her and blamed himself, and told himself – over and over – that he couldn't help himself. It was gratitude he'd felt for his wife, that she was still there.

She was eyeing me shrewdly. "Sometimes, Mr Beacham, it's better to have a wife who hates you, than any number of empty affairs."

"You haven't convinced me you could have killed him," I told her.

She laughed. "You wanted motives."

"Which means," I said, "that you've relaxed. And that's because you believe there's no motive for Lennie to have done it."

"You *do* understand."

"Then it does no harm to give you this." I reached into my pocket and produced the key with the yellow tag.

She reached out, then withdrew her hand. She had become very pale.

"It's the key to your flat in Manchester?"

"Yes. I've got its twin. But where did you get it?"

"Lennie was in Manchester so often for one main purpose. Your husband thought he'd be needing the flat very soon. That *you* would. And there was a woman installed in that flat."

She moaned softly. "In my flat!" One she didn't know about?

"Lennie had been trying to get her out."

"For *that*," she whispered, "I *would* have killed him."

"And Lennie succeeded. Finally, he got her to leave. He locked her out and took away her key. That was why Lennie was in Manchester that evening, and that was why he was so eager to see your husband. It was good news he was bringing him, and he was excited. Even less reason for Lennie to have killed him, you see."

I placed the key on the table beside me. She appeared reluctant to touch it, but she couldn't take her eyes from it.

"How did you come to have it?" she asked at last.

I shrugged. Detail would be extraneous. "Lennie had it in his brief-case, which was in his car, so it found its way to Virginia Trent."

"Virginia knows?" Her eyes flew open wide.

"No. She thought it fitted an entirely different lock. She gave it to me – I won't tell you how or why."

She sighed. "I lied to you, Mr Beacham, when you came before. I want to apologise for that. If I'd known then, about *that*," she nodded towards the key, "I'd have had something different to say. How dare he use my flat! How dared he!"

It was at last at an end. I got to my feet. She said: "I didn't offer you anything. What can I get you?"

"No! Oh no. I must rush. Shall I see myself out?"

She came with me to the front door. I walked rapidly to the car. The quartz grandfather clock in the hall had told me it was 8.58. She didn't wave, just stood there sadly as I drove away.

I was miles from Kaye, miles from the town, and that to drive through. I pushed the Fiat, but it had seen better days, worse drivers. I cursed it, but it went sluggish on hills and accelerated with its years heavy on its shoulders. I parked it in Macklin Centre, locked it, ran for her outer door. It was open. I pounded up the stairs, and she heard me coming.

In the doorway, she was, calm and cold.

"Oh God, Kaye! I'm sorry."

She must have seen some of my distress in my face, and she was very quick, very receptive. The ice melted. Her face became radiant.

"Ken!"

"Darling." I kicked the door shut behind me.

After a few moments she pressed me away from her. "Kenny?" I tried to smile. "You're shaking," she said, accusing.

"It's been such a day." I walked away from her, not wishing her to realise why my eyes were so bright.

"Come and sit down."

She took my hand and led me to her settee, took my face in her palms, gently ran her fingers down my cheeks.

"What's this?" she asked gently. "I do believe you're crying!"

"I spoilt your meal."

"No you haven't. And nobody cries for *Sole Mimi*."

"I expected fury, and you . . ." I gestured. "Oh hell!"

Then she laughed. "You're an emotional idiot, and I love you. Now you just sit there and I'll pop it in the oven. Twenty minutes, that's all it takes. I've done the sauce. Then we'll have a glass of sherry . . . I got some in, specially. And a bottle of white wine."

She said all this while walking away from me, out into the kitchen. I recovered enough to look round. She had tidied the room. The table had a cloth on it, which was probably a special treat for Kaye, and two stumps of candle stuck with their own wax to place mats, her idea of a bit of fun. I couldn't help smiling. After a couple of minutes I got up and drew the cork from the sherry bottle. Good stuff. She'd gone mad. I took a glass into the kitchen for her.

"We have it on cold plates," she said, "so that the sauce doesn't melt, and there's Peach Melba to follow."

I touched my glass to hers. "Congratulations on the exhibition."

She grinned. "I haven't done the paintings yet."

"But you will. That's the point, isn't it! You set out to do something, and you do it."

She moved me back into the room. "And poor old indecisive Ken can't last long enough to do anything."

"Heh. Hold on!"

"We'll have the lights off and the candles lit," she told me. "We'll have to eat quickly, though."

"Why's that?"

"There's no more than 20 minutes left in the candles." She giggled.

I could sense every movement of her slim and mobile body, feel every thought maturing and know how it would end. It was delicious to bask in her presence, and see in her eyes that she felt delight in mine. The knowledge made me self-conscious and uncertain. Even shy. I smiled, but could have sworn it was stiff. I wondered for a moment whether she liked my smile. Was it perhaps ugly? She danced round me and cried: "Your time's up."

"Time?"

"To stare at me and strip me naked."

"I was doing no such thing!"

"Then you should have been doing it." She was pressing me down into a chair at one end of the table. "Light the candles. Matches there. I'll bring it in." Then she tossed over her shoulder: "I was."

"What?"

"Stripping you naked."

I lit the candles and put out the main light. In the shadows I dared to call: "And what did you see?"

"Just a man," she said indifferently, walking in with the dish hot in her oven gloves. "Trala!" We stared at it. It smelt delicious. "Just a man I happen to love," she said. "Pass me your plate, I can hardly see a thing."

Just as well. My eyes were bright again.

We sat, at the end, finishing the wine with the light on, because the candles had smoked themselves to extinction. The meal had been wonderful, its setting ridiculous and romantic.

"I didn't know you were such a good cook," I said.

"Oh, I'm not. I just did what it said in the book."

"The story of my life. I just do what it says in the book."

"Perhaps you ought to open a new book?"

"Yes." I hesitated. She had not asked me about my phone call to Lena, and seemed uninterested in its outcome. No, not uninterested, I decided. She was simply waiting until I told her. "Kaye, I was offered a transfer back, today."

"Is that what you want?"

"It's what Lena wants. Wanted. I don't know now. I phoned her because she asked me to, but really I wanted to tell her. To relieve her mind. It's been a disaster here."

She pouted. "Oh? Thank you, kind sir."

"You know what I mean. But she wouldn't listen. I don't think she understood a word I said."

"So now what do you do?"

"I don't know. She's clearly distressed and unsettled, and I . . . Kaye, when you live with someone for years, whatever happens, there's still something left, because you've shared so much. I don't know. Really, I don't know."

"It's very simple," she said, with all the cool awareness of her bouncing youth. "Do you still love her, Ken?"

I reached and put my hand on hers. "Everything's so cut and dried for you, isn't it? Love, you say, and it means something to you. Something positive. God knows what it means to different people. But it changes, you know. At the beginning, it's mainly the sex aspect, but that fades, or takes on another shade, and isn't the main thing. You fall out of love with the body and into love with the person. Yet if that person changes . . . then you're in trouble. But sometimes you love the person at once, before you even know the body. One look, and you know, so that both aspects come together, and the sex is a reflection of the person, the person an element of the sex. Do you know what I'm saying, Kaye?"

"Yes," she said. "Of course."

"I do admire this confidence of yours. Wait till you're my age."

"I knew at once."

"That *isn't* what I'm saying. I'm saying that Lena is my wife, and love doesn't come into the decision any more. Not the love there was. Or I suppose there was."

"So you're going back to her?"

"I'm older than you. I'm stuck in my ways. The Civil Service mentality's part of my life. The alternative to Lena frightens me. It's too big."

"Me? Too big?" Her eyes danced.

"What you mean to me is too big. What you mean to me is . . . well, everything tossed into the air – my home, my job, my wife."

The smile hovered. To Kaye, life was the joy of attacking it and living with it to the full. It was an excitement and an experience. We had spent one night together. We had met three times – was it four, a hundred? – and we had not discussed serious matters. She had always gone alone. A man, any man, had been temporary, as her love for Lennie now appeared to have been. Now I had slapped her with cold reality, and she could no longer smile, could only gulp to swallow an emotion, put her glass to her lips but not drink, grope for a napkin and dab away nothing.

Then at last she whispered: "You're talking as though you're thinking of doing this for me?"

"I'm telling you the alternatives I've got to consider." I looked away. "It was a risk I had to take, telling you."

"You thought I'd laugh at you?"

"I value your advice. But laugh if you like."

"But I'm selfish, you know. Did you realise that, Ken? I live just for my own pleasure of creating things and achieving something. And up to now that's been enough. But now . . . oh hell, Ken, you've ruined everything! I can't do it alone any more. I've got to have somebody to show my silly little triumphs to. Somebody who'll share them. So if I advise you to go back, and you do, then I'll have no reason left for any of it, and all the fun'll go out!"

Now it was she who was close to tears. I pushed my chair back. "Weren't there some sketches you wanted to show me?"

". . . of everything," she breathed. She looked up into my eyes. "If there's nobody who understands."

It was not simply that I needed her. She needed me. Trotter had been way out. He was the one who didn't understand.

One touch and she'd have gone over the edge. I said: "Sketches." When she looked at me it was with a rueful smile.

"We'll clear away first," she decided.

"I'll help you with the washing-up."

"You're my guest, Ken."

"Oh Lord, as formal as that, is it?"

Then we were past it, and I thought I knew where I stood with her. And she with me. Thought. But you can never be sure. What on earth goes on in their heads?

The sketches were pen and ink, with splashes of water colour to indicate what she had in mind as to treatment. She was thinking in terms of pattern. I liked them. They gave a sense of peace.

"You work from imagination?" I asked. "These are all landscapes."

"I just put down the shapes and designs I want, then I

go looking for a scene that nearly fits, and push things round a bit. That tree over there, the old mill farther to the left, you know."

"You move nature to suit yourself?"

"Everybody does it. You just try matching up a Constable with the scene as it really is."

"It must give you a great sense of power, picking up a church and moving it."

She laughed.

"And these little beetle things?" I asked.

"They're people. Where I want them to be."

"Breughel?"

"Like that. Everything you can think of, it's already been done. I'm just messing about with the perspective."

"Clever girl."

She put them away. Eight towards her set. She'd made a start. Give her an objective, and she aimed straight for it.

We went to do the washing-up. Waving the cloth, I said: "What're you doing tomorrow, Kaye?"

She glanced at me, eyebrows twitching. "I ought to do some work. Have you got something exciting in mind?"

I polished a glass carefully, my eyes on it. "I can't go on hiring that Fiat. I need my Cortina. It's supposed to be parked in the drive of our place at Acocks Green, but of course . . ."

"You want me to drive you there?"

"I could make it on the bus and train."

"It'd be a day out."

"Not the whole day. I could pick up some of my things, though."

She was silent for a few moments. I was indicating that a decision had been taken, and that I wanted her to share in bringing it about. A plate slipped from her hand, but I caught it on the way down.

"Your reactions are good," she commented. "If we're

going to do that, you'd better stay the night. Hadn't you?"

I had to admit that it was probably the most convenient. So I stayed the night.

Chapter Fifteen

Kaye was not a very good getter-up. For the first half an hour after dragging herself from the bed, it seemed that she was drugged, her brain inert and her body not reacting. I never feel too bright, myself, so we suited each other. We sat morosely at her table, fumbling tea cups to our lips, pushing cornflakes around in bowls. With me, it's the shave that does the trick. That I was using shaving kit obviously left behind by a former overnight-stayer – surely Lennie had never been able to accomplish this? – did not worry me at all. Kaye seemed to recover by splashing her face with cold water and spluttering.

We left the Fiat locked up in the car park square, but I took my briefcase from it. If any vandals were again tempted, I couldn't afford to lose that.

"Can we stop at Mrs Zalusky's?" I asked. "A clean shirt, a change of socks."

"Just tell me where."

But I think she knew that I had to see whether there was a message from Lena, or maybe a letter. There was neither. Mrs Z said she thought she'd lost me, and I galloped up the stairs. Clean shirt and pants. Clean socks and my other pair of shoes. I was down in five minutes.

"Going to collect my Cortina," I shouted, then I threaded my way through the greenery.

Kaye glanced at my face, and gave me a pert little smile. "Nothing?"

"Nothing," I agreed, fumbling with the seat belt. "Are we in a great hurry?"

"None at all. We've got all day, haven't we?"

"Then I wonder . . . would you mind if we call on Mrs Trent?"

She drove away from the kerb, not replying.

"You wouldn't need to meet her."

"It'd seem strange, going to his home." She sounded doubtful. "Is it important?"

"I suppose not. But I had a sudden thought. We never worked it out, but she was there, outside your flat, when she'd come to give you the key. She knew your name and address. So . . . how? Surely Lennie wouldn't have told her."

"Of course not. But it isn't important, is it? Which way do we go from here?" She was short and abrupt.

"To the Trent's place?"

"It's where you want to go, isn't it!"

I'd upset her. Her voice was tight. The car was slowing as we approached the junction.

"I'd like to know, that's all," I said.

"Which way, damn it?"

"Left, then."

She turned left.

"If it's going to upset you . . ." I began.

"It's just that I thought this was going to be *our* special day, and now she has to go and interfere. She did know, and that's that."

When she began emphasising words, it meant her emotions were involved. I decided to cancel it. Any time would do. "I mean . . . consider Mrs Lorimer," I said, trying to justify myself. "With her it was different."

"We're not going to see her as well, are we?"

"I was simply mentioning her. She told me she always knew when Lorimer had got himself another woman. The way he acted with her."

It was something Kaye could join in. She nodded. "Oh – she would."

"But even she, all experienced in things like that – and she spoke as though she'd had plenty of experience of it –

even she was never certain who and where. Yet Mrs Trent, with Lennie trying his first excursion . . ." I didn't know how to finish that without becoming too personal. "It *was* his first, would you say?"

She threw back her head and used the jocular tone that meant she was teasing herself. "It took somebody like me to lure him from the straight and narrow."

"And there can't be many like you."

She laughed. "You were saying – this marvellous bit of deduction you were making."

"I was just making the point that it's strange that Mrs Trent knew where to go. She didn't strike me as being the sort of person to follow him. And anyway – didn't I get the impression he usually called to see you on the way back from one of his visits?"

"It was easier for him to find the time," she said negligently.

"So I wondered how she knew. That's all."

"I can't see it's going to get you far."

"I'm not getting anywhere not knowing. It's the right-hand turn at the top."

We coasted to the kerb in front of Mrs Trent's place. I said I'd be only a few minutes. She was staring ahead through the windscreen, refusing to look at his home, afraid that she'd see Virginia Trent in the garden.

"Go for a little walk, if you'd feel better," I suggested. "I'll wait."

"Or we could simply drive away."

"Ken! Get it done – please!"

I left her. I was away 15 minutes, five of them having been thinking time. I got back into Kaye's car. She had been sitting with her head back, eyes closed, possibly dozing. She jerked nervously when I opened the door.

"Finished?"

I nodded. "Next stop Brummagam."

She took off at speed, missed her turn, and was agitated

until she re-discovered the road to the by-pass. Then at last she relaxed. After a few minutes:

"Well?" she demanded.

"How well did you know Lorimer?" I asked.

"Phil Lorimer? I never even met him. He was my brother's immediate boss, that's all I know."

"Did your brother speak about him at all?"

"Oh – very often. What're you getting at?"

"An opinion of Lorimer. An outside opinion. Your brother is the Production Control Manager. He'd be close to Lorimer. So – what did he say about him?"

"I don't use that sort of language in mixed company."

I grinned at her. "Like that, was it?"

"Like that. Now are you happy?"

I was far from happy. I was beginning to realise how little, in my job, I ever managed to scratch beneath the surface of people. In this Trent case I'd probed deeper than I'd ever done before, and believed I'd been doing well. But even now I knew nothing. Lorimer was a cipher, known, ambivalently, only through his wife. And now – through Mrs Trent.

"Aren't you going to tell me?" Kaye asked sharply.

"You're not going to like this, Kaye."

"I'm not liking it already."

I sighed. "All right. Hey! Watch the roundabout!" We clipped it. "Lennie was a buyer. Right? Not a salesman. Salesmen are out all the while, but buyers . . . I reckon they can do most of their work by phone. But as we know, Lennie was out a lot, and we know why, don't we!"

"Ken," she said, "you're waffling. Do get on with it! Lennie was out a lot because he was trying to get Lorimer's latest woman out of that flat."

She spoke disparagingly of Lorimer's woman. I suppose that Lorimer's woman was an entirely different proposition from Lennie's woman, from Kaye's point of view. I had a little, secret grin to myself, and went on: "So Lennie

211

was away from the district quite often – and *you* weren't complaining."

"Ken!" she warned.

"But Mrs Trent *was* complaining. She didn't even suspect there was such a person as you, Kaye. All she thought was that Lorimer was working Lennie too hard, when you'd expect, being brothers-in-law, he'd help Lennie a little, ease his burden so to speak. So what did she do? She went along to Lorimer about it. And she went along on the afternoon of that special day in January."

"Oh."

"Yes, oh. You can see what's coming, can't you? She accused Lorimer of working Lennie too hard, and he wasn't the sort to take accusations lying down. He told her – and this she said to me in all sincerity. She's a simple woman, Kaye, and she wouldn't lie. He told her that he'd given Lennie a very free rein. He wasn't accountable for every minute to Lorimer. And it wasn't Lorimer's fault if Lennie spent a lot of time out of the factory, it was Lennie's, because Lennie was having an affair. And if she didn't believe him, she should go and have word with a certain Kaye Trotter at such and such an address. The two men had obviously confided in each other."

"Why – the rotten bastard!"

"Yes. My feelings exactly. So what did Mrs Trent do? She certainly didn't go along to see you."

"Oh God, no!"

"But she did wait by her phone until Lennie called her, as she expected him to, to say he'd possibly be a little late because of the weather. And then she told him it'd better *be* only a little, because she knew where he had his woman and what her name was. She told him she knew, Kaye! And she told him where she'd got the information."

She was driving too fast and too wildly. I was about to protest, but one glance at her face warned me. You don't shock a sleep-walker, and she was driving purely by instinct.

212

"But Lennie didn't say," she cried, glancing sideways at me for far too long. "He said absolutely nothing. And Ken! He told me he was going to phone his wife and tell her he was stuck halfway, and then stay the night with me."

"He intended to call her bluff," I decided. "I think he was so angry he probably didn't know what he was doing. There he was, all triumph from having saved Lorimer from *his* domestic disaster, and he'd found that Lorimer had pitched him headfirst into it."

"Poor Lennie. That was why . . ."

She stopped. I waited. She was regaining control of her driving skill. When she went on, she was calmer. But there was a cold, distant passion about it.

"He was strange, all tensed-up. You know Lennie, all fun and go. I couldn't make him laugh that evening. He smiled, but it was stiff. He had to see Lorimer by nine, he said, but he let nine o'clock pass, and it seemed to give him some pleasure. 'He can wait,' he said. 'I remember now. And when he told me he'd finally got that woman out of the flat – I *thought* it was triumph and pleasure, but he was all tight about it, and he wouldn't let me kiss him."

"He wouldn't be in a kissing mood."

And then I dropped it, because I wanted to think, and didn't particularly want Kaye to carry on the reasoning to a logical conclusion. Without all the detail I knew, it was unlikely she would. I sat back, believing I could pursue it quietly, but at such times your expression speaks for you, and Kaye had never needed much of a hint. She might have driven a mile, two miles; I wasn't noticing. But suddenly she spoke.

"And where does all that get you?"

"I don't know."

"You do know, otherwise why would you be sitting there all miserable, as though the cat got the canary."

I turned and stared at her. "It's years since I heard that."

"And why can't you give me a straight answer?"

213

"Because it uncovers a damn good motive for Lennie to have gone out and killed Lorimer."

"A motive? And you think that's the end of the world! If everybody who had motives went out and did something about it, there'd be a lot fewer people on the streets. So what does it matter?"

"I was hoping against hope that this wouldn't happen. The motive was all that was missing."

"All! But you didn't know Lennie. There wasn't an atom of violence in him."

"There's violence in everybody, Kaye. You wouldn't believe! I had a case – three men arguing on a night shift, in a factory where they had a shunting siding. One of them was found in that shunting shed with his head off. He'd been lying across the rails. His two friends were the mildest characters . . ."

"You keep evading the issue!" she said, her voice shrill.

"Lennie reached Lorimer's office, Kaye. I've tried and tried, but I can't get round it. We know he reached that office, because those order sheets, which were in his pocket, were under Lorimer's arm, which was under his head. The same sheets, Kaye, not a set of duplicates that might have come along later by post. The police proved that to me. I don't know how much spare time Lennie had, and for the life of me I can't imagine how he'd even know what a nail gun is, let alone know how to get hold of it."

"He was a buyer," she tossed at me.

"What?"

But she had seen where I was heading, and in her contempt for my theory, was prepared to assist it along, for all the good it might do me.

"He was a buyer. He was responsible for buying everything in the factory, including machines and stores. So he'd know about the nail gun."

"You're a great help," I said miserably.

"Clearly, it's help you need. You were saying?"

"I was saying that I didn't know how he found the time,

214

but he must have reached Lorimer's office with the nail gun at a little after nine. Now don't you interrupt! Your brother was there until about nine. And it'd be natural for Lennie to stand at Lorimer's shoulder while they looked at the figures on the orders. The gun doesn't *fire* the nails, you know. The muzzle has to be actually pressed against . . ."

"There's a café up ahead. Shall we call in for coffee?" she asked acidly.

"If you like."

She swept into their car park, applied the handbrake, and sat back. No longer could she drive, because now she had to consider every word carefully, and mark its effect.

"What you're saying is that I lied to you."

"No I'm not."

I'd have preferred that she'd continued to drive. Her eyes were so hurt when she turned to me that I flinched.

"I told you, quite distinctly, twice if I remember correctly, that Lennie left me at around 9.15. He was dead ten minutes later."

"Your clock . . ."

"It was not wrong. It's a quartz, and it's *still* right."

"There must be something!"

"Do you believe I was lying to you, Ken?" she demanded, her eyes dark, a frown very nearly cleaving them apart.

"Of course not."

"It's what you're saying."

"It's what the evidence says."

"The evidence! You're acting like a police detective, and you're just a poor, plodding Civil Servant. What do *you* know about evidence?"

"A little."

"That wretched case is more than you can handle, and you know it."

We were quarrelling. Our first quarrel. Oh, I was an expert on quarrels, but Lena had never been reasonable in her taunts and challenges, so that always I could reserve to myself the tiny, comforting thought: but she's wrong.

215

With Kaye it was different, and it cut so much deeper. She was not wrong. I was lost and out of my depth. I mumbled something. She said with decision:

"What you ought to do is dump it on your Manager's desk and say: 'I've had enough.' And that'd be that."

I laughed, a nasty sound of sardonic amusement. "Oh no it wouldn't. It'd mean a decision that Mrs Trent wouldn't get her pension, because Lennie had reached Lorimer."

Her eyes blurred and she bit her lip. She had no reason to like Mrs Trent. She shook her head. "That'd be a shame." Then she was ashamed because the words carried an unpleasant tone of sarcasm.

"And all I'd have to set against it would be something I can't even put in the file, that I believe as truth what I was told by a young woman, because it was said just after the first time we made love."

"Oh, damn you, Ken!" she whispered, and she clenched her little fists on the steering wheel.

"What about that coffee?"

In answer, because she couldn't speak, she started the engine, and we swept out of that car park a damned sight faster than we'd gone in, and she said not another word until the signposts started saying Birmingham too urgently to be ignored.

"You'll have to guide me," she said evenly. She'd recovered.

"It's easy from here. We're on the right side of the city."

It seemed strange, approaching the house with a different woman. Ridiculously, I felt a sense of uneasiness, as we parked on the circle and I asked Kaye to come in. My Cortina was where Lena had said it would be, on the drive. The house seemed deserted. I hoped it was. A fine scene there'd be if Lena was there, or if she turned up when we were. And it was for Kaye I felt nervous, that she'd be subject to attack.

The garden was showing life. The daffs had done their

best and the tulips were now standing proud. Very soon the roses would be showing colour.

"You like gardening, Ken?" asked Kaye. I felt her nervousness.

"Not the work. The results."

"There's a garden at Ewr Felen," she said brightly. "Did I tell you? There *could* be an acre, all told. It goes back up the hill, behind the house, in kind of terraces."

"Like paddy fields?"

She laughed. It hadn't been funny. I slipped in the key.

"It should do well," she said. "It faces south."

"That's good."

There were cardboard boxes in the hall. Lena had been doing some packing, but had abandoned it. The boxes seemed forlorn.

"The sitting room's through here." I pushed open the door.

"It's nice."

"Not much at the back, though."

"A good set of weeds."

"Nowhere near an acre," I admitted.

"Ha!" she said. "Is that your typewriter?"

"It's only a portable."

She looked at me, one eyebrow cocked.

"Better take it, I suppose," I said, gripping its handle. It was the first physical step I'd taken towards removing myself from that house. But I felt its portentous weight, and suddenly the room was flooded with memories.

"The kitchen's not much," I offered.

"I can't say I find kitchens exciting. I hope the pictures aren't yours."

Children with huge eyes. "No, they're not mine."

"Where's your book?"

"She seems to have packed them."

"*Your* book. The one you're writing."

I laughed it to extinction. "What! All three versions? In the bedroom."

217

"You're not going to leave it!"

"A chunk of my life? Certainly not. Besides . . ." I stopped. "Besides, I might give it another go."

She grinned then, her gamin grin.

I went up to the bedroom. I did not invite her, but I couldn't ask her not to follow me. Strangely, I didn't want her in the bedroom. She plodded after me, though, head down, so I couldn't read her expression.

The bed had been stripped, the mattress leaning against the back wall. That was Lena, destroying the image of the matrimonial bed.

I said: "There's stuff I need."

In the centre drawer of the dressing-table were all the legal documents I'd need. Insurance certificates, car tax details, bank statements, my passport from the holiday we'd managed in Greece, my income tax code details.

She was looking out of the window, over my front garden, carefully not watching.

"When the house is sold," I said, "and everything's paid off – the mortgage and solicitors and things – there'll be a few thousand left. I reckon I'll have to split that with Lena, but we can manage on the rest."

"I don't want to know," she said in a thin voice.

"Well you should. It's important to you. You *ought* to know."

"If you think . . ."

"Money. I know, it doesn't matter. But we'll need to live on something."

"If you think I need your money . . . if you think that's the only reason I want you, Ken . . ."

My, she *was* in a mood! "Kaye," I said gently, and took her face between my palms. "Kaye, I'm only trying to be practical. One of us has to be practical. Admit it."

She managed a tight smile, tight because my hands were compressing it. I laughed. "You do get worked up!" I yanked open the wardrobe door. "Here's the great opus."

There was about 8 in of it, on scrap A4, and it weighed a ton. I lifted it out and dropped it into her arms. "There! You can trot down to the Cortine with that. Here're the keys. I'd like to hunt out what clothes I've got, then I'll be down."

She seemed relieved to get out of the room. From the window I watched her go to the Cortina. The bounce was back in her walk.

I had two suits in that wardrobe, one old, one new, two sports jackets, four pairs of slacks, and four pairs of shoes. In the drawers of my dressing-table – we'd had one each – were seven shirts and various pants, vests and so on. Quite a load to carry down. I was no longer feeling the oppression that accompanies the end of something solid. I saw it only as a move towards hope.

Lena had slashed every item of clothing I possessed. She had hacked at the shoes with a strength I thought could only have come from fury. The shirts and underwear had simply been gripped with two firm hands and torn apart. I could only imagine she'd persuaded Harry Burnett into driving her round here, right after that phone call. I wondered whether he had watched. I wondered what he had thought.

In just such a fury, Lennie Trent could have placed that gun against Lorimer's temple.

It was ten minutes before I was able to go down to Kaye. She was sitting, knees up, on the passenger's seat, with part of my handwritten manuscript on her lap.

"But Ken, it's wonderful . . ."

She stopped. I was holding open the door.

"Where's your stuff?"

I shook my head.

"Ken? What is it?"

"I'm leaving it."

But she'd put my book aside, and slid out of that car like an eel. "Tell me."

"She's destroyed all my clothes, Kaye. I don't know . . ."

Expressions flickered across her face. A dark anger,

lingering, a pale astonishment, horror, sympathy. "Oh . . . Ken . . .!" Then, practical as I'd never known her. "Can I repair anything?"

"No! Leave it." My voice cracked with anger. "Leave the damn stuff. What's it matter? Let's get away from here."

She hesitated. One finger came up and touched her lips. "Are you all right? Can you drive?"

"Away from here? Yes."

I led the way sedately, curbing my raging urgency. Kaye's car sat firmly in my rear vision mirror, solidly. I felt she was there in the Cortina with me. Then after a while the violence that Lena had used on me – through what was mine – settled into a dull ache. Dull aches you can live with.

We stopped for lunch. Once well clear of the busy city outskirts, I was eager to find a place to stop. I needed Kaye's company. But we ate silently. It still weighed heavily on us. In slashing through anything that might still exist between her and me, Lena had managed to wound what lay between Kaye and me. And we couldn't pick it up and soothe it.

In train again, we returned to Mrs Zalusky's. We got out of our respective cars. "I'll phone you," I said, and she nodded. We touched fingers. She walked away from me and I decided to call after her, but she'd gone before I could put it into effect.

It was only three o'clock. I went up to my room and found small comfort from Polski's uncritical friendship. Gradually the shock receded. Suddenly I found myself wondering why Lena had not destroyed my book. But of course, she'd been completely uninterested in it, and it wouldn't occur to her that it mattered to me. Very nearly, I ran down to get it from the car, a warm feeling of possession gripping me.

Then I realised it was Saturday afternoon, and I would be able to return the Fiat. The snag was that it was parked outside Kaye's. Snag, did I say? But Lena had struck deeper than she could have realised. Whereas it had been a shock to me, to Kaye it must have seemed that it was she who'd brought Lena to those pitiful depths of malice. To Kaye, the distress would be growing, and any attempt on my part to prove that she was not the pivotal point of Lena's hatred could only endanger the strength of the tie between us.

Therefore, I parked the Cortina beside the Fiat – sheer luck, this, as the shopping centre was busy – and slipped off with it before I was noticed. I'd call in when I got back, I decided.

I handed in the Fiat and settled up. They told me the insurance people were definitely going to write-off the Mini, so I'd have to write Lena about that. Hell, there were dozens of things I'd have to write Lena about.

To get the bus back to Kaye's I had to travel first to the bus terminal, and the one from there went past Crayshaw's. I hadn't realised that. On impulse, I got off at the stop just beyond the gates.

There was no sense to it. I had a marginal reason, but no genuine excuse. But the place haunted me, and the small question of Kaye's truthfulness stood hugely between us. I would have liked to go to her with the whole thing cleared.

Chapter Sixteen

I strolled to the gates with my hands in my pockets. No black briefcase at that time, "E11R" on it, nothing to authorise me. But the gatekeeper was the same Geoff, and he knew me now. He seemed to land for all the easy shifts. Experience, that was.

"Hello there," I said. "Anybody around at this time?"

Know me, yes. Trust me, no. He pushed back his peaked cap. "Depends who you mean."

"Oh . . . the storekeeper, or Mr Trotter perhaps. Maybe the Production Controller – Stone is it?"

"The top brass, eh? Never want to talk to the real workers, do you?"

"Not," I admitted, "at this moment."

"Well, you picked a good time. There's all hell going on in there. A machine-bearing burnt out. All *your* lot are there, the MD too."

"That's fine."

But I wasn't as confident as that sounded. I was toying with an idea. Lennie Trent had been a buyer – stores, the lot. He, in other words, would have bought the nail gun. He might have bought a replacement, and have had it with him that night. Oh yes, I know. Clutching at straws.

"I'll just wander in, then," I said, having no authority, nothing but a smile to ease me on my way. He nodded. "You know where."

I headed for the small door I'd used before.

It was still daylight, but the storm clouds Mr Z had felt in his bones were massing, the light fading. With the door shut behind me, it could well have been night. The high, booming corrugated iron roof had a few nominal glass panels in it, but up there they were not likely to be cleaned. Very little light penetrated, and again the focus of attention was a concentrated flush of light, somewhere in the middle. The heavy, jagged shadows of machinery stood between me and that objective, the small group of diminished humanity that argued around a derelict machine. Voices echoed high into the steel rafters, and tools clashed emptily on concrete floors. There was anger, abuse. I approached slowly, feeling my way in a wavy, uncertain line.

Now my idea seemed futile. To these men, lamenting over the bearings in several hundred thousand pounds' worth of machinery, any enquiry regarding nail guns would seem paltry.

My steps slowed.

And what was I really proposing? That Lennie had somehow arrived at the factory with the nail gun already in his possession, and afterwards faked a break-in to cover its use? You will see how desperate I was to prove the truth of Kaye's statement. But did it prove any such thing? Of course it didn't. He still wouldn't have had the time.

I found I was no longer moving. I stood in a smell of slurry beside a towering machine that I could barely recognise as metal. Beside me – my fingers touched its rim – there was a bin of curly swarf, the distant light catching glints in its white, new surface. I stood, decided to go back, and turned.

A shape moved in the shadows beyond the machine. A foot slurred on oil-slicked concrete. I threw up an arm because he was coming at me, and then a black cloud flew at my face as a hand jerked out at me. Instinct had my eyes shut, but there was no time to protect myself from the grit reaching my mouth and nose. I knew that a fist or a weapon had to follow, but more strongly was the certain knowledge – an association subconsciously of various ideas – that the cloud had been carborundum powder, and that I dared not open my eyes to attempt to see or my mouth to call out.

The blow was from a fist, full in the face. I fell over into the swarf bin, sending it clattering, then sideways against the sweet oil-smelling machine, as my senses faded.

I opened my eyes to the pain of a blast of light. My eyeballs felt burned and scarred, my lips harsh, my nose blocked. An arm was round my shoulders. Trotter's arm, because it was his voice.

"Keep 'em shut. Your eyes – shut. Cough. Cough hard!"

I coughed. My throat rasped, and agony ran through it. He raised his voice. "The eyewash. Anybody got the eyewash, for God's sake!"

He now had me in a sitting position. Panic was fighting inside me, that I was blind, that I would never dare to take another breath. Something thrust itself against my teeth, metal, mug-shaped.

"A mouthful. Wash it round. Spit it out. Good. Do it again."

I did. Things were feeling better. Somebody was gently wiping my lips and nostrils with a wet cloth. Then Trotter told me: "Head forward. Right forward! I'm going to put this over your eye. Right eye. When I tell you, put your head back and open it. Right eye only. Okay?"

I couldn't reply, felt the eyebath on my right eye, flung my head back, and opened it. Of course, both eyes opened. Light again tortured me. I blinked a few times, then he thrust my head down and took it away.

"Good. Where's the other eyebath? For pity's sake, Frank, the other one."

I waited. We repeated it for the left eye. Then I sat up and I could see, though my eyes were still sore. We repeated the process. My face was streaming, some of it tears. Peterson, the night foreman, was crouched beside me, wet cloth in hand, wiping my face. Trotter sat back on his heels, grimacing.

"Fine. You'll do fine. There's tea coming up."

Somebody's flask tea. Horrible and wonderful.

"It's all right to swallow," said Trotter. "Won't hurt your belly. Can you breathe okay?"

"I can breathe."

"Blow your nose. Hard. Several times."

It's what the little hairs are for, like a car's air cleaner. I blew. An ounce or two of carborundum powder had been up there.

"Now try standing."

I could stand. Sundry pains established themselves. My jaw was stiff, my slacks ruined, my left elbow painful.

A man I did not know stood watching me. He had an air of authority, and his examination of me was critical.

"Who is he?" he demanded. "Is this our man?"

"Hardly," said Trotter. "He's from Social Security."

"Then what the hell's he doing here?"

That I would've found difficulty justifying. I shook my head.

"I don't like it," said this man, obviously the new MD. "Better send for the police."

"Would I throw carborundum powder in my own face?" I demanded. Maybe it was the dust, perhaps my anger and exasperation broke through. It came out as a rasp of indignation. He turned away.

Trotter said: "I'll run you home."

"I need you, Trotter," the MD said. To his second-in-command he might have used the mister, I thought.

Trotter flashed him a look of intense dislike. "I'll run him home!"

"Phone Kaye," I cut in quickly. "I can walk. I'll wait in the gatekeeper's hut."

But Trotter asserted his independence by walking me there, and waited while I phoned Kaye myself. Then he nodded, and left.

"Have you seen yourself in a mirror?" Geoff asked.

He had a mirror. Well, he would, wouldn't he, in order to admire his air of smart neatness. I stared into it. I might just as well have been down a coal mine.

225

By the time Kaye arrived, I'd cleared a lot of it off. My eyes were still red, but didn't feel gritty, and my breathing was operating, so my instincts had saved a lot. But I wondered whether I'd ever get my nostrils clear again.

"Oh God, Ken!" she said, "What have you been doing?"

My voice was all right, too. "I was attacked. Let's get away from here, Kaye. This place is unlucky for me."

She bundled me out into her car. "Get you into a bath. Clean clothes. A good job the seats are plastic." I let her get on with it, talking the distress and concern out of herself.

"And what were you doing in that place?" she demanded.

"Oh . . . a stupid idea. I was trying to prove he could've got there – Lennie – and shot Lorimer, even in the short time you gave him."

She bit her lip. She blamed herself for having given Lennie such a short time, and thus having brought about my present pitiful condition.

"Why can't you drop it!" she whispered, her voice uncertain.

"There's the motive," I appealed. "There's a motive now, but when you look at it you see it's not any motive for Lennie to have gone breaking open doors and getting nail guns and calmly going to Lorimer with murder in his mind. That's the trouble. Time or not, that motive's for Lennie to have charged into Lorimer's office, probably flung the order sheets in his face, and Lorimer's blasted key after them."

She hadn't been listening to one word. "A nice, soothing bath," she told me. "My bath oil and a lovely, smelly new cake of soap I've got, and a change from the skin outwards. Did you know your chin's swelling?"

"I feel gritty all over. But no need to race, Kaye."

"Race? I'm not racing." She screeched to a halt as lights changed to red. It gave her time to glance at me. "I saw the Cortina. Why didn't you come up to see me?"

"I thought you were upset. What Lena did. I reckoned you might need a bit of time, alone."

"Men are so stupid," she stated. "With you in my life, the last thing I wanted was to be alone."

A nice, soothing bath, she'd said. A nice, soothing tongue was better than all her baths, smelly soap and all.

She parked. The area was now more clear. At the top of the stairs she showed me the bathroom she shared with the other flat, on the landing.

Then, inside her flat: "Now, off with your clothes. I'll need to dump that stuff of yours in a plastic bag, till we can give it some thought. You'll have to borrow my dressing gown, unless you want to risk it naked. Sylvia won't mind, anyway. Oh, and give me your keys." She held out her hand.

"Keys?"

"I'll have to get you something to change into. I suppose your Mrs Z won't mind?"

"Not if you explain nicely." I thought she could've used her own car, seeing it was warm, but I gave her the keys anyway. "You have to double de-clutch from third to second. Can I keep the pants on?"

"Don't be coy. It's only just along the landing."

I trotted along the corridor and the bathroom handle stuck. Sylvia came out to investigate the noise – 50 years of jolly, fat Sylvia – and as Kaye had said, she didn't mind. Then I got inside with the soap and the bath oil, and it was like entering a haven, the previous steam still on the air and a smell of clean women.

The trouble with soaking is that there comes a time when no more hot water will run, and it seems warmer out of it than in. The last speck of irritant had been washed away. I was ready to dress, but Kaye had not returned. I was dry, and she had not tossed in my clothes. There was nothing to do but risk another trip along the corridor, which I did, and that blasted Sylvia once more didn't mind.

When Kaye returned I was making coffee in the kitchen. She came in and laughed. "You're all pink!"

"What've you brought?"

227

"While I was at it, the lot. I didn't know what you'd want, and Mrs Z asked me to say it didn't have to mean you'd left it vacant, whatever that means. It's all in your car, on the back seat."

Oh, she was clever! You can see what she'd done; she'd created a situation in which I could move in with her, and yet she had not forced it on me by bringing it all up to the flat herself. The choice was still mine.

"I can hardly go down like this and sort it through."

"Just say."

"For now – pants and vest, my blue shirt and the grey suit to go with it. The brown shoes – the only shoes – and brown socks to match. No tie. If you would."

"At your service, sir."

As she grimaced and turned away, I added: "I'll fetch up the rest later. If you don't mind."

She clattered happily away down the stairs.

By the time she returned I had the coffee ready. Her arms were loaded. Ridiculously, I felt I couldn't dress in front of her, and took it all into the bedroom. She came and sat on the edge of the bed, coffee in her hand. I wonder why that seemed all right?

"She's nice," she said.

"Who?"

"Mrs Z."

"Did you meet the cat?"

"Claw marks on my shoulder to prove it."

"Yes, that's the one."

Then we went and sat in her living room and stared at each other.

"Any more sketches?" I asked.

"When have I had time?"

"After you got back."

She pouted. "They'd have been all angry purples and furious reds."

"Yes. I suppose so."

She stirred. "I suppose I could go down for two plaice and chips."

"Do they have mushy peas?"

"Too classy. It's scampi these days."

"My life seems empty."

Then we sat some more. She put on a record, but I couldn't concentrate.

"In a mood," I said, "to throw the keys in his face."

"Who?"

"Lennie. That night, when he left you. I said it earlier . . . remember? Not in a mood to hunt out a nail gun and calmly plan murder, but to bang into Lorimer's office and throw the keys in his face."

"Do we really have to talk about that?"

"So . . . why didn't he?"

"Are you listening to this, Ken?"

"Not really."

"It's Segovia."

"It'll be there tomorrow."

"And so will the other!" she said tersely, getting up to put it off. "Always it'll be there, in your mind, because you can't accept my word that he didn't have time for anything."

"Lennie might not be on my mind tomorrow, my sweet, if you'll just humour me for a few minutes."

She was mildly sulky, flinging herself about, flicking her hair out of her eyes. "I thought we could have a quiet evening. Your jaw looks stiff." She peered at my jaw above her glasses.

"It hurts."

"Then don't talk."

"Kaye . . . please. Why didn't he throw the key in Lorimer's face? There was no mention of a key in that room. The order forms were there, under Lorimer's arm. And the keys . . . apparently in his brief-case, which you snuck down and popped into the back of Lennie's car. Kaye! Are you listening?"

229

"Trying not to."

"Oh – come on! Can't we just talk it through?"

Then she smiled. "You're stubborn, d'you know that! Pig-headed. Come on, then, talk."

"All right. I'm trying to recall what you said about that key. Lennie was here. He suddenly remembered he'd got to see Lorimer. He fetched the order forms out of the brief-case, then he dug down and came up with the key. Then didn't he say something like: 'I've got to give him this'? Or these?"

"Oh . . . this. Singular."

"And you thought he meant the order. Singular."

"Well yes."

"But there were quite a few sheets to that order. He'd surely refer to them as 'these'. Plural. If he said 'this', then he could have been referring to the key."

She laughed. "D'you know, you'd do lovely in court, cross-examining. I *suppose* he could have meant the key."

"Then why did he put it back in the brief-case, and leave it behind?"

"I don't know, Ken. He was bending over the brief-case, on the floor, holding the flap open and looking up at me with that strange look I told you about, and he lifted the key up, just to show me. I suppose all he did was let it drop again."

"This is supposition?"

"Well, I didn't actually see. That look in his eyes – I tell you, I didn't like it. Not Lennie at all, that smile he gave me. I looked away."

"Oh dear," I said. "Oh dear me!"

"What is it?"

"Lord, I don't know!"

But I knew it was something. My nice clean skin was prickling and the hair on the nape of my neck was standing on end. I wished I'd been alone, so that I could've thumped something, if only for the pain. I'd been such an utter fool, playing around with images that hadn't been presented to me.

"You might let me in on it," she said quietly.

"Can I use your phone, Kaye?"

"Of course." Her eyebrows were nearly into her hair-line.

I dialled Mrs Trent's number. She was an eternity answering.

"Mrs Trent? It's Ken Beacham. That key you had with the yellow tag – you told me it was in your husband's things. By that, did you mean his brief-case?"

"Well . . . no."

My chest was beating. "Will you tell me where."

"They . . . they sent everything back, eventually. As a matter of fact, the brief-case came separately, because they found it down behind the seat, at the scrapyard they towed the car to."

By this time Kaye had her head pressed against mine, now completely involved with it. I whispered: "Yes?"

"The police had brought round all the rest. Including his jacket, though it was all torn. But they left it to me to clear out the pockets. The key was in the right-hand side pocket."

I breathed out at last. "Thank you, Mrs Trent. Thank you indeed. Good night."

I hung up. Kaye stepped away from me. "Right-hand side pocket," I said. "All ready for bringing out into the light and throwing into Lorimer's face. If Lennie had got there."

"*Now* you're sure he didn't? I don't understand."

"The order sheets were in the inside pocket and the key in the outside one. The orders got there, but not the key. Therefore, Lennie didn't, otherwise he'd have delivered both. The orders got there, but not the key. Lennie knew he had both. Somebody didn't know that."

She was red with excitement, but in her eyes was an uncertainty I didn't understand. Now it was I who was carried along on a wave of wild and enormous decision, and she was not used to my lead. For a moment she even seemed afraid of my enthusiasm.

"How soon can we leave for Wales?" I asked.

She caught her breath. "Tomorrow. Tomorrow, if we try."

I laughed insanely. "I'm all packed. Shall I leave you to start on yours?"

"Leave me?" she demanded. "Now?"

"Not for long. Just one thing to clear up, then I'm free. I'll need my keys, though."

"They're over there." Making a gesture, but with her eyes not leaving mine. "I don't want to be left, Ken. Not here, waiting."

"Then come along, sweetheart." I was trying out endearments for one I could make permanent. "It'll be about an hour."

"Where're we going? Do I need a coat?"

"In my car, to the office. As a special treat – and you must realise that members of the public are strictly forbidden – as a special treat, as the special woman of the Inspector of this parish, you shall enter with me and see where I work."

"Oh . . . lovely!"

"Used to work," I amended.

"I can't wait!"

So I drove her round to the office, which was all dark in a darkening street, with the rain beginning to slice down, leaving the Cortina at the kerb and running for it to the shadowed porch. The hedges in the little gardens each side were smelling of wet dust. With the two keys, I opened the door, conquering an insane desire to whip her up and carry her over the threshold.

She said: "It's just like an old, haunted house."

It *was* haunted, by Lennie Trent and Philip Lorimer and their women. But one of the women was very much alive, and determined to denigrate my work and what it stood for.

"Oh, I must see where all the useless toil goes on!" she cried.

"You will come and sit by me, and you will be very quiet and serious," I told her.

Which she did, for a good five minutes.

Chapter Seventeen

She was nervous and tense. I could almost feel the suppressed emotion vibrating through her. I unfolded a chair for her, and sat her down on the other side of my desk, opened my filing cabinet and got out all my 17 files. That was a fair enough current load. 18 with the Trent file.

"Now what're you doing?" she asked.

"Just running through them, to see whether there're any comments to make."

"Then what?"

"A final minute for the Trent file, two more short notes, and we can lock up and go."

She stirred restlessly. I concentrated. She bounced to her feet and walked round the room.

"Is this where you usually work?"

"Yes."

"It's a bit empty and solitary, isn't it? Like a monk's cell."

I raised my head. She was walking her fingers along the top of the filing cabinet. "I'm more out than in. And it's quiet. Usually."

"It's spooky."

"All right, it's spooky. Can't you let me get on and finish this?"

"Isn't there something I can do?" she complained.

I thought about that. Go and wait in the car? No. I was going to have to live with her restless presence around me, so I might as well get used to it. "If it's open, the room next door's a kitchen. Try whipping up a cup of tea. How about that?"

She looked at me thoughtfully for a moment, then she nodded and went out. I got my head down again. The notes I had to make were minor, more in the way of suggestions. "Perhaps a visit to the employer?" "Wife might be upset if we pursue this line." That sort of thing.

She put her head in. "That cupboard's full of stuff. Which lot's yours?"

I sighed, and sat back. "Bottom left. Box of tea bags and a bag of sugar. Use the milk at the bottom right. That's the Manager's."

"Oh goodee! Top grade milk."

She was gone again.

The 17 files took me 20 minutes. I stacked them neatly on the edge of my desk, and placed a note on top. "Manager to see."

She came in with two mugs of tea. No tea bags in them, so she'd used somebody's pot.

"Are you nearly done?"

"The difficult bit's next," I told her.

She sipped. "It's a big place, isn't it?"

"Have you been wandering around?" I realised it had taken her a long while to make a pot of tea. "Where have you been, Kaye?"

"Oh . . ." Shrugging. "Looking round. Seeing how the bureaucrats live."

Lights on all over the building – we'd have the police there. "Did I detect a note of envy?"

"Oh . . . brother!"

I rolled a sheet of A4 into my machine, and began to type.

"Oh my God!" she said, "is that the best you can do?" She was certainly on edge.

"I'm not a typist. Damn it, Kaye, can't you find something to look at? And *not* those files, please. It was you who wanted to come here."

"What're you doing now?"

"If you come round here, you can see."

So it was with Kaye standing at my shoulder that I continued to peck away. There would be recorded somewhere the correct wording for presenting resignations. I didn't feel like looking it up. I typed:

1. Manager
2. R.O. (Estabs)
3. Regional Controller

Please accept this as my resignation. I am aware that it is customary for a month's notice to be given, but the same circumstances that make the resignation necessary also prevent me from offering notice.

K. Beacham. E.O.

She touched my shoulder. I turned up my head and grinned at her, then wound in another sheet of A4.

Paul,

I am sorry this has happened, and even sorrier that you'll find yourself in some amount of staffing difficulty for a while.

"Who's Paul?" she asked.

"The Manager. Isn't that obvious?" I returned to the keys.

I think you will find that all current files are noted up to date. Perhaps you will be good enough to pass on my resignation to the appropriate authorities.

You will find that the Trent file is minuted up to date, and that I've recommended allowance. A further point arises from this, one we've discussed. Mrs Lorimer withdrew her application for Ind Death Ben, but it now seems that this would be for allowance. Perhaps you will see to it that she receives a new application form. Another office will be responsible, of course, but my opinion is that Lorimer's death can be accepted as an industrial accident.

It is a pity we shall not have the opportunity of working together. I think we would have enjoyed it.

    Best wishes,
      Ken.

"But you detested him," Kaye said.

"I was getting to understand him. With some people, it takes a time."

"There's some more tea if you want it."

"No, thanks. I'd better get on with this."

So she took out the mugs for washing up and I dug into my final minute as an Inspector. When she again appeared at my elbow, I was well into the Trent case.

Manager,

    This case has raised difficulties because of an apparent contradiction, which I was not able to resolve until now.

    Leonard Trent was employed as a buyer, and though it was not part of his normal duties he was bringing back a set of order forms for his MD. As the MD – Philip Lorimer – had asked him to do this, I think we can accept that Trent was in the course of his official duties in complying. However, the point arose as to whether he had, at the time of his death, completed this duty and left the factory premises, and thus taken himself from the sphere of his employment, or had not reached the office, and was still within it.

    As evidence of the former were the order forms, which were found beneath Lorimer's arm when he was discovered dead in his office. As evidence of the latter, I had verbal evidence that I could not dispute.

    I have now discovered that Trent had reason to be extremely angry about an action Lorimer had taken, when at the same time he – Trent – had done Lorimer a favour. This favour involved a key. I feel that Trent, had he reached Lorimer's office, would have been in a mood to throw that key in Lorimer's face, and the fact that the key was still in Trent's pocket after his death indicates he did not reach that office. This I maintain in spite of the presence of the order sheets in the office.

Mrs Trent's claim is therefore recommended on the grounds that Trent's death arose out of his employment, his instructed duties to deliver the orders not having been completed – and in the course of his employment, because he was still travelling on the way to complete his assignment.

The presence of the order sheets in Lorimer's office therefore needs explanation.

At this point, I was aware that Kaye was standing beside me again. She touched my shoulder. "The ladies? Can you tell me . . ."

"Upstairs, on the right."

She disappeared, to let me get on with it.

Lorimer had been waiting in his office. He had expected Trent to arrive there before nine. But the weather was bad, and perhaps Lorimer's mental attitude was influenced by this. In any event, Trent had not arrived when Trotter left Lorimer's office at nine. Trotter then joined the gatekeeper in his shed, until, at 9.23, Trent crashed his car close to the gates. There was no specific evidence as to the direction Trent was driving – away from or towards Lorimer's office.

I hesitated, wondering whether to mention the brief case. But it was a side-issue of my conclusions. It was I who'd allowed myself to be confused, and I didn't see why I needed to admit it. Trotter, by drawing the gatekeeper's attention to it, had given the impression that he thought the order sheets would be in the brief case. Clearly, now, this had been intentional. I carried on, not mentioning it.

Trotter and the gatekeeper then went to Trent's aid and tried to get him from the wreck, though he was dead. Trent's jacket was torn at this time. In his inside pocket – if he'd been going towards Lorimer's office – would have been the folded order sheets. It was because those order sheets were found in Lorimer's office that Lorimer was assumed to have died after Trotter left him at nine, their presence implying that Trent had been there, after nine.

But Trotter knew that the order forms were being brought by Trent, and would have known very well what they looked like. He would have recognised them protruding from the inside breast pocket of Trent's jacket. Trotter went from the car to the gatekeeper's hut, ostensibly to phone Lorimer, and said he got no reply. Lorimer was dead at that time. Trotter therefore ran up the yard to Lorimer's office, and reached it just before Peterson, the night foreman, did. Peterson has stated that when he arrived in the doorway Trotter was just backing away from Lorimer's desk. As he would have been if he'd taken the two seconds it would need to slip the order sheets beneath Lorimer's arm.

Lorimer, I believe, had been dead when Trotter left him at nine o'clock. I believe that Trotter, seeing the order sheets in Trent's pocket, had thought to use them in order to make it appear that Trent had killed Lorimer, and at the same time provide himself with an alibi, the time of death appearing to fall within the period he was with the gate-keeper. Trent, being dead, could in no way dispute this.

Kaye, I saw, was now sitting opposite me again. It'd been the grate of her chair as she returned to it that had attracted my attention. She sat, modelled in palid porcelain, staring at me.

"You've been reading this?" I asked. She was so long responding that the porcelain image became disturbing, and I almost clapped my hands to break the spell.

At last she nodded.

"I'm sorry," I said gently.

She cleared her throat and looked away.

"Do you accept this?" I persisted. "Would you say it's reasonable?"

She spoke as though her mind was far away. "I didn't lie to you, Ken."

"I thought you said you'd read it. I'm saying that you told me the truth, and I'm able to prove it."

Her eyes sparkled. I saw that her lips were pale. "But that's the point! You *had* to prove it."

"Not for me, Kaye. For them. For the Department."

She stared at me broodingly, and her eyes clouded again. "He was very angry with me, for having told you the truth."

"You should've told me that."

"How could I?" she burst out. "He's my brother. I love him. What he is now, I've done for him. Encouraged, persuaded, bullied. I got him as far as he could go – it was only his idea that he could go further." She stopped. The thought of her brother's anger was disturbing to her. He'd owed her something better than anger. "He shouted at me, Ken. I was supposed to say that Lennie left me at 8.50, but nobody asked me until you came along."

"No. Yes. I see." I found it difficult to watch her struggling with it, but I remembered she hadn't answered my original question. "But you didn't say . . . do you find my summary of it reasonable?"

She shrugged. "I suppose."

"Well . . . I don't. There's more."

240

"It's *your* idea." She lifted her chin. "What don't you see as reasonable?"

I smiled at her. If I'd been an artist, that was how I'd have tried to catch her – eyes defiant, hair untidy, chin jutting; all her determination and forcefulness was caught in that pose. But I'd have liked to catch what lurked behind it, her quick sympathy and understanding, her warmth, her vitality.

I said: "That gatekeeper – Geoff Arblaster – he was very graphic in describing it. The crash, the way they ran out to Lennie's car, the struggle to get him free, the fear that it'd go up in flames. The way Lennie's coat was torn. And the way your brother said something frantic about where was the brief-case, and then ran away to get help. What I can't believe is that during those few hectic seconds – two minutes, perhaps – your brother found time, and a portion to spare in his brain, to work all that out – how he could distort the picture and provide himself with an alibi by taking those order sheets up to Lorimer's office. Nobody's brain's that quick. It sticks in my mind, like a lump."

I waited and at last she answered me quite steadily. "I phoned him, you see. The moment Lennie left me, I phoned. And at night all the calls go to the gatekeeper's hut, and David happened to be there. I told him, because I knew the strange mood Lennie was in, and Lennie was very unpredictable. I said David ought to be in Lorimer's office when Lennie got there."

So Trotter had had ten minutes or so in the gatehouse to appraise the situation. The car crash was a bonus. Even as he ran towards Trent's car, he'd have been wondering how he could fit this in, and use it to his own advantage.

"Will you need to put that in?" she whispered.

"I think not." I smiled, and returned to typing my last or vital minute.

It is in no way within my duties as an Inspector to produce motives for murders, but in this case the motive for Lorimer's death bears heavily on the result of any future claim by Mrs Lorimer for benefit, so I have to consider this. It is known that Lorimer had been trying to discover the culprit of the apparent sabotage of machinery at the factory. My information was that it had never been proved that the breakdowns were the result of sabotage, but a recent attack on me at the factory was done with carborundum powder, which is highly abrasive to metals, and I therefore believe that sabotage must have been taking place.

Trotter had resented the appointment of a new MD, as he resents the present one, because he believed the post should have gone to him. He might have expected that the reduced output caused by sabotage would reflect on Lorimer's future prospects – as Lorimer believed it would – and Trotter was in an ideal position to perpetrate this. There is therefore a possibility that Lorimer discovered the culprit that evening, and that it was Trotter. When Trotter stated that he was standing beside Lorimer at his desk, it was not simply because they were expecting Trent, but because Lorimer was dismissing Trotter from his duties and threatening legal action. This would have meant the end for Trotter.

In these circumstances, Trotter, having obtained the nail gun because he knew he'd been detected, would have the means, the opportunity, and the motive for murder.

Kaye's tiny, artistic hand was like a vice biting into my shoulder. I didn't look up.

As I was already aware that Lorimer was employed under a contract of service (his board held a right of control and a right of termination at the end of his contract period, also he was paid by regular salary), the only matter to pursue was whether his death was an industrial accident. He was in the course

242

of his employment, because he was at the factory in pursuit of his duties. The accident arose out of his duties, because he was killed while pursuing an act of sabotage at the factory he was managing. I recommend that any claim by Marjorie Lorimer for Industrial Death Benefit should be for allowance.

K. Beacham.

Inspector.

I rolled it out of the typewriter and tagged it into the Trent file. Then I rolled in my personal note to Harkness and added:

After having read my minute on the Trent file, I'm sure you will apply to HQ for permission to inform the law enforcement authorities. There are no written statements from either Mrs Trent or Mrs Lorimer, but I'm sure these will not be difficult to obtain, especially as benefit depends on them in both cases, and, in the case of Mrs Lorimer, also her private insurance difficulties in respect of her husband's apparent suicide.

Paul – I wonder whether you would ask the Inspectors who visit these ladies to give them my best wishes. I'm sorry I can't do this myself. One pleasure of my duties has been that I promised myself this, always.

K.

I sat back. For some reason I felt exhausted, but elated.

"All done," I said.

"Then . . . we can go?"

"In just a few seconds."

I had to leave Harkness my keys. Four of them. Front door key, the one that switched on the burglar alarm, the key to my filing cabinet, the key to the cabinet in benefits section. I peeled them off my key ring and put them together with a

2in Treasury tag. Then I put all the files in my cabinet, and snapped the lock with my thumb. I sorted out all the mess of leaflets and forms that'd gone dog-eared in the briefcase, and tossed them into the wastebasket. All that was left inside were my personal, legal documents. I tossed the office keys in my palm, and hefted the brief-case in my other hand.

"Ready?" I asked. "You didn't leave any lights on?"

She shook her head. She was moving stiffly now, as in a dream, in which she was struggling to fight her way back to reality. "Aren't you leaving the keys?"

"Got to activate the burglar alarm as we go out. I'll pop 'em through the letter box."

She led the way. In the hall, I looked behind. No, no lights left on. She was standing on the top step, well in so that the little porch would keep off the worst of the drifting rain. I slammed the door after me, and turned the burglar alarm to on. The keys were still in my hand when I turned, attracted by a sound she'd made. It could have been a choked warning.

In a raincoat black with water, neck open, head uncovered and streaming with rain, David Trotter was standing at the foot of the steps. The street-lamp behind him burnished his hair but shadowed his face. My feet were taking the steps down towards him, because that was what I'd told them to do and shock had prevented me from cancelling the instruction. Now I succeeded. I stopped. His features were distorted by some strong emotion – hatred, revulsion, fear? I couldn't tell. In his hand he was swinging something heavy and hard.

I turned. Kaye was standing above me. I knew then that she had not gone to the ladies, she'd gone to the telephone room and got herself a line, and warned him.

"You—" I began, in complete confusion.

Her eyes were wide with horror, her hand flew to her mouth, and she screamed: "No!" But her cry was not to me.

I groped towards her. I knew that Trotter needed the

keys. With them, he could reach the evidence. I took a step upwards, and a blow struck the side of my head, glancing off my shoulder. Kaye had run past me, but I was down on my knees and blinded with pain. I heard a struggle and a cry of agony. Then her voice was raised again, into a shrill cry of warning and terror.

"Ken!"

My hand was reaching for the letter box, keys clutched in it. Another wild blow nearly took off my ear. His grunting effort was close behind me, and I knew he was intending to kill me. With me dead, and the keys in his hand, he'd have only Kaye to deal with.

Therefore, my lurching brain insisted, only one thing would defeat him, my ability to post the keys.

I was in the porch now, on my knees, head low and shoulders hunched in for protection. My hand groped for the letter box. The weapon crashed into my forearm, and I dropped the keys. Rolling, groaning, I twisted, kicking out, fighting back, and caught his knee-cap. It gave me a second. My left hand found the keys. He rushed at me again as my fingers fumbled in the flap. Then I clung to the open slot with both hands, refusing to be forced away from it, and slowly eased the keys through.

They fell with a clatter inside as his hand rose above my head, then I slid into unconsciousness.

I believe that the cold rain on my face brought me round. A wind was whipping hair across my face. I had no way of knowing how long I'd been unconscious, but there was no movement in the street, and no sound of a retreating vehicle. My Cortina stood waiting, dripping as dismally as I, but not feeling my pain.

I tried to move. Every bone seemed to have been affected. One by one I tried my limbs. Each moved, but one arm and my shoulder were rapidly stiffening. I felt very cold, and was shaking. I knew I had to move. My head rocked when

I tried, and one side of my face was sticky with blood. I fumbled for the briefcase.

Using the rails, I hauled myself to my feet. The first step down was an experiment, and sickness flooded me from the pain. Another step. Better. Not good, but better. The Cortina shimmered, and seemed to withdraw itself into the distance. Two more steps down. I was on the pavement, a gulf to be crossed, and shuffled to the car, groped the door open with my left hand, then fell inside.

After a few moments I switched on the engine and the heater, and sat. I couldn't marshal any thoughts. All that was lodged in my brain was a hollow despair. I allowed hot air to pour over me until the shaking eased, until the smell of warm, wet clothing was like a fog in the car. The windows steamed. I wound down the one at my elbow, having to reach across with my left arm. The right one still wasn't operating too well.

Then, tentatively because my eyes wouldn't focus, I drove away. Through the town. Be careful. Watch the traffic signals. Not much traffic, so it must have been getting late. I didn't know. My watch was a blur when I looked at it. On through town, out the other side.

To Mrs Zalusky's.

A little rest, now, and I'd be able to make it through the garden and the conservatory. Mrs Z would have a pot of tea ready, you could bet. My mind focused on that. Whatever the time, however small amount of warning I gave her, she'd have a pot of tea.

There was a man sitting quietly in the car parked in front of me. Blinking, I managed to recognise his shape. I'd seen the car before. A Chevette. Harry Burnett. By craning my head – a painful contortion, that – I could see that there was a light on in my room.

I could well have been confused. For the life of me, I couldn't imagine what Lena could have to say. I've mended your clothes? Will you be Harry's best man? I ached for the comfort of that room, to feel its peace, but Lena's presence defiled it.

I started the engine again and backed up, giving myself room to pull away. At the end of the road I hesitated. Then I turned right and drove to Macklin Shopping Centre.

Her Escort was not where I'd last seen it; her flat was dark. I groped my way to the front door, and it was open – the light was on in Sylvia's flat.

My limbs were rapidly stiffening, and it was painful negotiating the stairs. I reached her door, and it was closed. I touched it. She'd left the catch up, and it swung open. Reaching in a hand, I located the switch, then I moved inside.

There was blood on the carpet. I stepped round it. "Kaye," I whispered, but she would not answer, of course, not from a dead flat. Moving stiffly, I crossed the room. On a low table were a pile of library books and two keys, holding down a note.

"Sorry I couldn't give notice. Here are the keys.
    Kaye Trotter.
  P.S. Will you please return my library books?"

There was a spot of blood on the note, too.

She had stripped out her personal and treasured items, her guitar, record player and records, her painting equipment and sketches, canvases, paints. Not much more; there hadn't been time. I was thirstily reading signs. Blood appeared everywhere, in spots, in a pink rim to the washbasin. It spelled out a panic race to get clear, before I followed her.

She had not stayed with me at the office. Perhaps she had feared to face my condemnation, or perhaps she'd not been able to stay, but had been dumped on her doorstep by David Trotter. Certainly he'd hurt her when she'd tried to restrain him.

There had been no time to clear out the less personal items. She had not stripped down the bed, or taken spare linen from the cupboard. Some of her clothes were still there. She didn't have much. Her crockery, her cooking utensils. The plastic bag with my soiled clothes in it.

Three trips down to the car did it. I stood in the flat, looking round. Empty now. No evidence of Kaye's presence. Only her pot plants. I hesitated, then began to take them down.

Sylvia watched me from the landing. Then, without a word, she helped me. By this time the Cortina was very crowded. We found a corner for the azalea. Then we stood, Sylvia with a rain hood over her head, me with the water running down the back of my neck. At last she spoke.

"Tell her . . . give her my love."

I nodded, and got painfully into the car.

"You saw her come home?" I asked, the door still open.

She nodded. "I heard the squeal of a car's tyres, and looked out. Somebody pushed her out of the car door. I heard a man shout something about her getting lost."

"She was . . . all right?"

Sylvia smiled weakly. "Yes. Her hand to her face . . . or I'd have gone to her."

I touched her hand in gratitude and drove away. Which way to Wales?

I had a few clues. It faced south to the Severn. It was clothed in rhododendrons, which would soon be in bloom. Every blasted mountain in Wales is clothed with them! But I still had a chance. You reached the place through a farm-yard. It was called Ewr Felen. It stood for yellow acre.

A week to find it? A month? I had any amount of time.

My clothes were drying, my eyesight clearing, and I could see some distance ahead. I didn't think anybody would be able to trace me, but after all, I had stolen a black government briefcase, with "EIIR" on it in gold.

As a fleeing criminal, therefore, I headed for Wales.
K.B.
Ewr Felen,
Wales.